PRAISE

Lovel

'*Loveland* is gripping, insightful an
these women with me for a very, very long time.'

EMILY MAGUIRE, author of *Love Objects*

'Heartbreaking in its emotional reach: a tender, slow reveal of doomed marriages and a damaged past.'

GAIL JONES, author of *Our Shadows*

'*Loveland* is a book of such tenderness and precision: it is radiant.'

STEPHANIE BISHOP, author of *The Other Side of the World*

'In Robert Lukins's *Loveland*, each perfectly crafted sentence compels you to read on to the next. Equal parts surprising and inevitable, *Loveland* is a novel that is as gloriously satisfying as it is achingly beautiful. A must-read.'

PAIGE CLARK, author of *She Is Haunted*

'There's a fairytale-like quality to the beginning of *Loveland*—a hero sets out on a journey to a dilapidated castle. The poisonous kind of love that Lukins probes at is one that's usually only alluded to in such stories. It takes a masterful writer to tell an ugly story so beautifully. I couldn't stop reading it.'

ALLEE RICHARDS, author of *Small Joys of Real Life*

'A chilling and visceral portrait of families and submerged violence, the cascade of shame through generations.'

KRISTINA OLSSON, author of *Shell*

PRAISE FOR

The Everlasting Sunday

'Striking. Lukins' great achievement is to have created an atmosphere that is at once very much of this world, and musical and timeless. Everlasting indeed.'

MICHELLE DE KRETSER, Miles Franklin
Award-winning author of *The Life to Come*

'Robert Lukins' powerful, assured writing cuts like a knife into a world crackling with secrets and tension.'

LUCY TRELOAR, author of *The Times*
Book of the Year, *Salt Creek*

'A remarkable book. David Malouf said it was one of the best novels he had read in recent times . . . I want to add a personal recommendation.'

STEPHEN ROMEI, *The Australian*

'Extraordinary . . . *The Everlasting Sunday* is a beautifully written, subtle novel, dealing with loss, forgiveness, love, redemption and the complexity of our natures.'

JOHN PURCELL, Booktopia

'Lukins achieves something delicate and spare.'

PETER KENNEALLY, *Sydney Morning Herald*

'Both savage and tender, *The Everlasting Sunday*, is a haunting debut novel.'

Better Reading

Robert Lukins is a writer living in Melbourne. His debut novel, *The Everlasting Sunday*, was published in 2018 and was nominated for several major literary awards. His writing has appeared in *Meanjin*, *Crikey*, *Overland*, *The Big Issue*, and other odd places.

LOVELAND

ROBERT LUKINS

ALLEN&UNWIN
SYDNEY·MELBOURNE·AUCKLAND·LONDON

First published in 2022

Australian Government | **Australia Council for the Arts** — This project has been assisted by the Australian Government through the Australia Council, its arts funding and advisory board.

The writing of this novel was supported by a travel grant awarded by The Neilma Sidney Literary Travel Fund, The Myer Foundation, and Writers Victoria.

Allen & Unwin
83 Alexander Street
Crows Nest NSW 2065
Australia
Phone: (61 2) 8425 0100
Email: info@allenandunwin.com
Web: www.allenandunwin.com

NATIONAL LIBRARY OF AUSTRALIA — A catalogue record for this book is available from the National Library of Australia

ISBN 978 1 76087 984 6

Set in 12/16.5 pt Adobe Caslon by Bookhouse, Sydney
Printed in Australia by McPherson's Printing Group

10 9 8 7 6 5 4 3 2 1

To Easy

BEFORE AND AFTER

All the structures of the lake were ablaze. The big house, the amusements, the boardwalk. The Ferris wheel had caught finally. Towers of black smoke and the women standing in the shallows. One stayed in the shadow of the boathouse while the other was lit a flashing gold by the fires. The baby was inside, asleep in her cot. The man had come to curse them and make demands, screaming that all was gone. The women stood, calm and unmoving.

The performance of death came inevitably, as all things do. The water, the stars, the flames. The man showed a knife and then a red line was drawn across his throat and he fell forward. Life was pouring out of him but against the reflection of flames the colour of the water changed only a little.

1

With the lake finding its level against their shins, the women then spoke and touched hands. The people of the town would be drawn by the fires. They would discover the violence of this man. His inevitable acts. The flames and the blood and the blame.

It had all come so quickly in the end.

Chapter One

None of this is real.

May was stuffing crackers into the face of little Phoebe while fighting to keep her shopping bags from yawning their contents onto the concrete. The grey footpath alongside the grey road buzzing under a grey sky. These dusk storms that Queensland was too proud of. The rain was close to beginning and May was maybe five seconds away from concluding that Karl had missed his chance, so it was four seconds later that he came dumb-smiling his way around the corner. That great arch of teeth May had been victim to all her life. The smile which meant that her impatience now cooled to irritation.

None of this is real.

Not the traffic or the shopping bags or the yellow of Karl's teeth.

〜

There are collections of particles in some particular and temporary arrangement and we assign them values for a time. We call them a shopping bag. The smile of a man. We might call the arrangement of our neural response love. May had been seventeen, listening to her first counsellor, and this was his opening salvo—all this on the temporary arrangements and them not being real—and he had looked so pleased with himself. He'd talked much more than her during those six mandated sessions, and May couldn't remember much of the rest of his theories, but this idea of the absence of reality had stayed with her. It had always been a relief.

〜

'I have no time,' she said. 'Really, no time.'

'I'm late but I have doughnuts.' Karl shook a paper bag. 'No kiss?'

May settled her shopping and the child enough that she could lean in to his cheek.

'And who are we?' Karl asked, bending at the waist so that his excessively round face was too near to that of the small girl.

'Phoebe,' May said. 'The infant you're menacing is Phoebe. Please, open the door.'

'She wants a doughnut. Isn't that right?' He stayed bent until his back could no longer maintain. 'Does she talk?'

'She talks and she'll have a doughnut,' May said. 'Please, the door.'

He produced a grenade of keys and began to riffle through for the one that might recognise the lock to his office. Karl's business was sandwiched between a tattoo parlour and Red Lantern Massage, and an overflowing bin on the footpath meant his doorstep was all coffee cups and chip packets. The unreal sky was darkening further, becoming the skin of a mouldy orange. A bus honked its tuneless horn.

'No-one has time for niceties anymore,' Karl said. 'Everything's big talk now but small talk is the grease. That's what keeps the machine of civilisation from sticking.' He waved them through.

'The shopping,' May said, struggling to push Phoebe inside. The child was crying and reaching for Karl's bag. 'And the doughnut, Karl, please.'

He took a folder from the unstaffed reception desk and poured onto it three of the cinnamon-sugared rings. Karl handed this all to Phoebe and patted her softly at the crest of her French braid. She opened her mouth and filled her cheeks.

'Slow,' May said to the girl and raised a finger. 'Breathe.'

Phoebe allowed herself to be lifted onto one of the chairs at the office table. May took the other and cringed at the girl's furious hunger. Karl still wore that grin which seemed to sit an inch in front of his face.

'May, how are you?'

'Why do you have a reception desk? You've never had a receptionist.'

'You don't need a receptionist. You just need the desk. Sorry I'm late. Just had a doctor up to his elbow in my prostate. Insufferable organ. I hate it and it hates me. The only thing we agree on.'

May's shopping bags ceased supporting each other and their contents tipped onto the linoleum floor. May stopped a tomato and a tin of beans with her feet.

'We couldn't do this over the phone?' May asked. 'It's just I'm working. Damn, where's my phone? Did you see me put it down? My phone.'

Phoebe signalled for her drink bottle.

'Couldn't be helped.' Karl, who had been rummaging through the documents piled haphazardly on the table, seemed to find the necessary cache of papers. 'Now, *Casey*.'

May paused in the search through her shoulder bag. Her grandmother had died the year before. Nine months? It must have been nearly twelve. They had cremated her—this *Casey*— and scattered her ashes in the foaming water of the Pacific Ocean. Her grandmother had always refused to go anywhere near the beach. Awful places, she would say. All that sand. Karl had stood beside May and her mother as they fought with her grandmother's dust against the wind.

'Casey's will,' he said now.

'You need to talk to Mum.'

'I have.' The levitating smile had retracted and Karl's tone was one of serious calm.

'Did she owe money? She can't have. I thought this would have been sorted by now. Is it debt? I thought you couldn't inherit debt.' Phoebe was now clawing at May's neck. 'Pencils, Karl? Something?' She took the pen from his hand and the topmost papers from a pile. 'Phoebe, darling, will you draw me something? A rainbow?'

Phoebe looked into the tip of the pen.

'A black rainbow is fine, sweetie. Draw. There are black rainbows.'

'Casey appointed me executor.' He put his elbows on the table and brought his fingertips together.

'Very impressive.'

'The executor is a very responsible position.'

'I don't doubt it. I should ask, though—can suburban solicitors without receptionists be appointed executors?'

They exchanged smiles of condescension. May had known Karl all her life. All of it that she could remember. Since her father had quit the family and Karl stepped in to help. They had even moved in with Karl and his wife for a few months until they sorted out a place of their own. He had been her father's closest friend and had spent the years since making up for it.

Casey had *property*. Karl said the word as if it deserved May's attention. There was land. A decent chunk of land and a house. *Property*. May was struck by the continued use of this other word: Casey. She was Grandmother. *Casey* was some dead woman.

May made the point that this property couldn't be real as her grandmother had collected and actually used those vouchers on the back of supermarket receipts. Hadn't bought a new dress in her life. Money was the great, bonding worry of their family. Karl agreed but only said again about the property. A house and twenty-four acres of lakeside Nebraskan property.

'*Nebraskan*. Now I know you're shitting me.'

'I am not shitting you, May. You, I will never shit.'

Phoebe stopped drawing at the sound of this fun-seeming new word. May adopted her best poker face but knew she would be dealing with it for the remainder of the day.

'So she had money?'

'No,' Karl said. 'Well, a little. Three thousand and sixty-eight dollars in a savings account. A little jewellery.'

'And twenty acres of Nebraskan property?'

'Twenty-four and a house. There's nothing particularly strange about it. Unbelievable as it is, people die every day, then their stuff gets handed out. There are inheritances. People inherit. It's not just in Dickens. It happens all the time.'

'Not to us it doesn't.'

The sound of the traffic penetrated the office door. People say that if you live near a busy road you grow deaf to it, but May had lived on busy roads all her life and she still heard the noise. That static like her dying fridge. A repulsive appliance. Late at night, lying awake in bed, she would have deeply sensual fantasies of pushing it off a motorway overpass. She and Karl had arranged to meet at five o'clock and with him being late it would be half past by now. The noise. The endless drone of metal and plastics: workers busy in the combat of fleeing work. Phoebe was due back at her parents' by six, when the kid's father would be getting home. The father who was May's employer and derived too much pleasure from referring to May as the nanny. May preferred babysitter, which seemed more like the temporary situation of a teenager and not the unintended career of an adult. But before she could dump the child and begin the half-hour's drive to the Tavern there was this matter of the property. Nebraskan.

'Mum knows about this?'

'She knows,' Karl said. 'As the executor of Casey's will—'

'*Executor.*'

'Yes, wise guy. As the executor, I identified and informed the beneficiaries of the estate.'

'What does that mean?'

'Your mum. The property's hers. I started on the paperwork straight away because it's hell on earth. The grant of probate and state and international legislation and tax and blah, blah, blah. You don't want to know any of it, I promise. The long and short of it is that the worst of it is done, and we're going to need your help getting this down the home stretch.'

Phoebe had begun to draw on the leg of May's chair. The traffic was now more obviously angry through the door's inch of particle board and faded oak veneer. May's thoughts locked in to the vibration while Karl's dumb smile widened. The noise became a disturbed bees' nest. Bees the shape and size of lorries. Are bees really all male but the queen? It sounded nightmarish. She could look it up. She wouldn't.

'Your mother's intending for you to have it, May. That's where we stand. She's said right from the start she wants to sell up and pass the proceeds on to you.'

Thoughts circling her mind and not finding a place to land. She focused only on what part of this was the trick. Where the sting was going to come from. 'I don't understand.'

'I know.' The smile again. The plumpness of his eyes.

'How am I just hearing about this?'

'It wasn't my place to tell you.' Karl took the document from the desk and began to turn its pages slowly. 'This is how your mother wanted to handle it and I'm only her solicitor in this instance; I have to follow her instructions. I think she thought it would just make more sense coming from me. Keep things official.'

Phoebe was sobbing with tiredness and slapping at the desk, so May snatched the remaining doughnut and threw it into the corner. The kid bounded after it like a dog.

'Mum mops floors. Scrubs people's toilets,' May said. 'I raise awful people's children. I don't understand.'

Karl went to speak but all that was released was the wet sharpness of his voice cracking. He had always been quick with his emotions. May had seen him cry a few times over the years. He had certainly cried more than she had at her grandmother's funeral. He was a good man. More than good. She couldn't bear unease to register on that beautiful, dumb face.

'It's just a surprise,' she said.

They held each other's stares, gave nods of surrender, then both turned to watch Phoebe, who was sitting against a pot plant amid the dust and hair of the unswept floor. The plant was surprisingly healthy. She pointed this out.

'It's plastic. May, look, I'm sorry. It wasn't my place to say.'

'I know. You're the executor.' She stood and walked around the table to him and kissed his cheek. 'And with that comes much responsibility.'

'This could be something great for you, May. A new start.'

His voice was strange with neutrality. She hated that he was trying so hard. She poked him in the belly to extinguish the effort.

'Why do we carry on, Karl?'

'Just in case the world doesn't end.'

May thought briefly of the planet engulfed in flames. Time itself reaching its end. She checked her phone.

'Oh damn,' she said. 'I'm really late. I have to go.' Phoebe was now sleeping noisily on the floor. 'Her parents already hate me.'

May took her shopping, upset the child and hurried outside, flinging goodbyes over her shoulder. She rushed them through the car park of Cotton Tree's public library, where she saw Ima, the librarian, closing up, checking the lock of the automatic doors. Ima had been at the library forever. The kids made awful jokes of her name.

May reached her car and it reluctantly agreed to action. There were five missed calls on her phone. She pushed the vehicle into the dull flow of traffic, which was backed up all the way to the Plaza, and it was no better going around the headland. The child cried. Ahead was an endless arc of headlights beneath the black of the storm which had arrived with a spray of angry drops on the windshield. There was no escaping any of it, so she sighed into the wind. Turned the radio up above the crying.

Her mind should have been full with this dubious idea of a Nebraskan property. Twenty-four acres and a house; it should be seeming like a lottery win. All the things she should have been thinking. Of her grandmother and what the woman had kept hidden. Her mother and her silence on the subject. What selling up should mean. The complications and simplicity.

May, though, thought only of what Karl had said of this being a *new start*. The thing he had hinted at so many times before in his not-meddling-but-definitely-meddling way. He was speaking of May's husband. *New start* meaning that May could take her son and leave Patrick.

The road remained locked tight as far as she could see. Just the blazing red of brake lights into the distance, white lights behind, and the man in the stationary car beside her watching porn on his phone. May's stomach was all knots and raging acid. Somebody honked.

LOVELAND, APRIL 1955

It was a perfect life. Casey reminded herself of this before opening her eyes that market day. Easter was behind them and so the morning air was sweet with oranges and cinnamon. The week before she'd removed the bedroom's windowpanes from their frame in the wall. She realised this made no great sense, as she then needed to hang netting from a ceiling hook above the bed to protect herself from the mosquitoes, but it was how she wanted things. To invite spring's air in through the open square of the wall. A canvas awning would keep out the worst of the rain.

She lay like this for some time, listening for the movement of birds to confirm the day. The scent of oranges became confused with grass and the disturbed dirt from the neighbouring farm.

The farmers would be at toil and so she too would set to work. Casey put on a cotton dress—the one with a pattern of plum blossom that the previous year had hibernated in the wardrobe for at least another month. The season could not wait. A perfect life, she remembered.

It was a decent walk into town so she took her white sunhat from its peg and her trolley from its place at the front door and set off along the road. Reaching the crest of the hill, she turned as she always did for a glimpse of her home: the dark wooden square sitting with its feet in the lake. Bluegrass coloured the few hundred yards to the boundary with the farm. The perfect life.

At the market, she went first to the juice stand. She stood to the side of the cart and drank her orange and ice. The cold of it shocked her tongue. She chewed on the ice and watched the older ladies at the vegetable stalls. They were fussing over artichokes and the seller laughed at their complaints. They bought their bundles and the seller was given a slap to his backside for his cheek and he made promises to behave. There were locals who Casey recognised, and some obvious visitors pointing to baskets of flowers and honey jars. The air above shimmered as if off a hotplate. On the other side of the open square a musical trio began to play and insects hovered in excitement.

She thanked the juice seller and returned her glass. He seemed to engage in conversation and so Casey pulled at the brim of her hat and showed the man a palm of farewell. The familiar weight settled on her chest. It was, though, all so perfect. The scented air, the warmth and the happiness of the dragonflies. She hoped always for just one morning in which the spell would not be broken, but here was the weight on her chest. The heavy acid.

Casey bought her vegetables. She smiled in response to the comments on the weather and the crowds. She listened intently to the musicians, willing them to calm her heart and occupy her senses. They played on, something befitting a carnival, but it was being taken on the wind and a nearby couple's arguing became impossible to avoid. One was asking the other why they had come at all if they were going to be in such a lousy mood. Casey moved on to the fruit stall and was reaching for a plum when she caught sight of the husband. He was sitting on the edge of the central fountain, eating an apple.

All she ever wanted was one morning without the spell breaking. Her chest. She struggled for breath. It would pass. The air was still so sweet with flowers and spice. Those oranges and cinnamon. She straightened and made the last of her purchases. Bread and cheese and oil. Her trolley was full and she wanted to be home before the sun gained too much height.

The juice seller waved as she left the market and she smiled. There was nothing to be gained by blaming this man. This young man with his juice and ice. She would maintain the peace between her and these people, because without this she would truly have nothing. Casey had this market. The storekeepers of the town. The strangers on the road. She would maintain though the ache in her chest was worse than usual. It had been the damn couple's argument before the sight of the husband.

She began the walk home, closing her eyes against the dust blowing from the road. There would be no cars coming this way through the low hills. She could make the journey without opening her eyes. The only danger would be if the neighbouring farmer brought his truck to the market, but he would have been already. So Casey walked with her eyes shut tight. The daylight pushed in hard through her eyelids. The universe was the colour of a pale peach.

The goddamn arguing of that couple. Their failure to be simple and happy. It was unfair of her, she knew, but this was her feeling. The couple could so easily have forgiven each other's shortcomings. They could have gone and listened to the trio. Danced if they had wanted to. She continued home and spoke her daily truths. Each morning she would speak plainly to herself so that she would not forget.

Her name was Casey.

She was nineteen years old.

She was a prisoner in her home and permitted to travel only to the local stores and market. The word prisoner was never used but it was how she came to understand herself. There were rules. Some had been explained and others she had learned by the husband's reaction. She was permitted to speak only pleasantries and generalities with those she met. The town had a name, L——, but she was not permitted to utter it because the name angered the husband. The husband would always be watching and listening. She was not permitted to read newspapers or watch television. She would be alone but for the husband. Rules. Rules and those things she had learned.

Casey opened her eyes as she started up the final incline. The pain in her chest had eased by the time she saw the square of her home, but an involuntary glance over her shoulder revealed the silhouette of the husband a hill behind. He was keeping close that morning. She would continue with her day and tell herself again of her life's perfection.

She would speak the truth and live this lie. This simple and perfect life. If she told herself often enough it might become so. She had so much to be grateful for. The ancient beauty around spoke of the coming of spring. The oranges and cinnamon.

Chapter Two

Forty-two minutes late. Phoebe's father had been waiting, silently furious, and had pulled the child away from May at the doorway. He had pointed for May to leave the shopping by the wall and had spoken only to say that the mother wasn't home yet. His tone made clear this was something May should be thankful for. She left and drove to the Tavern as quickly as the storm traffic would allow, parked and ran through the rain. Pushing the side door to the pub open, drenched, she looked around the room and saw Patrick sitting at a table with a half-finished beer.

'The roads,' she said, conjuring laughter as she sat opposite. 'I could kill everyone, honestly.'

He stretched his fingers out across the laminate. He had dried stripes of paint or plaster on his cheek and his eyes stayed wide, expectant.

'I'm sorry,' said May, 'I had the kid. And the traffic was terrible in the wet. Sorry.'

The Tavern was always busy, and with the rain pummelling down everyone had abandoned the outdoor tables and crammed inside. Behind May a table of men in footy jerseys were laughing and pouring from jugs. Music was playing beneath the shouting. Something people might have danced to in other lives.

When Patrick spoke it was too quiet, so May had to strain to hear. 'Forty-five minutes.'

He drank steadily, coming to the end of his schooner. Another empty stood to the side. In the past she would have feared what this calm foretold. Wondered at what would rise from beneath the still water's surface. Now she only waited.

'How was work?' she asked.

'You're funny.'

He ran a finger around the rim of the glass. Date nights had been her idea, arrived at after the last big thing and agreed to in his days of contrition after he had reversed his van over and over into the mailboxes at the front of their building. The man in Apartment 1 had called the police. So she and Patrick met at the Tavern on Monday nights for their dates, just like they had never done when they were young. She thought of her grandmother and wondered how far her ashes had travelled.

Traffic, bees, pot plant.

Property.

May wondered why she wasn't telling him.

'How's the job at the Big Top?'

They lived on the eastern crest of Buderim Mountain, ten minutes from the old Big Top shopping centre—as good as laid to waste with the coming of the sprawling Sunshine Plaza—where Patrick had been doing a job on a back office renovation. Plastering. Walls, mostly. Worked for his brother.

'Finished,' Patrick said.

'That's good.'

May showed her teeth. He inhaled slowly and tapped that fingertip to his schooner glass. It was quieter at the near bar, so May went around to the far side, where she thought it might be worse. She gave herself these miniature holidays. She consciously filled her lungs deeply—one, two—and calculated how many minutes she had bought for herself. She had hoped for four but her turn to order came too quickly when a man coughed a XXXX fog into her face while insisting, *Ladies first*. She ordered and looked past the bar to where someone was having a birthday. More footy blokes, making a show of dancing together. Broncos jerseys stretching taut over beer guts that brushed navel to navel. She wished they hadn't changed the laws and people still smoked in pubs. She didn't smoke herself but longed for that grey shroud in which to lose herself. She walked back to

Patrick and as he watched her put his beer down on the table she wondered why she still wasn't telling him.

After, back at the apartment, Francis was eating cereal on the couch with his long, spidery legs folded up beneath him. May didn't try with another *hello* and went to the kitchen where the meal she had prepared for her son sat untouched in the fridge under its plastic wrap. She might usually have attempted a light-hearted complaint. Like the complaints mothers make on television shows that only prove the familial bonds. The ones that end with mussing up the kid's hair and the hiding of smiles. She went and stood against the wall while Francis looked up from his bowl, almost formed an expression, then returned to his show. Some reality television thing. A man and a woman, both topless, argued in a spa bath.

He had turned seventeen the week before. On the night of the birthday he had gone out with his friends and returned home with a cut under his eye and a lump like a half-egg above his temple. When he was little Francis would close his eyes and jump from the couch, horizontal, with his arms held tight to his sides. He said he was just testing to see if he could do it and May was always envious that he could hold his nerve. After the third trip to Emergency and his second concussion she had covered the living room floor with blankets and towels and he cried at the danger being removed. Now, his wounded eye and forehead were just a haze of rough pink.

The word descended into her thoughts: *Nebraska*. She didn't know where it was. America, but where? The top? Did it snow? That new start. She would search for it. Find a map.

Francis drank the last of his cereal and she wondered why she wasn't telling him either.

'My May, she only told me after her kidney.'

My May was what mother called daughter when the child needed soothing. Nightmares, hospitals, the rest. *Her kidney* was the grandmother's cancer. Francis had gone to sleep or at least his room and May had gone to her bedroom and called her mother. Patrick was still at the Tavern, where she'd left him with a fresh beer.

'My May, it's yours,' her mother said. 'What would I do with all that now?'

'Stop working, for starters.'

'And what then? This is for you and Francis.'

May wiped at her oily face. Tissue boxes stood in a neat column on her bedside table. It couldn't be real: *Nebraska*. Her grandmother had been born an American, she knew that. In Maine. The place with lobsters. The place where May's mother was born. The pair had moved to the Sunshine Coast a year later. The husband had died: the wife and daughter moved to

Australia. This was the story and no-one had ever spoken this word *Nebraska*. She could hear Francis through the wall; he was either gaming or watching videos or both. There was a strain to her mother's voice and May wanted it to end. They were both so tired and all she wanted was for her mother to rest. She would do as her mother wanted. Sell the property and be done with this. Figure the rest out as it arrived.

'My May, this is for you and Francis. She only told me after her kidney.'

Listening to her mother's chest tightening and her son not sleeping, May resolved to bypass any mystery or comprehension and navigate the most direct path through this. She wouldn't question how this came about or why it had been kept from her. Everything was merely as it was and she would maintain the generations of silence. She would tell her mother what her mother wanted to hear. She would do what was needed to sell the house, but when the day came she wouldn't take a cent. Not a cent. Somehow, though, something might be fixed in all this.

The lock on the front door made the sounds of Patrick returning. The man always pushed too soon and the doorframe shook. His boots fell onto the floor and May felt her stomach clench. She resolved to tell them both. With that something might be fixed.

—

The scene had moved to the street and a set of eyes had appeared at the near apartment window. May had done her work and convinced Patrick to return to the pub. His van's engine was running and he threw a flannelette shirt inside to the passenger seat. The man in Apartment 1 was at his parted curtain and making no attempt to hide. May had sent Francis back inside but he was lingering in the stairwell.

'We'll need to get this done,' Patrick said as he leaned out from the driver's seat and held her by the shoulder. His smile was his worst one. 'Quick and done.'

An hour earlier, she had made him his cup of tea and peanut butter on toast and told him flatly of her grandmother's will and Nebraska. The house. The property. She imagined him reaching out his hand to meet hers but it never came. There was no pause of disbelief. No hanging moment. Only him clarifying details.

Yes, it was left to May's mother but she intended it for May. *Yes*, she was sure. It would be made legal. It was twenty-four acres. *Yes*, twenty-four.

She had said nothing of her intention to insist her mother keep the money from the sale of the house. He had leaped so quickly on the prospect of an inheritance that her resolve stood no chance. He had asked if she was sure and she heard herself say *yes*.

Now, in the street, she tried to shrug off his hold on her shoulder.

'How long did the lawyer say?' He had started to drum with his free hand on the steering wheel. 'How long?'

Francis appeared in the unkind streetlight, hanging back by the final concrete stair. Patrick had spelled out plainly what was to happen. May was to give him the solicitor's phone number and email. It would be hurried along and the property sold and he would see to it all. May would be spared the hassle; she wasn't good at handling these kinds of things, he reminded her. Finances and admin, he said, weren't her strength. He would sort it out and he would spare her.

The van's engine revved and the neighbour stood at his window. Patrick was going back to the pub thanks to May's secret urging. Her practised, delicate encouragement. He was drunk already, and loud, and after she had told him of Nebraska he had begun his agitated spiral, growing more heated and unpredictable and twisting himself tighter like a rubber band. She knew what a rubber band did when released so she would send it outside. She reminded him how hard he worked. How he deserved his rewards. It was well before closing time at the Tavern and maybe his brother would meet him. He was soon in the street accepting the van keys.

One hand on the wheel, the other on May's shoulder, there was a moment when Patrick's suspicion seemed to overcome the alcohol in his blood. It was so brief, just the flash of his eyes locking focus on hers, and she felt his grip tighten. But she wouldn't let a thing show. The engine was running, he was so close to gone. She wouldn't falter now, even as his fingers dug in so hard between her bone and muscle. She couldn't stop from flinching, just a jolt, as his thumb pushed in deep under her collarbone.

'Enjoy yourself,' she said.

'That solicitor's number. Remember.' He spoke quietly, steady. 'I'll be calling him first thing. You won't need to worry about it. I'll sort everything.'

He maintained his grip and she knew already how her skin would look in the mirror. The impressions left by his long fingers would be a hot red before she went to bed.

'Thank you,' she said, and this released her.

She waved as he drove away then walked back inside. The curtains closed. The bruises would be a deep blue by the morning. She would wear his stripes.

LOVELAND, SEPTEMBER 1955

She had walked inside from sweeping leaves off the verandah when the memory came. It was often that way. At the end of a day when she was so close to forgetting everything. It was when she had some feeling of being satisfied that the sensation would return to Casey of her earliest times in Loveland. Of arriving after a journey in the back of a bus that had lasted three days with the changes and sleepless nights in hired rooms. Of being led into her new home.

There had been those first months, perhaps two seasons.

The husband had been nervous. She had put it down to this, nerves, and this had explained enough and lent her a kind of protectiveness over him. He was older and yet had become so unsure and rigid, and it would be her job to bring out their happiness. He wasn't the same man she had met the year before and from whom she had accepted love and a wedding proposal, that was clear, but this was his nerves at the great adventure they were embarking on and so it was her job to help him return. She had written letters of reassurance to her family and he had taken them to be posted.

He spent so much time out with his work. On the property and away. They would come together for the night's meal and he would hold his fork in his fist and bounce the tip of its handle against the table. She would check on his day and ask the questions she had prepared.

The days passed, the nights and meals, and he only grew more tightly wound. Those nerves. Casey would probe gently at the edges of this but it would only lead to greater distance. He would take his plate outside to finish. Work later or stay away longer and return without even a motion towards explanation. So, then, she would keep the house and herself ever neater and abandon her questions. She would bring out their happiness.

～

They had met for the first time over the dinner table at Casey's home in Maine. A place where her family name had once meant more. It still carried something, conjured some air of fond remembrance, but not what it had. Moses had been seated directly across from Casey and it was clear from her parents' preparation and gesturing what they meant for the pair. Moses, for his part, was charming and wise and handsome. Quiet. Certainly quieter than the boys Casey knew, but that was because Moses was a man. Two decades older. His quietness was what happened when you quit saying dopey and hopeless things like the boys Casey knew.

Moses would visit now and then, to discuss the prospect of business with Casey's father, to join their family dinners, only to leave again for weeks at a time, and this made Casey think of *The Age of Innocence*, that romantic novel she had read in school. In truth, Casey had not read the thing closely, but she remembered the images of courtship from a distance and looks across tables and simmering urges. Her parents expected her to marry well and young and they had never made a secret of that. It was the old way of an old family, and though Casey knew it wasn't the way of her generation, she would admit to herself that she saw something appealing in the idea. Living in that old time of romance. Here was Moses across the dining table and it truly felt like that innocent age.

This went on for six months. Moses took her out alone to a restaurant twice. Then once for a walk around the downtown area, and when they reached the Two Penny Bridge he asked her if she would marry him. She knew enough from her memory of that romantic book to make him wait for an answer. But she knew immediately what her answer would be, as did he. Six weeks later they were married at the Sacred Heart Church. Moses had been so handsome on that day. So quiet.

⌒

Those two seasons into their married life, at the end of a day on the cusp of spring, Moses had returned from three days away to the sight of her in an unfamiliar dress. It was pretty but modest and the colour of a new lily. A dispassionate pink lily. Her hair had been cut. She had been to the nicer place in town and had her ends seen to and the woman had taken more off than Casey had asked for. She liked the cut, though. She admired herself in the mirror at home but worried at the boldness of it. The gesture. And it had been too much. It was the hair as much as the dress in the end. Perhaps alone they might have been accepted, but together they seemed to reinforce a message in the husband's ear. She wondered later what he heard.

Casey led her husband to the dinner table, sure he must be tired and hungry from his trip. She urged him to sit, and as she brought out the food and cutlery and wine she saw him looking at the dress. The hair. The hair that she'd admired and knew to be too much and which that day triggered something in him. She sat and his voice never rose above a steady murmur as he explained the way things needed to change. To return, he would say. To return to how they should have been.

The marriage could only live on by becoming what was intended. Marriage was a vow to create and honour boundaries. This was the only arrangement that could ensure their happiness. And wasn't that what she wanted for them? She had wanted to be a wife and so he explained how a wife would be. The respect that she would need to show. She must surely understand how hard he was working for them? She would need to work too and her work was this family of theirs. Her job was their happiness, and wasn't this what she wanted?

The rules would come later. The ones explained and those learned by the husband's reaction. For now he only explained the vision of a wife. That thing she had agreed to become.

His voice never rose above that steady murmur as he described how fortunate she was. It would be a perfect life. He delivered his explanations with such ease, no different from how he had informed her of the day of the rubbish collection when she arrived. The place to leave the linen so that the staff could take it to the laundry. The husband had made real what so many wished for: that the nuisances of a marriage be transformed into something more certain.

She would wonder about her family and the story they were being told. She'd heard no suggestion of them visiting. There had been no letters. She wondered about the ones she had written and which of them, if any, he had actually posted for her.

That night he had taken her from the dinner table to their bedroom and lay with his weight along her body. He had already removed his trousers while she was still in her dress the colour of a lily. She told him it was hurting and he told her to hush. She whimpered and he raised a finger to her lips. He brought both his hands around her biceps, squeezed, and the pain was more than anyone had ever made her feel. Gripped her so tightly at the hips that she would wear the bruises of his fingers for weeks. He wanted assurances again of her virginity. He said she didn't move right for innocence and that he could never trust her. She closed her watering eyes, gasped, then felt the natural rhythm of her breathing end. It would never return.

⌒

The leaves had been swept. The day ended. She would walk across the threshold of her little house on the lake and the memory of those early times would return. She would sometimes be brought to laughter by the absurdity and this would always be followed by the worst of her pain. On those sleepless nights, if she was alone, she would fetch the longest knife from the kitchen and lie with the handle sitting on the highest point of her belly, the blade's tip resting against her throat.

Chapter Three

May checked her phone and there was a queue of messages from Patrick so she attended to them in order. He wanted the solicitor's number. Wanted her to confirm the arrangements. It was a Saturday morning and she stood at the front door with a hand raised, keeping her son from the day.

'I only want one minute. Please.'

He made a display of inhaling, then lowering his shoulders and stepping back. He walked to the table and sat.

'One minute,' he said. 'So is this where we get to the bottom of things? Nut it out with a heart-to-heart?'

She sat opposite and waited until he took the hand she offered.

'I'm doing my best,' she said. 'I always do my best. We can figure out what we do from here. You and me, Francis. A fresh start and all that.'

'Just watch it go to hell,' he said. 'You're a magician. You'll find a way. You always do.'

She squeezed his hand tighter as he tried to reclaim it. The melodrama of it all.

'What about Dad?'

'What about him?'

'That's what I thought.' The boy's expression aged twenty years and became exactly that of his father. 'Forget about the figuring out. Just leave the thinking to us, okay? It's not your strength. We'll spare you.'

He left. Not theatrically, not violently. Just walked out and left the door open, swamping the apartment with the noise of traffic and a humid, salty wind.

So this wouldn't be a time of them coming together in some neat little coupling. She'd never really believed that it would be, but she'd let herself hope all the same. Maybe it was her job now to make something of this. This house. This mad house of *Nebraska*. The son and the father were a pair and so maybe she had to make a pairing of her own with this house.

May waited for her chest to ease, then put the breakfast dishes into the sink and wiped the table. She ran a cloth down the fridge and hit the thing's side to quiet its buzzing. She put her hand to the stitch in her stomach and made the apartment clean.

—

The mother called. They had been talking more often and May would hear the woman using an unfamiliar tone that sounded like an instructing parent. May grew to welcome it and thought it seemed closer to the mothers and daughters on television. The mother said that May needed to go to Nebraska to settle things with the house. Go to that place only conjured into existence a fortnight earlier. She spoke about this as if it were already decided and May only needed to make the arrangements and cease her resistance. It was happening. Her mother was far too old and far too tired and busy to deal with it herself. This would be May's job and the proceeds would all go to her. These were the mother's instructions. The three thousand dollars of the grandmother's had been transferred and May needed to book the flight. *You do what you need*, the mother kept saying. *Go and do what you need.*

'And Francis?' May asked.

'He'll survive.'

'I can't leave him.'

'Why not? He already hates you.'

They laughed, pathetic with living. Holding the phone in one hand, May stretched out her other arm and watched her trembling fingers.

⌣

May had first seen a counsellor when she was in secondary school. It was her contribution to a negotiated truce in the wake of some episode of trouble. A build-up of after-school detentions, truancy and then a fistfight. Then, it had been a matter of admitting to her anger and making the appropriate promises.

Later, at nineteen, well clear of the beige prison blocks of Kawana High, it was May who sought out Dr O'Connor. Dr O'Connor who insisted on being called Emma. At that first appointment, May had been married for a day under six weeks.

Generalised anxiety disorder, Emma diagnosed.

It meant a lot and little. There were many causes and as many ways forward. Emma encouraged couples counselling. It would be complementary. May said that this was something she would look into but it wasn't possible just then. Maybe later, though. Definitely later. Emma asked more about Patrick and the marriage, and May contained what she could but her expression must have betrayed her. Her hands. Emma would ask if May was fearful or in physical danger. Told her that things could be done. May smiled and made assurances and tucked her hands between her thighs.

This impulse was something May would only find the right name for years later. In this small, white room, a woman whom May had grown to like and trust was offering her the chance to explain things and seek help, but still May smiled and reassured. The right name for it was shame. Much later, when May found this word, it brought a real relief. It explained so much and meant May didn't need to go on wondering. She felt shame and so she wouldn't reveal it. Not to anyone. Certainly not gentle, kind

Emma. Anyway, how could it be solved? Something so vast and impossible.

May only wanted her shakes gone. The sweating, the insomnia. This woman was a doctor and so should be able to address these illnesses.

If May was in danger, then things could be done.

May talked about the trembling hands, the heat and tightness in her chest.

In time, Emma would teach her ways to bring on calm. Strategies. The making of space. Emma started with the usual suggestion about three deep breaths and focusing on the movement of air. It had never worked for May as she could never make it to the third breath. Emma suggested a song instead. May should choose one she knew well, that she could sing silently to herself to remove her focus from the physical. It was only a temporary measure, to make that space.

It was the summer of 1997 and May had been stuck on Elliott Smith and *Either/Or*. Patrick hated the album, said it was moaning rubbish, and so it existed only within her headphones.

There had been that one song in particular, 'Ballad of Big Nothing'.

So she began to sing this to herself. Silently. Filling her mind and leaving her voice unspent. She sang inside and her pulse did slow. The panic eased and her hands became still. The world eased and for a time disappeared.

So then, this was the song.

⌣

Phoebe's parents had been understanding. The father had nodded and only made noises of *mmm* when May had explained about needing a break from caring for the child. *Work*, she should have called it. A ten-day break. Two weeks at most. *Leave.* It should have been called *leave. Would that be okay?* She had worked for the parents for eighteen months and never missed a day. *Mmm.* It was a full twenty-four hours later that Phoebe's mother sent a long message to May's phone explaining that she could certainly take leave, and in fact not return, as her employment was terminated *effective immediately*. It was the lack of notice, she said. Lack of professionalism. The abandonment. The disregard for the child's needs and wellbeing. Phoebe's feelings. It had been an informal arrangement with no agency or contracts and so it was done.

May laughed in disbelief at the message, directly into the face of her phone, and felt a surge of relief. There was some thrill to this. The girl, Phoebe, was a dear thing. A dear thing and May worried for her, but in that moment of being fired May knew that she would not truly miss the child. The truth was that she did not particularly like children. This thought arrived whole and undeniable. Children. Didn't like them. Her own son was something else but *children*, the category, no. The parents would hire through the proper channels next time. They were rich. They would say wealthy, but they were rich. The house at Sunshine Beach with all its unused levels and rooms. The artworks too big for the walls. The silver under glass. May's mother had been their cleaner and made the connection when she heard they were looking for someone to look after the child. Next time they would find someone appropriate and Phoebe would have an appropriate life. The parents were awful people, so Phoebe would have that to contend with, but she would no doubt discover that straightforward trick of becoming awful herself.

May was the daughter of someone who now owned a house and twenty-four acres of lakeside Nebraskan property. Maybe May was a rich girl now too. Perhaps she would become an awful person. A girl could dream. May let a clouded memory of her grandmother's voice speak and its message settled in her mind. That new start. Unrest might be replaced with something better.

Her grandmother had died and wanted this.

May let the words fall in a peaceful place. Maybe this was simple after all. A child would follow the instructions of her mother. May went online and booked her flight to Nebraska. She sent her son a message about his dinner, an apology, and told him what time she'd be home. The whole procedure took maybe fifteen minutes. She heard herself laugh again. Watched her hands.

The plane's engines reached their highest pitch and the craft began its propulsion down the runway. It had all come into being so quickly. Too fast for May to have had sufficient doubts or to be troubled by reason. So May was buckled into the seat of a moving aircraft.

May had flown six times in her life. To and from Sydney, once. To and from Cairns, twice. Each a family holiday that would be christened with Patrick's disapproval over the size or state of the hotel room. He had always been the one to book. Then there would be the escape of the pool. The pool where she would shut her eyes and think only of the beaches of home. The days of closed eyes and sunscreen and clinging to plastic loungers. Patrick would move between the water and the bar. Her son would be back in the hotel room.

May had been in Karl's office as he'd called Patrick and told him about the flight, as she'd asked. She stood at his shoulder, her stomach raging. Karl told Patrick that it was regrettable but necessary as, yes, only May could act on her mother's behalf. There had been the formal handing over of power of attorney and it was the only way it could be resolved, yes. Karl had booked the flight for May to Nebraska. Yes, so soon. Non-refundable. The quicker this was resolved the better. Better for everyone. Karl had hung up the phone and turned to May and told her it was done. He smiled that dumb smile. May kissed Karl's cheek and wondered what it would be like to be with a person whose smile wasn't doubted. Whose smile didn't terrify.

Patrick had been two years ahead of her at school, with the awe and mystery that this brought. She would talk with her friends about him, and early on the girls had jostled as if he might fall into any of their laps, but May had always felt some strange confidence about it. A confidence she wasn't familiar with, that this good-looking boy with the soft hair and muscular arms would be hers. They held eye contact. They recognised something in each other that they thought missing from themselves. This was what they would say.

May's mother had recognised something in Patrick too, and she'd fought with May against him from the start. May was seventeen and in the fog of this boy with the quiet ways and a job and an apartment of his own. She defied her mother and knew that her friends' objections were born of jealousy.

May would look back at when she had joined with Patrick and think it all so minor. Knowing what would come after, the passion of that early time would never seem nearly enough. It could never be a love great or ferocious enough to explain what it became.

When May first realised that there was something else to the relationship, something misaligned, she was too deep into its flesh. She had burrowed in and found herself alone. She said nothing at first, out of embarrassment. That emotion so prized by the young. She had made so much of defending Patrick and their love against her mother. There had been so many arguments and tears, May just couldn't walk back on all she'd said, so she persisted. Burrowed in further.

We just become how and who we are and no-one is beyond that. He had been handsome and charming, but when she looked back it was never enough. The story could never explain itself. She came to realise that the marks on her body were not the worst of it. There is physical pain and it is unbearable in the moment but the moment is at least brief. It was the unending struggle for air. This was the worst of it and the thing that never passed. The fear that stole her every breath.

The flight attendant was instructing everyone to switch to flight mode or turn off their devices. There had been a succession of messages from Patrick, all repetitions of what he had been making clear in the days previous. To attend to his plan for the house and the way it needed to be administered. For her to call if she became confused and to let him know as things progressed. To call him the moment she landed.

She thought of Francis. Her son, whom she had last seen three days before and who hadn't spoken to her. Wouldn't. And certainly not to say goodbye.

The plane gained speed and May became aware of the liquid of her body. The fluids and blood so close to the surface. She thought of Francis and his absence and it was a cold stream of poison running from her heart. How could she be leaving him? How cold a person she must be. Certainly not a mother.

And Patrick. What would register on his face once he realised that she had escaped? Because that was exactly what was happening. Only then, with the plane's wheels rolling under her, could she allow her mind to accept the truth of it. She was leaving him. He couldn't know but it had already happened. Her lungs screamed for air.

It was too, too late.

The wheels lifted off the bitumen and May made fists of surrender. The music played in her mind. Her Elliott Smith. She would sing. Her Big Nothing. May's stomach dropped and heart pined and she was consumed with the ecstasy of leaving the earth.

LOVELAND, APRIL 1956

It was late in the morning and the sun had overtaken the shade at the side of the house. Casey had been sitting on her wooden seat, holding a book open in her lap but giving her attention to the worker and his gardening. He had been pulling weeds from the slope between the promenade and the low fence at the boathouse boundary, working methodically, as he always did, going in sweeping lines and loosening the rogue plants from the ground with his trowel. This was Henry, whose name Casey only knew from it being called out between the hills and the big house.

⌒

The big house was the hotel, the grand building of the lake, but Casey had heard the staff using this cosier term and she'd taken it to her heart. The big house that looked like something she'd dreamed into existence. It was so clearly of an earlier, greater time and sat at the crest of a rise above the lake. Its pale stone gave it a permanent glare against the daylight, and in the mornings Casey would need to raise her hand against it as she looked up from the boathouse. The boathouse that was her home. Their home. The perfect square against the edge of the water that she would keep clean against the elements and from which she would look up at the big house and wonder about the talk and activity inside.

The husband had decided the boathouse would be their home. One of the workers had carried her bags directly down the hillside path and Casey had done well to conceal her disappointment. The husband had shown her the hotel that first day. He'd taken her on a tour of its five grand storeys and she'd seen inside some of its guestrooms and been led into the dining space and the balcony for tea and drinks. She hadn't seen any guests that day but she'd assumed that must have to do with the seasons. She knew nothing of the hotel business. It must have been the seasons. There were, though, the half-dozen staff with their neat white uniforms and chores. They greeted Moses as he walked Casey through the property and then scurried away to their duties.

The rest of the grounds formed that picture from a dream. The wooden promenade that hugged the lake's edge, the gazebo, the jetty, the Ferris wheel. The wheel was not as tall as the ones she had ridden in at fairs but it was a magical sight all the same. They went to the end of the boardwalk, and when they were in its shadow Casey could see that the Ferris wheel was in disrepair. Its white cloth was tattered and stained and its metal scaffolding was rusted. A heavy and old-looking chain anchored the wheel to the ground and kept it from turning.

It was all to be fixed, Moses told her. The wheel and the rotten planks of the promenade and the leaking walls of the hotel. In his parents' day, the place had been a jewel and the best families would come here to holiday and see it shine on the hill. It was his parents who had let it fade. His mother had died suddenly of something with her lungs and his father had then lingered with his melancholy and inaction for enough years to see the place go quiet and dark. It was left to Moses. Everything. The dust and the debt. This place that had been such a wonder its name had become that of the town. Moses would see it return, just as he had returned after his years of absence. The ageing and neglect of the generation before his would be undone and the grandeur would return to Loveland.

She found herself wondering about the husband and his war. He'd never spoken to her of what happened in those years and she knew only that he had been there, somewhere. Over there with the fighting. He spoke of it only in terms of what it owed him now. What fate had taken and what was due in return.

He had accompanied Casey back along the boardwalk, and as they went she began to notice more clearly this degeneration he talked of. The cracks and the rot and the pieces missing. He walked her to the steps at the side of the boathouse and told her that the staff and their noise and work wouldn't bother her down here. This was to be their home, and before they could step inside he waited and she thanked him.

~

Casey watched Henry the gardener shake the soil from the roots of the weeds and then throw them into the nearest of a dozen heaps. When he was done, he piled them into a wheelbarrow and brought the plants to the flat space where the lake began to turn. He built a great, final stack which he would later set alight and tend until it was just a smoking black circle on the earth.

She watched Henry work and admired his sweating face. The way he stopped at the completion of each weeded arc and ran a cloth across his brow and arms. She watched the man cursing as he struggled by the boundary line, where the fence ran down into the water. He fought against a clump of plants with flowers like purple crowns. Henry eventually triumphed but in the act of throwing them to his heap had lost one into the wire of the fence. She watched this discarded thing moving in the breeze. Henry made his bonfire then went over the hill, and this little rope of weed remained.

Casey thought the flower was quite beautiful. She had none of them on her side of the fence. The husband could be watching from the big house but what crime was there in collecting a weed? Without pausing to reconsider, she acted. She threw her book aside, ran barefoot down the outside steps and onto the bank, across the grass and dirt. In that moment she was a child and giddy with the pleasure of running. She went into the lake up to her ankles. She would rescue the flower from the wire because it was beautiful, and surely that couldn't be a crime.

Chapter Four

The planet rotated under the aeroplane. Stops in unknown, too-bright cities. May saw their airports and food courts. Auckland with its mirror-clean tiles and sushi. The shepherding and waiting and sitting. She saw a San Francisco runway through tall walls of glass and a man walked by in a cowboy hat that seemed like it must be a joke. People brought her trays of food and small drinks and delivered them with new accents. When it was too much she wedged in her earbuds and closed her eyes. The hours. The dryness and impossibility of sleep. The journey was so much longer than any May had taken before. She had imagined travel like this and knew it from films and had always imagined that she would savour it. Revel, even, in the exhaustion and dehydration. Here she was, though, and she couldn't find her place in it.

Nebraska came at dawn.

A couple in her row had asked for the aisle because the man had a tricky belly and might need to make a run for the toilets. So May was by the window and the washed-out landscape sweeping under them. The vision was a haze with the focus of the ground itself seeming off. All pink-yellow into an indefinite distance. They were into the landing descent, and so this haze must have been the industry of the city making the grey lines of roads and rectangles of factory tops. Then rivers broke in and May now understood why people always said they snaked. She supposed the ones at home did the same, but standing at the banks a person couldn't tell. These Nebraskan rivers were thinned-out straights and then bulging corners, as if some rat was working its way through the animal's guts.

'Coming home?' the woman of the couple had asked after they landed.

May had removed her earbuds and gone to speak but then there had been a commotion with the man and his tricky stomach.

Inside the terminal she waited for her suitcase and then stood at the car rental counter where the attendant bombarded May with politeness and warmth. Sunrise was still in the act of occurring while the customer service representative gushed directions and well-wishes and gentle concern.

She made it through the last of the terminal and outside. May had not slept for a moment of the flight and with every passing minute on land she grew only more tired, sore, raw, and this new world grew in volume. The United States of America was so far a place of only loudness. The arcades, planes overhead and luggage carousels. Voices, wind and grass. Insects. Even this sunrise seemed to make a long, scratching sound as it transpired above.

No, she was being unfair. Oversensitive.

May wanted sleep. A bed. What hour would it be for her son? Had he eaten? Yes. He had never not eaten. Jesus. She looked to the brightening horizon and heard its metallic creak. No, she was being unfair.

The car park was busy and efficient and she became aware of now being beneath the wide Nebraskan sky. She guessed there might be something novel and memorable about it if she were to raise her eyes but that was too taxing to contemplate. May loaded her luggage into the boot of the car and stood for a minute at the driver's-side door and wiped down her face and neck with the alcohol wipes from the customer service representative. No, Suzanne. Her name had been Suzanne.

May drove three slow laps of the car park and got an encouraging wave each time from a man who was filling gas bottles at the service station. This, then, must be enough of getting used to being on the wrong side of the car and driving on the wrong side of the road, so she drove onto the highway and joined the slowest lane, which still seemed much too fast. And the noise. The directions were on a piece of paper on the passenger seat; Suzanne had underlined *Loveland* on the final line and made the 'o' into a heart. May turned on the radio and couldn't work out how to change the channel and so the selection was the last driver's. Suzanne had said it would be a ninety-minute drive. Two hours if she stopped, as Suzanne said she must, at the most perfect little breakfast place.

Electricity towers. Steel cables to the horizon. The pink-yellow had become yellow alone. An overpowering yellow. Lorries. They would be called trucks here. Semis. Rigs. Great speeding things trying to suck her rental car into the monstrous left lane. She thought of the mother and the inheritance and the grandmother. Maybe the grandmother should be *Casey* here. That was her name then. It didn't seem strange here. Casey. May thought of her son. The phone call to her husband she was supposed to have made the moment she landed. The call she would normally be in a panic to make and yet now, here, she felt no compulsion towards. The husband was so far away. She imagined him speaking but no sound left his mouth. He was so far away. Then came the roar of a truck, discharging its horns as it filled the frame of May's shaking door window. The radio. 'A Horse with No Name'.

—

The breakfast place was exactly where Suzanne's directions described and it was a relief to pull off the highway. The woman at the counter and the man bringing the food and coffee fussed over May's accent. They asked her to judge their own renditions of this terrific word, *Australia*. May looked at her phone and did the sums to work out the time back on the Sunshine Coast. Imagined what Patrick would be doing if she made the call just then. The call she realised she wouldn't be making. It was that small in the end. A realisation not a decision. She hadn't called him.

When she couldn't finish her second slice of cherry pie they put it on a tray and then in a paper bag and sent her back out to the highway with serviettes and wooden cutlery. 'Mississippi Queen'. The screeching sky. Right lane, right lane, right lane.

Suzanne's directions came to an end and so May arrived at this place, Loveland, with its underlining and heart. There was a sign that announced the town, then the sight of its first buildings, all churches. Then the Loveland Volunteer Fire Department, which had chains across its giant doors, then more churches. The regular houses began and each with wide, deep porches. May thought of the television shows of her childhood. Those porches with their family scenes: a mother yelling for a boy to be home for supper.

Trees shadowed the length of every street. Some kind that looked like artificial Christmas trees. And pick-up trucks. Every driveway was loaded with these overgrown things that seemed like kids' toys become real. American flags stuck in lawns. Waving from flagpoles. Then other flags, red ones around the letter 'N'. GO BIG RED on a sign in a front window.

The car's clock said 07.31. There were more of these pick-ups on the road and people walking the footpaths as May found what must have been the town centre. There was a dark statue of a man on a horse outside a place that looked like the diners in films, so May parked in the lot to its side. That second slice of pie was still half-eaten in its bag but she ached for water. Water and coffee and a bathroom.

A teenage girl in a candy-striped shirt greeted May and called her *ma'am* and told her to take a seat, and two women in the next booth smiled as she sat.

The teenager presented a cup and saucer and began to pour black coffee from a jug.

'Could I get some water, please?' May asked.

'What's that?' The teenager tilted her broad, gentle face. Pointed at May's mouth. 'That voice.'

'Australia?'

'Thought so.' She finished pouring and set down a jug of milk. 'That's what I thought. Can I get you some breakfast?'

'Just the coffee.' May looked over her shoulder to the still-staring, still-smiling women. 'And that water, please. Coffee and water, thank you.'

'Coming up. Sing out if you need.'

May found the bathroom and after going in the stall, scrubbed her hands and, avoiding the mirror, drank from the tap. Back in her booth she fixed her coffee with milk and watched the street. Pick-ups and people walking dogs. She took some folded papers from her bag. The papers Karl had talked her through and she thought she understood enough of. Letters of Administration. A Certificate of Title. She found the page she was after with the address scored through with yellow highlighter.

'Loveland'

Loveland Drive

Loveland, NE

Below this was a map Karl had printed out and then drawn over. An elongated yellow oval at the edge of Loveland Lake. Karl had said it was an oxbow lake. Shaped like a horseshoe and left after a river floods, he'd said, and winked. He'd looked it up.

May had bought an adapter at the airport and was charging her phone from a point under her table. She searched an online map and again found the town, the lake, but not the house.

When she'd finished her coffee she turned to the women in the booth behind.

'Hi there. Good morning,' one said.

'Good morning,' said the other. 'How are you?'

'Fine,' May said. 'Thank you. I'm fine.'

'That's great.'

'That's great.'

'Fine day.'

'Fine day.'

The two women continued with a barrage of pleasantries, speaking over the tail end of each other's words. She assumed they were sisters.

May's exhaustion hit again, deeper, and she reached for her song. Told herself there are collections of particles in some particular and temporary arrangement and we assign them values for a time. She gave the coffee mime to the teenager at the register.

'Do you live here?' May asked the women. 'If you don't mind me asking. In Loveland, I mean.'

'Always have,' they said. 'Oh, you're Australian? We just love it. Whenever it's on television. We love that Hugh Jackman. We admit that. But you know about him. Keith Urban. Such a cutie. Nicole. Love them.'

They stared at her with an intensity that was frightening but May knew it was only kindness. Kindness and enthusiasm. She needed another coffee. She finished her water.

'I'm looking for a house.' May reached for her papers. 'A particular house.'

'Yes, yes.'

'I don't have all the information, that's the trouble.' She held up the page with the circled lake. 'Loveland, in apostrophes. I guess that's the name of the house? Loveland Drive. Loveland, Nebraska. I think I've found the last part.'

'Oh,' the women said. They looked at the map closely, then turned to each other and produced another neutral *oh*. Their smiles didn't dim, yet they seemed on the edge of something.

'I can't find a Loveland Drive,' May said. 'These roads by the lake don't seem to have names.' Her cheeks ached from holding a shape like a smile.

The teenager arrived with the coffee. 'And ladies, your eggs are a minute off. Top up? Are you lost, ma'am? Maybe we can help.'

'She's looking for the boathouse.'

'You don't want to go there,' the teenager said and began wiping the table. 'Unless you're official. You're from the government? Council? No? Well then, plenty of beautiful places to see in Loveland before you go down that far. To see the lake I'd go up by the old blue church on the south side. You don't want to go near the water, but there's a square of park that's still pretty at the back of the blue church. We call it the blue church because it's the prettiest shade you've ever seen. They say it was painted the exact shade of the spring sky so that you couldn't tell where the church ended and heaven began. They boarded it up a long time ago and it's not as blue as it was. Still, it's pretty.'

'Or Lakeview,' the women said. 'Take a picnic lunch out to Lakeview. You can't actually see the lake from there, but it's pretty too. Or the civil war museum? That's just near. Of course, the war didn't make it to Nebraska. Plenty of Nebraskans left to fight, though. Plenty. Proud of them. And on the good side, of course. We're proud of that, aren't we? The right side, it turns out.'

'That sounds lovely,' May said. 'All of it. I will need to find this house, though. The boathouse, you called it. It's mine, that's the thing. Well, my mother's. I mean it was my grandmother's and she died. Passed away. There's this house and some land. I'm not making sense. I'm here to settle things.'

May flattened out her map on the booth's table. The teenager let out a high, gentle *hmmm*.

'Can I trouble you for directions?' May asked. 'This thing is useless.' She tapped her phone with a fingertip.

'You're saying you're Casey Love's granddaughter?' the women asked.

'Casey, yes. It was Casey Lawrence, though.'

'And Moses Love was your grandfather?'

'That's right, but it was Lawrence, not Love.'

The teenager and the women went quiet. May's coffee spun slowly in its cup. Her muscles seized the opportunity to scream for sleep.

'I don't mean to correct you, but it's definitely Love,' the teenager said. 'Casey and Moses Love. Maybe she changed her name, after? It was Love back in the day though, no doubt about it.'

'I'm not sure I understand,' May said. 'How could you know that?'

'Because the Love family founded the town.' The sisters now. 'But you know about that.'

'I don't know any of it.'

'Were they miners? Smelters. Iron smelters. Built the town. Generations of the Love family right down to your grandparents. That was the end, I suppose. After the . . . difficulties.'

Through the tall windows daylight was imposing itself. The light and its great metallic noise. This was all too much to consider and far too much to comprehend. Her grandmother had always been a Lawrence. That's the only name May had heard and she'd never had reason to think any more of it. Now this *Love*. Iron smelters. Is smelting just melting? Too much. She would drink her coffee and ask again for the directions to the house. The boathouse. Too much. A thought of her son, a second's flash of his face, broke through and her chest compressed. She would keep moving. She would drink her coffee and take directions.

The road followed a long, bare curve. It had been ten minutes' drive from the diner. Ten minutes after the thankyous and good wishes and promises to return. Ten minutes, a last house and then nothing but yellowed grass before the road dipped and the lake simply appeared. The shape of a horseshoe miles wide and the colour of cheap soft drink.

The water shone more brilliantly than the sky. It was an almost phosphorescent yellow-green. When Francis was sick as a toddler, May would wipe his nose and the tissue would become this colour and she would take him to a doctor. The sting of her chest. She forced her eyeline up to see the opposite side of the lake, which was bordered with a line of golden trees. She drove on towards the inner arc of the horse's shoe, where she could then see a lone house at the shore. She continued till the bitumen ran out and pulled over into the loose gravel.

It was a sight that seemed artificial. Like a body of water had been dropped into a film with computers. It looked like medicine. She looked down at the small building and could see the lines of a chain-link fence. Maybe twelve feet high and a hundred yards clear from the house at its nearest point, it curved around until it met the water's edge on both sides. It was draped with rubbish and streamers of old plastic bags. Barbed wire ran along its top. At the centre of this wasteland was the house. The boathouse. Love house. Whatever it would be. It looked neat and well-kept, two storeys, square and built of dark wooden boards with a steeply pitched roof. Its windows and door were boarded over with sheets of ply.

May stepped out of the car and the hot wind and stench found her immediately. It smelled of what seemed to be salt and fish but overrun with some other chemistry. Burnt coffee was the nearest note she could fix on. But that was too singular. Garbage. It smelled like general, non-specific garbage.

Any plan of keeping this world from her senses failed. It was too much and too new. The place was beyond denying and so May opened her eyes fully. Accepted the light. Listened to the wind. She had arrived.

The hard ground stayed firm underfoot all the way to the fence. May shook at the metal briefly and an empty beer can came loose and fell at her feet. The boathouse. After the talk in the diner of her grandparents and the Love family's fortunes she had begun to wonder if she might be arriving at a house of some majesty, but this was no mansion. It looked only large enough for a couple of rooms. She walked along the fence line and ran her fingers against the wire. As she got to the shore she could see fully the lake side of the house and the two wide openings across the width of the lower floor. Twenty yards of earth lay between the boat bays and the foamy edge of the water.

A metal picket bracing a sign was lying face down on the ground. May found its edge and turned it over. WARNING written black and bold against red.

LAKE CLOSED
CONTAMINATED
TOXIC SUBSTANCES MAY BE
PRESENT IN THIS WATERWAY
NO WADING NO SWIMMING

NO BOATING NO ANCHORING
NO FISHING NO DOGS
CALL YOUR DOCTOR OR VETERINARIAN IF YOU OR
YOUR ANIMALS HAVE SUDDEN OR UNEXPLAINED
SICKNESS OR SIGNS OF POISONING.

The breeze swung around and blew over the lake. The smell was swirling and turning newly specific. It was of a particular communal toilet block at a caravan park where May had stayed when she was ten. Then like burning oil. The smell of her grandmother's sewing machine when she had finished her day's work. Finally, the scent that gathers in the decomposing litter beneath forest trees. The fallen leaves and soil and animal bodies becoming one within the moisture. All turning over and over. It was death but it was sweet.

May was so tired. Her skin was so dry. She wanted only peace or rest or to escape the sun. Lawrence or Love? Names. We assign values for a time. She let the sign fall back to the wet earth and returned to her car.

⌒

The rainforest began just behind May's primary school. She had learned from a library book about biomes and categories of living and drawn it all up on a sheet of curling cardboard to present to the class. Desert, bog, tundra, savanna. Swamp, woodland, rainforest. She drew arrows and titles and the creatures you would find. The teacher was so often unfair but this time told May what a good job she'd done. Got the class to applaud. So May knew about rainforests and was nine years old and so was qualified to call this dense magical place behind the school one.

A rainforest that was as good as private and almost a secret. She would sometimes cross paths with an old couple charging through with their binoculars and hiking boots, looking up into the canopy for birds. Sometimes, deeper in, she would discover high-schoolers moving in a huddle around cigarettes. May would hide from the trespassers. Leap off the faint track and into the ferns. She would find a log, a stump, and put her skinny body behind it and wait for the voices to trail away. This would be any afternoon after the final school bell and in the couple of hours before she would be expected for dinner or any of the daylight hours of those eternal weekends. This happened to be a Saturday morning, with all time ahead of her as she waited for the humans to pass. She found beetles in the soil and beneath the trees' bark and they crawled peacefully across her.

Running deeper and deeper in, under the call of the whipbirds and broken light, she eventually emerged into the clearing with the waterfall. It wasn't much, nothing to put on a postcard or a tourist trail, but this made it all the more hers.

A mountain of grey boulders began, high above May's four and a half feet. That tiny body. A stream fell from the cliff above. A constant, clear fall of water into the green bowl below that was made of stone with a shallow carpet of moss. She thought the high cliff looked like a loaf of bread that had been squashed in at one end on the drive home from the supermarket. The water came and came, whatever the season. She took off her dress and laid it where the sun would keep it dry and warm for after. Underneath it she wore her swimmers, the ones with the seashells.

The water was cold and it bit hard as she stepped in. She imagined it coming from mountains covered in snow and creatures with white fur. She thought of her biomes. The categories of living. May dived into the water without hesitating because she knew it was hesitation that hurt a person. Got a person thinking. Some sportsperson had said that on television. Allan Border. Martina Navratilova. Someone. May was bad at sports and so wouldn't watch it but she liked that one thing she'd heard. So she dived and hit the icy water before a choice needed to be made because once you're in, you're in, and you're beyond the situation.

She swam out to the deepest part of the pool where she couldn't touch the bottom and floated on her back, adjusting her position with the paddles of her hands. She looked up at the circle of sky. The treetops reaching in. She heard those whipbirds. The scrub turkeys. The beetles in the wet leaves of the ground. The water kept coming from that stone cliff and she slowly directed herself into the fall. Its noise overtook everything, rising louder until the water began to slap against her face, her chest, and for that time she was a part of this tumbling animal.

It was alive. It spoke, at least. It raised its voice above the others and May was in total, deathly peace.

In here there was no time before or after. No history with its sounds of fighting on the other side of a bedroom door. A father's absence being explained in a new tone of her mother's voice that became her lasting one. The direct, calming, tired one. The same as May's grandmother's. The explanations about money and the need for the adults to be working the days, nights and weekends. Yes, they understood that meant all the time there was. Under the fall there was no future in which May would become another of these direct, calming, tired women. Here was only the freedom of oblivion.

She came out the other side, the world returned, and May stretched out her limbs to make her swimming motions. She became aware again of the cold. She spun slowly around the cascade. Behind into the echo and shade of the cliff's overhang, then out into the broken daylight. She listened out for the oldies and teenagers but heard only the birds and insects so went to the water's edge and pulled herself up onto the flat rock. The whipbirds and scrub turkeys and beetles. She would make her own noises. The breathing of just another animal and the gentle slap of her wet hands against dry rock.

A breeze found its way across the water and May filled her lungs with it. It brought the strong smell of humus. She remembered this word from a library book. The floor of the rainforest where the fallen leaves and animals break down and turn to dark soil. It was always being added to and turned over and over. May thought of the death of all those animals and plants and decided it smelled sweet, like licorice.

~

Standing at the counter of the general store, May called out to the figure at the top of the ladder.

'Hello there,' the woman answered and set the last of a stack of great tins on a shelf.

'I need some tools,' May told her. The air smelled of grease. Sawdust. New plastic. 'Could you help me?'

'Hey, what's that voice?'

'Australia.'

'I love Australia.' The woman stepped down the ladder. 'Oh, your poor Irwin. That crocodile man. God bless him. Hardware, that's us. Hardware, lumber, feed, groceries, liquor.' She put two fingers in her mouth and whistled. 'What are you after?'

'I'm not sure.'

'Don't you worry. Tate'—the woman whistled again—'my Tate will help you.'

A boy came from the back where the shelves of food stopped and led into a space like a repair shop. Some men were there, making a racket with chains and lengths of wood. The boy walked with a slow, robotic gait and the woman slapped him on the hip when he arrived.

'Good morning, customer,' he said with an overdone charm. 'Welcome to Miller's General Store. How can I help you today?' He saluted, bringing the tips of his fingers to his temple through a curtain of oily hair.

'Tools,' May said.

'Tools,' Tate said seriously. 'Mom, the customer wants tools.'

'Well, help her then.' The woman smiled grimly.

'Follow me, customer.'

Tate marched towards the back with the same affected walk. The mother apologised to May and called out for her son to quit with the smartass routine.

'It's fine,' May said. 'I have one of my own.'

'A smartass?'

'A teenage boy. Yes.'

'Let me know if you need another,' the woman said and started back up her ladder.

The men were still making noise, pouring chain into the back of a truck at the building's open side.

'Customer—tools,' Tate said and fanned his palms towards two long aisles.

She was too tired, too aching. Altogether too everything. 'Your name's Tate?'

'My name is Tate. Tate is here to serve your every need.'

'Tate, it's nice to meet you. I'm May.' She stepped close and spoke in a calm, flat voice. 'I understand that you don't want to be here this morning. I don't want to be here either. The thing is, Tate, we're here. This is happening. Destiny has brought us together. So how about you quit the cute stuff, help me out and we get on with our miserable lives.'

He took his hands from his jeans pockets and stared into May's eyes.

She didn't recognise this voice she was speaking with. The tremendous space between this new world and her home. Some part of her seemed to have expanded already to fill it. She liked the sound of this new voice. How it felt in the jaw.

She looked back at the boy and the scattering of blemishes across his nose. His centre-parted hair had been badly dyed black. May didn't blink.

The boy smiled. 'What do you need?'

'I need to break into a house.'

'Lost your keys?'

'Never had any keys. I'll need something to get through a fence. Something to take the boards off some windows. And something to open a front door. I assume it's locked. Either way, I think we need some tools here, Tate.'

'If I help you here, May, am I going to get a special visit from the sheriff?' he asked. 'Because I do not require any more special visits from the sheriff. And trust me when I say my mother does not require it.'

'I just need your help.'

'Where's your house?'

'The boathouse at the lake.'

'You want to break into the boathouse?'

'I really do not have the life force necessary to give you the full background and history of this. Can we just not talk about it, Tate?'

He rubbed his hands together and smiled. He started to scan the racks, pulling off tools as he went and gripping them under one arm. A hammer. A crowbar. A plastic-wrapped set of screwdrivers. More.

'I'll need to clean, too,' May said.

In the next aisle, Tate collected a pair of buckets, spray bottles of cleaning fluid, sponges, rags, and put them into a plastic bin.

'Wait,' she said. 'I'll need to check the prices. We might need to—'

He held up a hand. 'You are clearly unfamiliar with the charitable nature of the residents of Loveland. When one of us is in need, we are all in need.'

He pushed the bin into her hands.

'Tate—'

'Accept the kindness, shut up and follow me.'

He checked for his mother and then signalled for May to stay quiet and hurry. The pair triggered the store's automatic doors while the mother worked at her high shelf.

'Mom,' Tate called out. 'I'm heading out. Rendering assistance. Full service.'

May tried to raise a hand but nearly dropped her bin and by then Tate was ushering her into the street. He kept calling out to his mother, smiling, waving, giving assurances. May recognised a look of familiar resignation on the woman's face.

'My mother understands the needs of her community. Where's your car?'

They unloaded across its back seat.

'I can't take all this,' May said.

'You're not,' Tate said. 'You're hiring me. The gear is complimentary but my expertise ain't free.'

'How much?' May leaned into the car's roof, looking across at the boy.

'A sixpack.'

'I'm not buying you beer.'

'Mother keeps count of the booze here. It's a shocking lack of trust.' He settled into the passenger seat and put his boots up on the dash. 'We can negotiate my fee on the way.'

May heard her son. Saw his long legs and the shape of his better smile. The kind, rarer one.

'I'm not buying you beer,' she said. 'How old are you, exactly?'

'How much do you need my help, exactly?'

Tate used boltcutters to make an opening in the chain-link fence the rough dimensions of a doorway and then bent away the sharp edges with pliers. Faded chip packets and shopping bags tumbled by on the wind. As they drove to the boathouse Tate had told May what he knew. That it had forever been a place where the local teenagers went to drink and smoke. To party, whatever. He hadn't been in a while, though. Bit out of the loop of things. His mother had partied there with her friends back in the day. Friday nights at the boathouse was a ritual dating back to the dawn of civilisation. Then it was boarded up again. The fence fixed again. And the kids found somewhere else to trash for a while.

'Damn kids.' Tate pulled at the front of his shirt.

The bottom floor seemed to be only an enclosed, empty space. She had looked through a gap in the timber walls and seen a dried mud floor with something in shadow, maybe furniture, sitting at the back under sheets. They scaled the staircase at the side of the house and stood at the sealed door on the second floor, where a verandah started and ran around the side facing the lake. Tate started to work on the door. He pulled away the plywood sheeting and poked at the lock. The wind turned and blew the smell of the lake over them; it had returned through its cycle to hot garbage.

'If you're staying, I'll help you put a decent bolt on this,' Tate said.

'I'm not staying.'

'It's too easy to pick these regular locks. Picking's not illegal, if you're wondering. I bought a kit online. A modern lock uses technology that's two hundred years old. Did you know that?'

May imagined the squalid den they would find inside. The punched-in and graffitied walls. Burger wrappers and discarded needles. A piss-wet mattress. Then something more Dickensian. She thought it was Dickens. Anyway, one of those television series. Rooms of gilded darkness with cobwebs and candlesticks and a pale, powdered woman attending to herself in the mirror.

Tate turned the handle and pushed the door open with his palm. He stood aside and May walked into the darkness and this mystery of her grandmother. She wondered for a second if it would smell of her perfume. This secret place of her family.

'I'll get the windows open,' Tate said.

The house was immaculate. With light from the open doorway May could see the bare but pristine state. Gleaming, waxed wood in every direction. Floor, walls, ceiling. A kitchen, a large open space and a small, closed room in one corner. As Tate went ahead and prised away each window's plywood panel the house grew brighter and became a richer shade of honey. Light, peach curtains covered the windows and May walked along, pulling them open. The daylight was crayon yellow and it hit the mahogany of the flooring and lit the room into a life-giving blaze. Tate was enjoying himself. He held two nails in the corner of his mouth and shook his hammer in triumph as the last sheet of ply pulled away.

The lake side consisted of more neat windows. At the middle were two glass-panelled doors which the boy had pushed open. He was carrying the plyboard through to the far corner of the verandah and sending each piece spinning down to the ground.

She came out to look at the scattered mess. 'Did we have to do that?'

'May, the planet ain't getting any deader. Can't get worse than dead. I could chuck every scrap of Nebraska's trash into this lake and you would not notice the difference. The thing is dead. Long, long dead.'

She heard her son's voice. Francis's relentless moan of *What does it matter?* May had always insisted that it did matter, whatever it was, for reasons she never actually believed. She secretly enjoyed his moaning because it reminded her of when he was a toddler. When he was truly untouched and hers. She leaned against the verandah's railing and Tate copied her. He had the same smell as Francis. Deodorant, milk and cola. She closed her eyes and listened for her son's angry noises through the wall. Her mother's weary conversations on the phone. Her grandmother's sewing machine.

'I'll pick them up later,' she said.

He shrugged.

'I thought it would be worse.' May walked back inside and ran a finger against the window glass. 'From the partying, *or whatever.*'

'It *is* worse, then. It gets totally trashed. But Jean swoops in after and cleans up. Gets the windows fixed. The fence, whatever.'

'Who's Jean?'

'I figured you knew her.' He went to the kitchen and ran water into the sink. He pushed his head under the stream then sent it back, spraying water up the wall.

'Who is she?'

'Just Jean, I don't know,' he said. 'She lives a little way back towards town. Old lady. Real old. You don't know her? Been here forever and been watching out for this place. I figured you were related.'

So now another name and another part of the story May didn't understand. Maybe understanding was asking too much. It certainly seemed it to her flagging, dehydrated mind.

The boy was pacing the room with his excessive teenage strides. He kept running his fingers back into his hair and then drumming on the wooden walls with his palms. May couldn't remember being this young.

He had arrived at the door of the final, closed room. He fanned out his lock picks and May shrugged and agreed. He began as May walked in a pondering circle. The house might be worth something after all. She began to consider an agent's banter. Period charm. Original features. A rare opportunity.

'Hey, the water's on,' she said, realising she should have been surprised at this. She walked to a brass switch on the wall and found it working. A ceiling light blinked in and out of being. A glass jellyfish shade, clean of dust.

'Alakazam.' Tate pushed the small room's door open.

May walked inside and enough light fell in from the main space to reveal a plain bedroom. The bed against the opposite wall was a narrow double, fully made up with bedding and pillows, all bound under transparent plastic sheeting. Two small nightstands and a dressing table were likewise wrapped. An old and shining lantern rested in the centre of a small table and May stroked it with a finger. Chairs were stacked in one corner to the side of an infant's cot, and hanging above the bed was a small painting of a red plain. A desert beneath a dark and vacant sky.

May sat on the floor and leaned her weight against the side of the mattress. Her body burned to rest. She could close her eyes and sleep. It could be that simple. Had this bed been her grandmother's? Casey. She was Casey now. As May shifted, the bedding's plastic sheet let out a disapproving squeak.

⌒

May, the child, had been at the waterfall again. It was right on midday, in one of the summers that stretched to meet itself again the year after. May's grandmother would have heard her hit the gravel driveway on her bike. May would build speed the length of Glasshouse View Court, never touching her brakes from where the decline began at the shops. When she rounded the corner before her house she would have to quickly aim her BMX at a precise point where the bitumen met the concrete lip of their drive, because if she got it wrong she would be sent off into the disaster of trees and thorny scrub. May knew the angle, though, and spotted her mark, so on this day met the gravel at full tilt, locked on the back brake and swung her tail out in a perfect arc. The stones sprayed the red bricks of the house. Some pelted against the glass of a window and May saw her grandmother on the other side. The woman could never be startled. May's grandmother had never flinched. May leaned the bike against the wall of the carport and when she got to the front door it was being held open.

'You've been out in the bush?'

'Yep.'

Her grandmother wasn't angry; she was never angry.

They walked into the living room and May took her place cross-legged on the floor in front of the lounge while her grandmother sat behind and began searching for ticks. The comb was in her left hand and the tweezers waiting in her right. You had to get them early or they could make trouble. May would close her eyes and wait for the scratch of the plastic teeth against her scalp. Her grandmother would start at the centre part and move her way slowly, meticulously to the ears.

'One,' she said and carried the tiny creature across to the saucer on the coffee table.

May opened her eyes to watch as the tick was broken in half with the tweezer tips. You had to get them early, before they burrowed in.

May closed her eyes and felt again the plastic scratch. Her grandmother's feet pushed in at May's hips and she felt the last of the water in her swimmers. They would soon dry. There was no point in changing.

'Two.'

'Grandma, did you have ticks where you grew up?'

The woman didn't pause. Just kept on with her parting and searching. 'No.'

'None at all?'

'Three. None at all.'

'So what did you have?'

A smell arrived of something in the kitchen. It would be one of her grandmother's slow casseroles. The ones that took a whole day, bubbling away secretly on the stovetop. May's mother would still be at work when dinnertime came, so later she would heat hers in the microwave and sit in front of the television, mute with the day and night's work. She would shower only after she ate, so for that while the room would smell of May's mother. Of sweat and bleach.

'Four.'

The tick went ruined into the saucer. This, *four*, was one of the few words that held something of the grandmother's accent. The one from when she was a child. American.

'What did you have then?' May asked again, knowing there would be no answer but asking anyway, to make some point. 'Where you grew up.'

The woman only kept on with her comb, parting, parting. She felt no need to fill the silence and so May imagined there had been some decision made a very long time before by her grandmother that she would never talk of being young. That could be the only explanation. She had made the decision to begin later, in a different place, and so would only respond with silence to these questions of youth. Still, May would ask them.

'There must have been something,' May said. 'What would bite you?'

'Stay still. This one's gone in.'

May steadied herself and dug her fingernails into her thighs. She knew not to resist, having been here so many times before. The quicker the better, always. The tick would have burrowed its head into her scalp and her grandmother would need to get the tweezers as flush against the skin as she could.

'Straight out, never twist.'

'Straight out, never twist,' May echoed.

If the body came away but the head stayed in the flesh it would poison her blood. May knew this, so knew to sit straight and still. Hair always came out with the creature and it always hurt. The pressure started and May pushed her nails in deeper. Straight and still. The pain came to a sudden end and she watched the ugly thing go to the saucer and lie dead amid the smears of her blood.

Her grandmother had taught her that the tick's trick was that you didn't feel them latch on. There was no first sting.

They worked their way in and if you weren't lucky enough to have someone checking on you then it would be too late when you did spot it. The tick would poison your blood and make you weak and one day there might be a sleep you never woke from.

'Did you get it all?' May asked.

'I did.'

'You're sure?'

'Brave girl.' Her grandmother patted May's shoulder and went to get the rubbing alcohol.

⌒

'This Jean,' May said. 'You know where she lives?'

Tate stared blankly. 'Everybody knows where everybody lives.'

'Show me.'

'We can stop at the liquor store on the way.'

'I'm not buying you beer,' May said.

'I guess I could write you up an invoice for all this.'

May gave her expression of exhausted resistance. The well-worn one.

A dragonfly perched on the bed beside her and May's first thought was to leap to her feet but the energy didn't reach her legs. Did dragonflies bite? Were they venomous? Maybe her grandmother had dealt with these here and would have known. Casey. It was Casey. A wind gust found its way in from the water and was enough to send the insect back into flight and out of the room. The odour of the air had lessened. They say you grow used to things.

'What is the drinking age here?' she asked.

Tate only smiled and paced, drumming his rhythm on the wall.

LOVELAND, MAY 1956

It had seemed a long day and so Casey was happy for the sun to have fallen behind the horizon and for the night's settling-in to begin. Moses walked the perimeter of their home. Clockwise. Always clockwise. He checked the rope on the wooden dinghy in the shallows. She had been out on the water again. Too often, she knew, but there were so many questions to be asked out there. Music was carried on the wind from the big house, where they were having another of their dinners. Moses finished his circling and came inside. He checked the door lock. He seemed to conclude that all was well as Casey caught the smell of the workers' meats roasting.

Moses adjusted the curtains of their bedroom window and looked briefly opposite to Casey's painting. The one he had bought in the first days of her arrival. She had seen it in town and talked of Australia, the place she had read about with its strange animals and outback. She wanted to go one day. It was a dream of hers. He had said the painting was clearly of a Nebraskan plain, and ugly, but had taken out his wallet all the same. He said he would do whatever was needed to make her happy.

He checked the curtains again at the open square where the bedroom window had been removed. He must have thought on this and wondered if he shouldn't have allowed it, but he kept a constant watch and he might in the end have thought of this as being one less barrier between her and their love. And he did love her. That's what he said. That's the word the husband used for this.

Love.

The Christian name given to him by his parents came to be left on the doormat. There was no more Moses and he was always and only the husband now. The words amused him at first and then became a source of contentment. They were Man and Wife, he and Casey, and so he had become the husband. Protector of Casey and their love. One day the glory would return to this place and he would lay a stone path from the hotel to the boathouse and it would remind them of their early times.

These things he said.

The husband would guard their love from the harm that threatened outside. It would remain full, waiting for her to recognise it. And when that time came he would ask for no thanks or apology. Their family and future would be enough.

All his names for this.

The sounds from the top of the hill came again. There had been only one set of guests that week. A young-seeming couple with a little girl. Casey had seen them having breakfast and later watched the child swimming for a short time before the dear thing was wrapped in towels and taken back inside. When the place was free of guests and there were no bookings the staff would come together and make a feast of the fresh food to save it from going to waste. They would sit at the longest table of the hotel dining room with the doors and windows pushed open. A banquet. They would play records and their laughter and talk would spill out over the water.

In the boathouse Casey finished in the kitchen and moved to the bedroom. There was a dragonfly on her bedside table with its wings tucked behind its body, at rest. Casey put out the lamp and felt for the breeze. The husband would allow the curtain of the window space to remain open. There would be nothing between them and a happy life but the still-warm air steeped with charred herbs and music. He reached for her and the muscles of her body turned to stone. She imagined the cold steel blade with its point at her neck. The wind arrived with its sounds from the hilltop. The family laughter that would one day be theirs. All his names for this.

Chapter Five

Jean's house was among the final few on the curve before the decline to the lake. Hers was the least well kept. Not a wreck, but certainly not the tamed exhibitions of the others. Tate had pointed out the house as she drove him back into town, where they had stopped outside the liquor store and May was relieved to see it not yet open. Tate had made her put her hand to her heart and swear an oath that she understood her debt. The personal, unbreakable contract into which they had entered.

A sixpack. Swear.

I swear.

Now alone, parked in front of Jean's, May closed her eyes and pushed her face against the car's air vents. Her shirt was stale with sweat. It was ten in the morning, surely a reasonable time to knock on someone's door. Tate had said that the woman was maybe ninety. A teacher or something like that.

'What was her story?' May asked.

'Couldn't tell you. An old lady. Keeps a lookout for the boathouse. Now you know as much as me.'

The heat here wasn't like that of home. In Queensland, the heat fell from the sky, but here it came from every direction. It rose up from the soil, out from the trees' cores, seeping through the hopeless glass and metal of her Volkswagen Jetta. Casey had lived in this. Wiped this glue of humidity and dust from her neck. May tried to remember photographs of the woman when she was young but could only picture the years of the woman's Australian life, when May's mother was already a young girl and Casey was in the embrace of middle age. The heat of the car's failing air conditioning reminded May of her need for sleep. Brought it back to the front page of her mind. Anything, *anything* for some goddamn sleep.

The gate to Jean's house needed a shove to open and May followed a paved path towards the porch. It was a narrow block with the house set back among a garden of flowering trees and bushes and the lawn was either absent or knee-high. Dirt or forgetfulness. She reached the door, pressed the bell and heard electronic tones making a song deep within the house. The neighbours in both directions were mostly out of sight behind trees. May tried to centre herself around some words. *Hello. Jean.* They had lost any meaning. Words seemed to do that here. Maybe Tate was full of it and the lady didn't even live here. Or if she was really so ancient then maybe she had died. Maybe she'd never existed and this was all just a name given to a teenage boy's misunderstandings. The sound of her son, again, through the wall.

The door opened. A woman held a telephone receiver to her ear and pulled her dress up at one shoulder. Her long, grey hair rested in a disordered mass above her face and she was pulling its stray threads together inside a band. She was nothing like the ninety years old Tate had guessed at. Sixty, maybe seventy. Her eyes connected with May's on three separate occasions within these flourishes and May raised a hand and mouthed *sorry*, pointing at the telephone. The woman stayed motionless for a beat.

'Alan, I'm going to have to call you back. Yeah, soon. There's someone at the door. No, *my* door. At my house, Alan. No, I'm at *my* house. Where did you think—Alan, I'm going to call you back.'

'I'm sorry,' May said.

'The man's an imbecile but he'll survive. Who are you?'

'May.'

'So you are. Wonderful.'

The door closed before May had parted her lips to reply. Not slammed, only closed, as if the woman had just finished returning a trapped wasp into the garden.

May pressed the doorbell and again heard its distant 'Greensleeves'.

'Hello again, May.'

'Jean?'

'Mm-hmm.' The woman put her hand again to the door as if to close it.

The heat. Teenage boys. The cherry pie beginning to turn in her stomach. Sleep or death: whichever answered first.

May put her hand above Jean's on the timber. 'I own the boathouse,' she said. 'Well, my mother. Down at the lake? It was my grandmother's. Casey Lawrence. Or Love. Casey. She was my grandmother and she died and left us the house. A kid, Tate, told me you've been looking after it and I'm wondering about that. What the story is.'

The loud roar of an engine came from somewhere through the trees. May gripped her shirt in fright. A leaf blower.

Jean hadn't moved. She just looked at May; vacant. Her consciousness had fallen briefly from its track.

'Casey died?'

'She died,' May said. 'My grandmother.'

Jean once more fell away. The nearby machine was roaring high as its owner swung it from side to side. The air rushed through hot and dry. Leaves tumbled by.

'I can't help you,' Jean said, and took an awkward gulp of air. It was pained and involuntary, like a child whose finger had caught in the hinge of a door.

The howl of the blower and then again Jean with this noisy suck of breath. She covered her mouth.

'But you've been in my house?' May asked.

The door closed. May heard Jean's steps moving away, then nothing. She pressed the bell and knocked and pressed the bell and knocked. In a front window she saw a set of blinds blink closed and then the man with the leaf blower appeared suddenly through a space in the trees and raised a gloved hand. May waved back when she realised this was required to release her. The machine roared on and no more movement came from inside Jean's house and so May guessed this must be finished.

Whatever this Jean was to the house. The house of nothing but confusion. So then, Jean could stay her mysterious self. What could it matter? Finished, then.

May turned and walked back to the street. The sky was ever-brightening and she raised a hand above her eyes. The grass was in clumps of orange and the lake, when it pestered its way into sight, was its infected green and the smell of a wound.

The coolness inside the boathouse brought no relief and May washed herself in the kitchen sink. She went to the bedroom and glanced only briefly back at the door she had left open and its screaming daylight. Nothing mattered, then, and what could she do, anyway, if it did? Casey with some surname. It was just a name. It couldn't matter and the woman was dead regardless. The house. May had things to do.

She took off her shoes and slid across the tacky plastic that wrapped the bed and placed her head against the hill of trapped pillows. Her forehead and its damp skin. Her sweat-heavy shirt. May thought of her son's clothes that he refused to let her wash. Then his rushed demands for something clean. The arguments he started and she would deflect. She reached in her memory for the smell of her son. The arguing. His breath. Deodorant, milk and cola. Her whole body ached. She banished the tug of living and sleep took her.

Jean leaned into the wood of the doorframe with the lines of her face drawn dark and placid. May had no sensations of having woken; she just knew that her eyes were open and this woman stood looking down at her.

'I knocked,' Jean said. 'I'm sorry. I called out.'

May pushed herself upright and swung her feet down to the floor.

'I'm sorry about before, May. It is May, isn't it? I'm sorry. It's just that I was surprised. Your grandmother. I'm so sorry.' Jean took a slow breath. 'I was wondering if I could make you dinner. I have wine. Do you have plans?'

The light behind Jean consumed her edges and the woman appeared semi-transparent.

'I have no plans,' May said. 'I don't have a thing.'

—

The sun had sunk below the horizon and as they walked up from the lake Jean handed May a set of keys.

'These are yours.'

The humidity had dissipated and left a gentler warmth. They made the flat of the road and Jean let out a comic sigh.

'Casey never mentioned me?'

'No.'

'Okay.' She smiled. 'I'm sorry about your grandmother. I hadn't heard.'

'You knew her.'

'A long time ago.' Jean laughed. 'Fifty years? Sixty. Jesus, that's too long. Too long for anything.'

'My place is a mess,' Jean said, leading May into her house. 'I can't explain it—it just appears. Let's go out the back. Wine, yes? I have red. Oceans of red.'

The house was dim and musty and the hall was lined with overfull bookcases and stacks of printed paper. Dusty folders. The rooms they passed were unlit and smelled of scented candles. Through the kitchen May was pointed to a chair on the deck and she sat among the stems and stretching leaves of potted plants. The air was cut grass and petrol and some music had been started inside. Elvis. May had always hated the sound of him.

'Drink.' Jean stepped outside. 'Drink, drink.'

May shut her eyes as the wine hit the back of her tongue. Patrick would tell her it made her a zombie. Tell her to mix it with water.

'I've got a box of this stuff,' Jean said. 'It just says *red*. I liked the bear on the label.'

They turned themselves towards the backyard. It was long and bare and finished with a parade of trees. They were lean and old and their branches broke into each other and hid whatever lay behind. Fences ran down each side. May wondered who should be asking questions. There was a house that she was only here to settle and so maybe everything else could be lost detail. A past that had ended. Jean had handed over the keys so maybe that was a full stop.

'You have a lot of books,' May said.

'All work, I'm sorry to say. I'm a teacher at the college. In the city.'

'What do you teach?'

'Early modern lit, mostly. I'm hiding in the English department. When they can scrape together a class it's Milton, Spenser. That bunch. Some from later. Dickinson. So, I'm in high demand, as you can imagine. Jesus Christ.' She refilled both their glasses. 'What about you?'

'I don't do much of anything at the moment, now that I think of it.'

'You're my hero.'

'This wine is magnificent.' May held her glass up against the dim sky.

'It's just terrible, isn't it?'

They drank and planes passed overhead. May watched a star begin to move among the others and it soon vanished into the trees. Maybe a satellite. How high did a firefly fly? All the things she would never know.

'What's happening at the lake?' May asked. 'I saw the sign and that colour. Will it kill me?'

'Who knows? I'm starting to think everything has us in its sights. The lake is sick, though, that's for certain. It's been a long time since anyone's pulled a crawdad out of that thing.'

Jean was in the kitchen burning meat. The deck was now lit by a handful of citronella candles with scents so rich they stung. Mosquitoes frolicked in the spirals of smoke.

'Oh hell.'

Jean set two large bowls on the table. One contained a salad of lettuce and roughly cut tomato and the other a stack of steaming, charred steaks. She followed with plates and cutlery and a bowl of orange liquid.

'Welcome to Nebraska,' she said. 'Have you had this? Dorothy Lynch. They say it's salad dressing but you can't be sure.' She speared a steak with her fork, dragged it on to her plate and then painted it thickly with the sauce. 'It's not right. I know that, but here we are.'

May's hunger came as a crash and she devastated her meat. A second steak replaced the first and she laid on stripes of the dressing. It was foul. Her mouth filled with ash and fat and the bear wine and eventually she remembered to breathe. She looked out and the stars were like those from children's books. Bright and perfect. She felt revolted and full and pushed away the last shard of gristle.

'I'm sorry you had to watch that,' she said.

'It was a privilege. I wish I could be that hungry for anything.'

'Terrible.'

'Magnificent. Here we are.'

May held the wine bottle and scratched her nail against the outline of the bear's mouth. Its teeth. Her husband's face. She pressed every thought down under the wine's surface. Down. She looked out at the stars.

'I know you're just being polite by not asking about your grandmother's house. Me and the house, I mean.' Jean was all nervous smile, unwrapping and wrapping her hair. 'Casey really never mentioned me?'

'She never did.'

'I'm going to neck this glass then and start talking because I'm not nearly as polite as you.'

Those lost details. May nodded.

'I started working for your grandparents when I was fifteen, so . . . so, that would have been 1958. Holy shit. 1958. I'm seventy-five now. Did you wonder? I find people wonder, so best just to say it. Seventy-five but I was fifteen once. Fifteen but I was a game little thing. Brassy, my mother would say. Knew myself, I say. I answered an ad and went to work for Moses and Casey. Moses was more than forty then but Casey was only a little older than me. Eighteen? We were as good as sisters and I swear it only took a week. I came out to work for them and within a week your grandmother and I made ourselves sisters.

Moses was always *the husband*. It's how things were back then. Well, how it seemed. This was 1958, remember. Truly, it was a different world. A little better and so much worse. After Moses died everything came to an end. So sudden. Casey left with little Rosie, and I don't mind saying it was the end of whatever drop of young blood was left in me. I'm seventy-five now but I might have turned seventy-five then, do you see?'

'And they were always Love to you?' May asked, sitting forward in her seat.

'Of course.'

'Because they were Lawrence to me. Casey and Moses Lawrence.'

Jean's hair went again, getting twisted into its bun and released. 'What do you know about your grandfather?'

'Nothing, it turns out,' May said. 'He was just the grandfather who died young, when my mother was a baby. I thought it was his heart and that it must have happened in Maine. That's where I thought Casey was from. I'd never heard of Nebraska. Never Loveland.'

Jean nodded and kept at her hair. She drank and looked out into the yard.

May wondered what could come of this. Learning the details. Well, she would let them come and whatever they brought in their wake and it could all join the night and humidity.

Jean stood and took the plates. She would clear the table and refused help. There was ice cream in the freezer. Just vanilla. Plain old vanilla.

The wine found May talking like she hadn't since those friends in school. Jean was brilliant and a nut and told her all the gossip about her college students. The affairs and excuses. Jean took little persuasion to stand and deliver a poem.

'Something, Jean. Anything. Give me something *early modern* so I know what that is. Something that doesn't make me sad.'

Jean agreed and called it 'Song on May Morning'. It was the usual hopeless stuff that failed to form sense in May's ear, like the Shakespeare from school, but Jean gave it enough with her purple-stained teeth that it became something sweet. *The pale primrose. Warm desire.* Jean asked about May's family, her friends, her life, and May answered with names and a smile and said again about the magnificence of the wine.

⌒

It was the night of May's thirtieth birthday that she understood she did not have a friend in the world. It was a realisation that arrived whole. It was just after midnight and she was drunk, alone at the kitchen table in her high-waisted black pants and turtleneck. Her best strappy heels. She had dressed as if she were going out. Earlier in the night, with music playing, she had taken her full-length mirror out into the living room where the light was better. Make-up, perfume. She liked the way she looked in these clothes. She was a person with taste and energy.

Patrick had an early start the next day and she hadn't asked about them going out for dinner. He had showered and gone to bed before ten. So she was home drinking vodka and lemonade and smiling at the thought that there was not a person alive she could truthfully call a friend. A smile was the wrong expression but it didn't matter. This was the point. There was no-one to see it. She was drunk and alone and so she could be truthful. She had no friends and a feeling in her stomach like death was coming.

There had been no severing incident. No proclamations from Patrick that she wasn't to see those girls she had been unbreakable with from school. It had all just been a creep. A slow, noiseless decay. At her kitchen table, May drank and removed a pill of cotton from the sleeve of her turtleneck. Friendships don't need to be killed in some great show. Unfed, they will just shrink and go. Die without protest.

There had been no fences erected between May and those girls. *Those girls.* She had to work to bring their names to the front of her mind. She smiled again. There was nothing she could point to. No great crime of estrangement. Patrick had simply steered their marriage to his way.

He was tired.

He had work early.

He said that she became a zombie when she drank and that she had a son to think of.

So she was thirty and alone, drunk in her best heels without a friend on the planet. Just a husband and wife in a tiny, eternal orbit. She was embarrassed by what they had become but couldn't pin the crime on him so it would stick. He would say she could do whatever she liked. She was no baby. She had only herself to blame.

The birthday girl poured another of her vodka and lemonades and knew her mascara must be running. What a cliché she must look. A woman and her vodka and smeared make-up. She drank and smiled because there was no-one to see. That was the point.

'Nebraska is a place of disappearing,' Jean said, drunk and theatrical and answering no question. 'You can't know it and no-one does. It's this flat line, right? The empty space in the centre. A big old nothing to no-one. The South has flavour, right? It's all rich and heaviness. And the coasts have their own, young kind of taste. But Nebraska's got this intense nothing. Generically Midwestern, I say. Full of the people you'd imagine if you'd never set foot in the place. If you had no imagination and you just drew yourself a generic Midwesterner. Meat, meat and college football. Unbearable summers and unbearable winters. More hours in the day than we have a right to. They say it doesn't have an accent. It's just this middleness. This viscous middleness. A person disappears.'

'It's really something,' May said. 'What you've done for Casey. Keeping up the boathouse. Really something.'

It was 2 a.m. They had been silent and content.

'She didn't know,' Jean said. 'I wrote to her about the house in the early days but she never wanted to know. Asked me to stop talking about it. Gradually the letters got shorter. And further apart. In the end it was just the weather and hoping each other were keeping well. I just couldn't stand to watch the house fall over. Then the kids started with their parties and I couldn't bear it. Dumb, I know. Meanwhile my place is a dump. Dumb.'

—

Jean had been inside to use the toilet. As she walked out to the deck she passed May her phone.

'You got a message as I went by. It buzzed. I'm sorry. I didn't mean to pry.'

> *Answer me you fucking bitch. Sort this out. Call me.*
> *I fucking swear*

Seventeen missed calls.

'Oh,' May said, setting the phone down. 'You've met my husband then? My glass needs a refill while you're up.'

'This is your husband? Oh, sweet girl.'

May used to imagine a thread running between her heart and Patrick's, then one to her son. She would wonder which was thicker. Measure it. At last she had an answer, and though it wasn't made of love, it was the thread to her husband. Thick and heavy as rope.

Beneath stars, hot with wine.

'So what are you going to do?'

'All the things I'm supposed to,' May said. 'I'll find an agent, sell the place, fill out the forms. Whatever I'm supposed to do. But that's for Monday and Monday's so far away. There's time. There is so much time.'

—

Elvis was still moaning and May still thought he was tiresome but she asked the name of the song. Jean answered but the name didn't stick. It was so late. The stars. The real question came easily in the end, like the night had only been a prelude.

'So what happened here?' May asked. 'With Casey and Moses.'

'How much of it do you want to know?'

'Whatever you'd like to tell me.'

May turned to look only into the sky, nodding to these new stars.

'Okay. Okay, yes,' Jean said. 'Moses died. Here in Loveland, in front of the house. Casey's house. Your house. He was standing in the water up to his ankles and he died, just there, standing in the lake, and it wasn't his heart. I guess I know why they told you that but it wasn't his heart. He did it himself. Is this okay to say? Okay then, he did it himself. To himself. Moses had a knife and he cut his throat right there in the lake. I was there. Casey too. We watched him do it and we couldn't stop him. After that Casey just couldn't stay. She left with her beautiful little Rosie and that was it. I stayed and looked out for the house. That's all. I'm so sorry, sweet girl. That's all, I'm so sorry.'

May sat with the thought for a moment, to be sure, then took Jean's hand to reassure her. There was nothing to be sorry for. It had been like listening to the news and hearing of an ancient war in an unknown country. May thought of these figures standing in the water and she felt nothing. These were those lost details. They weren't hers.

Jean showed May to the spare room. They were both loaded and exhausted and so didn't speak. Jean tucked May in, left her.

LOVELAND, JUNE 1956

Casey had soaked the bed in the night. This was the phrase she'd picked up from her mother. The children at school said wet the bed, but for Casey's mother it was always soak. It seemed to carry more weight this way. That it was done with more purpose.

It was still dark in their bedroom and the husband was asleep. The sheets and her nightdress were cold and heavy and she reached her hand out and felt where it became dry just beneath the man's leg. Casey lay still and thought of how this could be escaped. There was nothing for it, though, and no way it could go undiscovered. So she just kept still and scratched slowly at the itch on her thigh.

At thirteen she had woken in this same way and gone to find her mother. It hadn't occurred to her for a moment that this was some error on her part. She had shown the sheets to her mother and thought the woman would be as curious as Casey had been. It had been a time of special worry for the girl and it seemed this could happen at such times. The mother had been so embarrassed. It was a surprise to the girl and she had burst into tears at the shock of being scolded. Casey was told to strip the bed at once and take the linen into the laundry. The mother stood over her. She told Casey to fill the tub with water and add the soap powder. A girl of this age soaking the bed. It was beyond belief. It was appalling. She was told to rinse and hang the sheets, and the mother did not want to hear another word on this. Casey would see to it that the bed was remade that afternoon.

Casey lay supine in her marital bed. Goosebumps raised on her legs and arms. Later, when the husband woke and discovered what had happened, he didn't show even a flicker of rage. It was only confusion and then disgust, and he said nothing in the end. Just checked himself and left to shower. There was no doubt of his disgust, though, and there was no attempt to shield her from this. She stayed in place and listened to him dress and then leave the house without breakfast.

Casey thought on this after and settled the mystery of why he had displayed no rage. It was because she was a woman and this was just another of these messes born between a woman's legs. The blood and piss and fluid that came with her sex and was solely theirs to repair. This was just another of these foul aspects of women and so he would only be repulsed and shower.

He left her to sort her trouble so she was on her knees, pushing the sheets under the suds of the washing basin. The times of worry. It was a bright and clear morning with the promise of heat. She would drag the mattress out to the deck. The bedding and her nightdress would dry quickly on the line. She would see to it and have it all repaired before the husband returned.

Chapter Six

May checked her phone with its blinding green screen: 5.32 a.m. The light shone on the bed and the wall and brought the confusion of being in Jean's spare room. The phone's battery was at six per cent and there were thirteen new messages from Patrick.

> *Call me.*
>
> *What the fuck*
>
> *call*
>
> *?*
>
> *Whats going on? I know the plane landed. call me*
>
> *Your son is a fucking headcase. Call*

???

Waiting

?

Call me

Fucking hell

?

I'm going to your mums

Five per cent charge.

May found the front door through the darkness of Jean's house, reached the road and walked along the faint white line at its centre. If a car came it would make no difference. One of those pick-ups and it would blast its horn and go right through her. It would make no difference. A minor Nebraskan statistic. *Nebraska*. A word with no meaning. None of this was real. A lazy dream at best. She might be finally, truly, mad. This was all a delusion then, and so she walked down the centre of the road and followed its decline to the lake. The worst lie of all. Against the dawn sky the water had become a deep red. The back of some poisonous frog. The smell of animals. All of nature that she had no defence against. Her mother, her husband, her son. Words without meaning.

She walked that white line and took out her phone. Found her son. It rang once, twice. The familiar chirp of him not answering. She didn't know the time there. It must be night for him, surely. She wanted him to wake and for her voice to be the thing he reached for.

Connection.

'What?'

'Francis, baby. I'm sorry to wake you. My baby. I just needed to talk to you. Are you okay? Tell me. It's late. I'm so sorry to wake you.'

'It's not late, Mum. My chips are coming.'

'Baby.'

'I've got to go. Hope you're having a great holiday. My chips are here. I've got to go. If you care. My chips are here.'

Disconnection.

Two per cent charge.

She had reached the end of the sealed road and the ground fell away. She thought of stepping out of her body and leaving it on the hardened sand. Snakes did that. Left the hurting skin behind and gave birth to themselves. Francis's voice had sounded so old. It was too much for her body and heart and so she shed them and stepped away.

May slipped through the gap of peeled-back fence and continued walking around the boatshed. Over the sheets of flung plywood and past the faded rubbish and nests of fishing line. Half-submerged house bricks. She stood at the water's edge and faced the house, placing her heels into the lake. The rim of scum and foam made no sound at her intrusion.

Where had Moses stood? It might have been exactly there. May wondered about the knife and if it had been something a hunter might use or an everyday blade from the kitchen. She had wondered this too about her husband's promises. As far as she knew Patrick didn't own an impressive knife for the job. A steak knife from the drawer would suit him. Something from their home, to make some point. This was what he promised would happen if she pushed him.

Kept pushing him.

Pushed him too far.

A throat would be slit. This warning he gave and would explain later as his temper. The short fuse she must know he had and must know meant nothing.

Here, though, Moses had made good with her husband's promise. May looked at the inch of water between her feet and imagined it splashed with her grandfather's blood. Hers. The man must have dropped to his knees to make a scene of it.

She went towards the house and its open arches. The level of the lake must have been much higher in her grandmother's day. So where had Moses been standing? And Jean. Casey. In the area under the house, just a little of the dawn was coming in between the walls' timber slats. The floor was a dirty, hard sand with coils of plastic twine. Rusted metal poked out of the ground and May decided it was the shaft of an anchor. This must all have been underwater once. She filled her lungs with the stink of salt and venom. Whatever had happened to the lake didn't matter. Just more lost detail. And Moses. Just some man.

Another message arrived from Patrick.

Francis called. What did you say to him? Says he hates you. Fucking call me. Sort this. Fucking call

One per cent.

She couldn't hold on to the thought of her son. Couldn't contain it. She had failed to build the right environment for him. This was the truth. She had put him into a wrong world. Failed to protect and failed to provide.

This was the truth and she couldn't hold on to it.

The temporary arrangements and the names she would give this. Patrick and his kitchen knife. The promises of leaving were weighed against the pains of staying and so she stayed. She had built this world. This was the truth. Anyone could see it. The names she gave these arrangements of her mind.

Under the house, against the darkest wall, there was the outline of something large beneath a cover. She found an exposed corner of the sheet that felt like an oily suede and lifted it to see a length of wood. She pulled the cover away and saw in full the shape of the boat. It was a small thing, almost a toy. Maybe ten feet long with a plank seat across its middle. It was striped beige by the invading light but seemed beneath that to be a copper colour. Two oars lay down its length.

She turned to look at the water. The sick, awakening lake. An impulse came over her to go out onto it. To find its centre and whatever was there, and if that was oblivion then she would disappear into it.

May felt the sand give just a little under her feet. She looked out at her lake and thought of impulse and time and falling water.

~~

It was a weekend morning when they drove by May's old primary school. She was then seven months pregnant with Francis and there had been silence after their departure from the hardware shop. Patrick had argued with the man at the counter over the price of the laundry taps, then put himself in their car's passenger side and thrown the keys to May.

As she drove by the old school she was deep in her distant place, so when the memory of her rainforest arrived it was to a May who was dreaming. In that moment she was again a young girl who showed her teeth and ran barefoot. She acted on her desire like she hadn't in so long, pulling over without a word. She opened the door, left the car and began to run, the smile of this younger girl on her face. She could feel herself. Heavy with her baby, May ran.

After a time she realised Patrick was following, calling to her. She pushed the car keys into her pocket and removed her shoes and socks when she reached the school's low chain fence.

She got herself over. She ran on through the empty playground and found where the school grounds ended and the path to the rainforest began. She ran on, despite the calling behind her. Despite the soft undersides of her feet against the stones and prickles. Enough of the dream remained.

Deeper into the rainforest she went and when she found the waterfall it was just as she remembered. Time hadn't reached it. She took the band out of her hair, pulled her dress over her head and walked out into the wide green bowl as she had done without hesitation as a child. The voice of her husband would arrive and grow loud but she pushed it up into the canopy. Into the rest of the noise of the whipbirds and beetles.

May went with her baby out to the middle of the stone pool where the falling water broke the surface. She floated on her back, pushed out with her palms and saw the water beading across her high, tight belly. She closed her eyes and made everything night and here the noises became one and was only this rushing water, from whatever impossible place it came. The baby kicked inside her but it would have to trust her. Her head went into the cascade and she introduced her son to the powers of nature. There might be something in this that he will come to recognise in life. Maybe it would be enough for him to escape. The fall was the place where all things were destroyed and born. With her child she disappeared behind the torrent. Where time and fear were escaped and a dream could be made real.

May put her hands to the boat's front and heaved its point around to face the lake. She had never understood the idea of instinct and how birds knew to switch continents with the seasons. How they knew the way. Or those tiny turtles that hatched under the sand and knew to climb and then dragged themselves to sea. Yet, there they were, and here she was. May pulled the boat out into the full daylight. Those turtles would get picked off by seagulls. She'd seen it on the wildlife shows and it was always so awful. One in a thousand made it to adulthood. Too awful, those sweet things.

She leaned harder in and felt a joy at the exercise of it and the foolishness. The lake was lethal and determined and she began to laugh at her eagerness as she neared the shore's edge. It might kill her and maybe that would be the cleanest solution. She could drown or her body would be melted away by toxins. The shame would go with it.

The boat began to buoy. The sun was clear and risen now and the water was a true, sick purple. It smelled of alcohol and toilet cleaner. She came around to the back and as she pushed the boat grew lighter. There was no living creature in any direction. Just that uninterested sun and whatever stirred beneath the ooze. She held on to the boat's edge and removed her shoes and socks, throwing them aboard. The lake was warm like a bath and its bottom felt slick against May's toes. The cuffs of her jeans sat beneath the waterline.

She left the shore and as she did she let it all release. Patrick and Moses and their knives and promises. Her tired, silent mother. Her boy. Francis. That boy who hated her and the world she'd made. What he'd inherited. The details of the past.

The boat tipped to one side as she clambered into it. Its edge dipped below the surface then righted itself violently and May was thrown onto her back. She grabbed at the sides and the rocking slowed. She laughed and heard herself as a child. The cost and thrill of living. That hatchling slipped from the seagull's beak. She laughed again that she was alive. She got herself seated facing the shore with the oars pivoting in their metal brackets.

A picture arrived in May's thoughts, complete and unreal, of Casey in her little boat. Her grandmother, then only eighteen, newly married and taking herself out onto the lake. Casey was laughing and free, free and young, making a direction for the future. May thought of her little turtles and their instinct and she began to row.

LOVELAND, JULY 1956

The husband wasn't due back until the early evening but she would never allow any of her excursions to run close. Her walks along nearby hilltops. The silent visits to the grounds of the big house. Certainly not these new moments on the lake. There was always the risk of a change to his travel arrangements. His business in the city might have reached an early conclusion so she would soon have to be back in the house, cleaning and baking, for what remained of the day.

Casey hummed as she lashed the boat's rope to its post—the post it was always lashed to and in the exact configuration the husband had left it. She was pleased with the way she was able to remake the complicated pattern of the knot, keeping the faded and younger surfaces of the rope as they had been. There would be no sign that the boat had moved. Certainly not that it had been rowed out to the lake's middle.

She was wet up to her knees and had her linen dress tucked up at her thighs. Back in the house she would wash it and hang it to dry. If she was caught in this final act she would say she had been washing the floors. She would always arrange the soapy bucket and mop in place before going down to the shore.

She had been going out on the water too often, though, she knew. The workers at the big house must have seen her rowing her way out on the lake. Perhaps watched her as she stayed turning in that place at its centre. They would wonder what the wife of Moses could be doing out there alone on the water. She doubted they would say anything to the husband. What reason would they have to report her secret? And, anyway, what could they suspect of her?

They had surely seen her, though. They must have. And she had been going out too often, she knew.

Chapter Seven

At the lake's middle the currents and winds united to have the boat stop dead. May's arms were sore so she pulled in the oars and straightened her back. The boathouse was directly in front, maybe two hundred metres away and to both sides the water bent in long curves. This desperate-looking crimson. It seemed to simmer.

She closed her eyes.

This is what we do to escape. Children find this trick when a cartoon lion jumps out from a television screen. It roars, we close our eyes and escape. How thick was the skin of an eyelid? One millimetre? That was her guess. Patrick worked and measured his life in millimetres. It was five mil this, and ten mil there. So May supposed the skin over her eye was one mil and this was all it took to be in a universe of one.

There were no husbands, mothers, dead relatives. No houses, teenagers, truck drivers and flying insects.

May was alone and she had, finally, given up.

After all these years.

She could at last stop and her arms shook with the rush of it. Patrick and his promise of a knife. He would kill her or himself and so either way kill the son. Francis was already dead, without knowing it. She kept her eyes shut tight and so kept herself in a perfect, empty universe.

The song came to her.

'Ballad of Big Nothing', around and around with its final notes touching its first. Her Big Nothing. The psychologist's trick for carving out space. Creating enough time to calm herself and bring forth the rational mind. So she sang the song of herself and it filled the world.

She had given up, finally and completely.

Big Nothing.

The boat shook hard, as if it had been struck, and May reached out to steady herself. She looked into the water but could see nothing below its disturbed surface, where dirty foam was now spinning in whirlpools and across the peaks of waves. The boat was still rocking from side to side, but it eventually settled. May's heart beat hard and her breath shortened. It was not fear but readiness. This was how animals fought.

Then came the pain.

A pain complete and so great she couldn't respond. It came from around and above and below, as if she were at the bottom of the sea. Muscles enclosing her, constricting, pulling and propelling her upwards.

May left the boat.

Left its seat and rose into the air with her arms pinned and legs crossed at the ankles. She couldn't even struggle. A wave of pressure travelled the length of her body until she hung still and suspended. She couldn't move her neck or tilt her chin to see how high she had risen. Couldn't judge by the wind or sound of the water because these had gone. There was just the pulse of blood in her ears.

This was impossible.

A sickness. Anything but real.

More pressure encircled her skull from its high point and moved down her face, clamped her jaw, then her throat and shoulders. So she stayed in that unreal place, high above the water, where the pain remained but quickly became stable, something to trust.

Her body stayed locked, but in time she realised she had a little movement again in her neck. She blinked her eyes into use and felt her sticky lashes. She tilted her neck as far as she was able and looked down at the lake far below. It was now a pale yellow and beyond that all was black. A black like outer space. That thing in science fiction films. Then a smell arose, with its overpowering sweetness. A sweetness she recognised but couldn't place.

May felt no sense of urgency. There was no instinct to panic. Her heart slowed and oxygen returned to her lungs. Whatever this was, she wouldn't hurry it. It could take the time it needed. Maybe there was no time here, anyway. The water below had become flat and May remained suspended, content, above her little rowboat on a perfect yellow plane and beyond that only darkness.

It seemed nothing but natural when the black began to replace itself with a picture of life. May thought of her apartment's television and how she thought it was far too big while Francis always complained that it was too small. Around her now she watched a vision take over the sky and it was of fire. Flames and molten earth turning over and coming to points of ash and smoke. The sound was still this rushing of blood.

The fire gave way to creatures. Animals filling the sky. Growing and changing as they swam and bobbed and crawled. Some grew legs and some felt no need. They ate each other and reproduced and died. Ate, reproduced and died. May watched and felt like she understood. She didn't question what of this was real, only watched and understood.

The dead rotted away. The flesh came free of its bones and oozed and released its gases but it was so fleeting. Death was so brief. It couldn't matter. Organs turned to a mess of fluid and flowed into the soil. A ground that was molten, then solid. The creatures reacted as well as they could and some blossomed while others tripped over themselves into extinction.

May watched and slowly recognised the vision becoming the land around her. The things with names like *lake* and *Love* and *Nebraska*. Seen at the right speed, the planet and world is a turning and impermanent thing. We only draw lines and give what's inside a name. These names are agreed upon by some for a short time. Lake, Love, Nebraska. They were once called nothing and later they would be nothing again.

May looked across the yellow water to the story being told in the sky and she accepted it. These arrangements that we give names for a time. And so May was released.

That tune again, Big Nothing.

Limp and accepting, she fell from the sky.

It occurred to May that the wetness of her jeans was uncomfortable. She would change into a new outfit when she was back with her luggage in the house. She would need to shower. The regular world had returned. She was a woman in a rowboat.

She knew now that she was gone in the mind. Truly gone like she had always wondered about. Touched in the head, her mother would call it. There was a particular sense of relief that came with it. To no longer be compelled to fight.

None of this is real.

There are collections of particles, in some particular and temporary arrangement, and we assign them values for a time. We call them a rowboat. We call them timber and their shape a house. Temporary arrangements and none of them are real.

May took the oars and put them in position and began to sing her song of ages. Not as an escape from anxiety. There was no need; she had given in and so knew no fear. Given in, completely. She sang because she liked the tune and it travelled in all directions across the lake as she rowed herself back to shore.

LOVELAND, AUGUST 1956

All the work Casey had invented for herself was done. She was letting herself grow too obviously idle, she knew. It was harder now to make a show of performing her duties. She would refocus her efforts the next day, she promised herself, but for now the day was done and Casey was by herself, watching the light dwindle over the lake and its far trees.

She had the bottle of liquor she had stolen the month before from the big house. It was an act so unlike her. She had been in the kitchen, left alone for only a moment while the cook went to fetch her regular box of provisions. Casey had seen on the counter the fresh delivery of wine and spirits and she had taken the nearest bottle. Held it between the folds of her dress.

Such risk. Put it in with her vegetables and flour when the cook returned. He must have noticed. Such unnecessary risk.

The night was truly coming now and she drank from her long glass of bourbon and juice. She had bought two bags of oranges from the market with only this cocktail in mind. Tomorrow she would focus again, put herself right, but for now she looked out at the lake like it were her lover returning. The lover she had imagined for herself before this place. Before the husband. The lover who would help her to see her own reflection more fully. She stoked these childhood ideas of romance and adventure. She looked at the lake and recognised the true shape of things.

She drank the liquor because it allowed her to be young again. Took her back to that time when she was without fear. It was not wrong to want to be young. It was not wrong to long for escape. She imagined a lover and thought of when she could next go out on the water.

Chapter Eight

'You're sure?' May asked.

'Couldn't be surer,' Tate's mother said and called out again for her son.

May had driven to the general store with a sense of clear purpose. Her muscles were free of their aches. The thought was reluctant to form, but she realised, as she stood and waited for Tate to emerge, that she was at peace. A ridiculous word. Something she had read on the sympathy cards that came with her grandmother's funeral. May thought of the lake and what she had seen. What she called Big Nothing because it didn't matter what name we gave something. Words were ridiculous. It was her mind's final collapse. It was a vision of all creation's truth.

She had seen that the land and its animals had come into being out of a tumble of heat and moisture and accident. Things settled where they did for a time. Or not. There was life. Sometimes not. Whether things lived or died or fought or flourished, they fell eventually into the grass and the soil and were turned over in the molten metals. There was no consequence to any of this. The pain would leave May's body and the tiredness and the need for water. Her phone had died but it would be charged in time and there would be more messages from Patrick and none from her son. Actions would occur. Things would settle and in their turn be folded into the planet's wet centre.

May hummed her song and smiled, waiting for Tate to emerge. His mother, who May now knew to be called Nancy, wondered aloud if the boy might be wearing his headphones and she swore that this time she would cut them up with the table saw like she'd always threatened.

'So, you're really staying at the boathouse?' Nancy asked, drumming her fingers on her counter.

'I am. My grandparents are both dead and so now it's mine to deal with. Their name was Love and I know nothing about them.'

Words came so easily. They weren't made of stone or anything needing tools to pull from the ground. They were made of air and only the names we give to things. If they came so easily then maybe the rest could too. So she would make herself comfortable in the boathouse, gather food for meals and watch the water. She would buy and drink wine. Maybe it was this uncomplicated.

At May's word, *Love*, Nancy's eyes flashed.

'You mean you don't know how the lake landed here? The Love family lake? No-one's got to you with that one yet? Oh, I am surprised. Telling it is a Loveland tradition. Will it bore you completely if I tell it?'

May only smiled deeper. More words. These weightless things.

⌢

It's 1877 and an ice jam is blocking a bottleneck of the Missouri. The jam won't budge and so the pressure builds. It keeps on and on, and by the high waters of midyear the river busts its banks. The mountain snows melt and flow.

On the eighth of July—and the Lovelander telling the story will always get that date just right—all at once a six-mile twist of the water, then going by the name Eagle Bend, was left an orphan when the river found a better way and made a new, straight path for its raging self. So Eagle Bend was a bend of the Missouri no more and was left as an oxbow lake all by its lone- some. That's the beginnings of the sick little spit we have today.

Then, the family Love.

They'd travelled in from the west ten years before and estab- lished a smelting works on the banks of the bend. White lead, pig lead. This was Judah Love and his kin. He set himself up a smoke factory on the water and they say the whole operation was about to be wrapped up and abandoned. Judah could set the earth itself afire but damned if he could figure out how to make it pay. So the investors were coming over the hills with their hands out when the river calls its own time and Judah wakes one day with the river now five miles down the road and just a lake at his doorstep. Go ahead a little while and Judah's made a new path of his own around this misery.

Judah happened to know what the rich desire, because it's all that he desired himself. And you know what the rich fancy? The rich fancy a little swimming. And maybe some ice cream and a dance at night and a morning promenade. The rich fancy whatever will best occupy their time and minds for those hateful long unoccupied days they have made for themselves. They want only to play the way they did as children, and so Judah built them the prettiest little playground. The good folk came to dip their toes in and live it up and fill Judah's pockets. He had found his way and this became a town. His name swelled out like an ink stain and that's how people came so many decades later to be standing in Loveland backyards drinking ice-cold Buds and looking up at a wide Loveland sky.

But the lake. The lake of all those summers. May's lake. The century saw to messing with the waters. People will mess with a river and the thing moved this way and that and then the rains don't come like they did and year after year the jewel of the lake at Loveland finds itself a little duller, and then duller still. The water begins to go down a little more, a little more, and then the unwanted colours bloom and the town wakes one morning to find its fish bent and floating. The Missouri didn't flood and those refreshing rains didn't come like they used to. The smell of all those dead fish. People from the government brought trucks in the end to haul them away. Fed them into chippers. The smell.

And the colours kept coming and each year the lake went down and they still can't decide who to blame. They think it might be Judah's ghost and the mountains he made from his smelters. They used to just bury the stuff and these hills are poison. Rivers flow underground all over the place. But who knows? They argue over the cause and the lake just keeps getting brighter and sicker and its level goes down and down. They put up signs. Tell the townsfolk they'll be fine if they just steer clear, but who knows? They keep arguing and the lake just gets sicker. And that's all there is to us: Loveland.

⌒

'Tate, I've been calling,' Nancy said. 'Or am I crazy? Have I been calling? Those headphones.'

'May,' Tate said, pleased. 'The customer has returned.'

'Child, I'm loaning you out for the day and I don't want to hear a word of complaint,' Nancy said. 'You're on that thin edge already. You're the Australian's for the day. Hear me?'

May had her arms folded and she nodded along with Nancy's words.

'I'll bring him back in one piece,' May said.

'Don't feel you have to.'

Tate plunged his hands into his pockets and shrugged. He looked between the two women, seeming unsure of which persona to deploy. May wanted the boathouse liveable and maybe even comfortable, and so they made a list and started with cereal, rice and sugar. She walked the aisles and handed things back to Tate, who carried their basket. Baked beans, SpaghettiOs.

'Baby corn,' she said and handed back two tins. 'I love these but I never buy them. Do you love these?'

'In Nebraska you go one way or the other with corn. I went the other.'

When they reached the dairy section May was reminded of her lack of refrigeration. Tate, speaking so it was under his mother's hearing, said they should head to Sargents. Sargents was the place. May paid Nancy and promised to have Tate home soon. Nancy leaned across the counter and kissed her son hard on the forehead.

A sun-faded billboard stood over the intersection: SAVE THE BABIES—HEARTBEAT 18 DAYS. Below, neon lettering blinking and useless against the sunlight in the front window of Sargents: HUNTING—CAMPING—GUNS.

Tate led them in and headed straight for the counter.

'Ricky, this is May. She's in need of some items of survival.'

The man, Ricky, eyed her reluctantly. Beside the cash register was a small television playing some sport. His eyes kept darting back to it.

'Okay then,' he said, watching the screen and the aftermath of a whistle being blown.

Tate leaned in, laying on his smile. 'I thought, *Ricky*, straight away. Ricky's the guy and Sargents is the place.'

The man seemed tired of Tate already and looked at May. 'What do you need?'

'This is a hunting shop?'

'Outdoor recreation.'

The three of them worked through her list, with the man grunting at intervals. May looked around the store as Tate put too much energy into his performance as go-between. Utensils. A pan. She wanted the lantern she'd found in the bedroom to work and in the end settled on new wicks and a bottle of lamp oil. This only wearied Ricky further, and by the time they got to *gas cooker* it was left to Tate to work both sides of the sale. He was on his knees at the back, asking himself questions about burners, while Ricky ate peanuts from a bag and watched his television. In the past this would have frustrated May, set her on edge, but now she was impervious.

Something of Big Nothing had stayed with her. This was her conclusion. A set of wooden shutters can be tilted open. A person can decide on their configuration being changed.

So what if this Ricky, with his nuts and sport, ignored them? What could it matter? Some stone and timber had assembled into a thing called a shop and some creatures and a debit card had found themselves inside it. The day before they would have been standing on the floor of an ancient ocean. Tomorrow it would be a scorched desert. So what of peanuts and television? May smiled and it wasn't out of malice.

Behind the counter was a wall of guns. She had never seen one in reality and she couldn't help but stare up at them dreamily. They weren't beautiful and gleaming, though. They had the look of toys. Plastic and rubber and some were painted in speckles of camouflage.

Ricky eventually relented and went to Tate and his cookers.

'See, I brought you business,' Tate said. 'I thought, I can do my pal Ricky a favour.'

'Don't think I'm owing you something now,' Ricky said. 'I can't help you.'

May looked through the glass of the counter and saw a row of gleaming knives. These had that miraculous look that was absent in the guns. The blades caught the dull orange of the overhead light and reflected back something more glorious. In one she saw her own reflection. Her eyes ran across its length.

'Ricky,' she said, 'let's take a look at these.'

He returned to the counter, unlocked the case and placed the knife she pointed to on the glass surface. 'Marbles Ideal, five-inch. Double-ya two. This one went to the beaches. Blade's a razor, tip's good. A high polish. Stacked leather handle, fibre washers, with your red, black and brass spacers. Bronze handguard. Aluminum pommel. The guard's a little bent, that's all. Got the sheath. A little damage near the throat. Keeper's missing. Battlefield condition. It's good. A good knife.'

'It's beautiful,' May said.

Ricky was rubbing the lower reaches of his perfectly spherical belly. 'You a hunter now?'

'You know what? That's exactly what I am.'

Tate took them to Green's, the second-hand store in the main street. The back seat was already crammed with an electric cooler, cooker and bottle of gas. The boot rattled with tins and jars.

A woman in an electric pink muumuu was dragging furniture out onto the footpath and patting her neck with a cloth. She had placed and straightened a mustard standing lamp and May was overwhelmed with the desire to possess it. Tate introduced the woman as Mary. Mary Green of Green's. The lamp was seventeen dollars.

Tate talked logistics on the footpath while May was drawn by the dark, dust-heavy pull of the store's interior. The conversation carried inside. Mary would have Wayne deliver it all. It was no problem. Wayne had his pick-up. No problem at all.

May ran her fingers across racks of dresses, all beautiful or delightful and all five dollars. She hit a seam of floral swing dresses that looked to be her size and put three over her arm—a tulip, a lily, a rose—then returned them to the rack. Shelves of cameras and tape machines. Five dollars and four. Televisions with coiled antennas and record players in awkward stacks. Musty books, fifty cents each. Accordions. A tall glass jar filled with wristwatches.

The feeling of money sat in May's guts. The mix of despair and worry and guilt. It was always this way, even when she stood waiting to pay for the family groceries. After she had kept so well to her budget. Checked and rechecked it. The money she earned went into an account only Patrick had a card for. He said he would do this for them. Like the rest, he said it wasn't her strength. The grocery money was transferred into her account each week.

When Tate came inside May was wearing a pair of heavy sixties sunglasses and looking into a wall of cracked mirrors. After paying for her flights there was still close to two thousand dollars left in her account from the money her mother had transferred. There was the car rental. Petrol. Meals to come. Two thousand dollars, though. Two thousand. It was a situation May had no reference for. The dresses, they were five dollars each. They were so pretty.

'Tate, you'll have to drag me out. I'll fight, so be strong.'

—

Mary's Wayne loaded the haul into the tray of his pick-up. The lamp, cooking pots, a round wooden table with folding sides and three near-matching chairs. The dresses on hangers inside a narrow wardrobe. A record player with tall speaker boxes and a crate of records. Tate had added a set of lime green crockery and a harmonica. May found sunglasses for him which he put on and declared himself the risen Jimmy Dean.

There was no good reason for all these purchases, she knew. May was furnishing a house and life she had no intention of maintaining. These were things, useless things, but they were beautiful. When she was in school she thought this might be her life: uncovering bargain prizes in a weekend flea market and taking them home without fear. On the lake she had seen that there was no before or after. Just things in motion from one state to another and everything would end up turned into the hot soil, so what could it matter? The pale rose dress was a waking dream and so May would have it. She bought the dress. She was free.

At the boathouse, Mary's Wayne had said yes to a glass of water but had necked it and edged back to the front door. Mary would be waiting. They thanked him as he left and then stood with their hands on their hips, looking helplessly down at it all.

'I'll get the turntable turning,' Tate said. He had been fascinated by the thing.

'Hungry?'

'Always.'

May left Tate to start with his ball of cabling and drove into town and the diner. The teenage girl was smiling at her register and asked if it would just be the coffee. May asked her name. *Gloria.* May left with pie, coffee, a milkshake, and two krautburgers, because Gloria had insisted.

'Beef, sauerkraut, onions, cheese and all the seasoning. You'll like it, May. If you like living, you'll like this.'

They pulled up the wings of May's new table and arranged the chairs around it. They ate and May listened to Tate slurping up his chocolate shake as she watched the cherry lake. The smell had softened further.

'These burgers,' she said. 'They're something.'

'Heaven.'

'My son would love them.'

Tate wiped his mouth with the front of his shirt. 'How old is he?'

'About the same age as you.'

She thought of putting her phone on to charge and retrieving its messages. There would be nothing from Francis. This thought brought no pain. It brought nothing. Again, the understanding that something of Big Nothing had remained in her. Wooden shutters tilted open.

'Listen up.' Tate pushed a switch on the record player, and there was a low sizzling. 'It's working. I think. I looked it up on my phone.'

The record was turning. He pulled the tonearm across and lowered its head. Crackle and hiss. The sounds buried in May deep and distant.

'My mom has this.' Tate held up the record's cover.

Tammy Wynette, *Your Good Girl's Gonna Go Bad*. It began through the speakers and May drifted to the open floor. The voice bounced around the wooden chamber of the boathouse. It was tough and urgent and May wondered at the woman behind it.

'I haven't danced since school. Tate, do they teach you?'

'They made us learn for a ball last year. I'll never do it again. Not once.'

She began to move to the tune. Her toes stretched out beyond her shadow. She danced across her Nebraskan home while Tate laughed. She laughed too and the polished floor squeaked under her canvas shoes.

Before setting up the camping stove Tate had checked the kitchen's old cooktop and found it operational. He lit its burners high and blue. They got to work, setting up the house as May wanted things. Tate dragged the narrow wardrobe for the new dresses. Whoever was nearest would drift to the turntable when a record had finished and take the next from the stack. Ella Fitzgerald. Loretta Lynn. Roy Clark. Names. Music hummed through timber and dust and May put her ear to the wall. The daylight in time became its purest amber and May poured glasses of soft drink and Tate told her it was called *pop*.

When they were done she drove him back to town and Tate asked to be dropped back at the hunting store. Business, he said. His mother wouldn't be expecting him so soon. It was fine, he assured her. He was out of the car the moment it came to a stop. He gave encouraging pats to the roof and she trusted him enough.

Back at the boathouse she went for the wine, filled one of her new crystal-looking glasses and took it to the balcony. She brought with her the old lantern from the bedroom and the oil and wicks from the store. This kind of procedure would normally not be hers. This would be Patrick on the balcony with a beer. She smiled down at the thing. Still-bright blue metal around a glass shade. May tinkered. Pulled at the hook at the top, the lever to the side, the knob and cap, until she decided she understood the thing and put in place the wick and lamp oil. She lit a match and brought it to the lamp without fear. She carried Big Nothing within her. She was free. The flame took and the lamp erupted with light and a thread of smoke which she took away with an adjustment of the wick. She hadn't set the house or herself on fire and everything was doing what it should.

She would drink herself to the outskirts of drunk and keep herself in that magical orbit. There was music and a house of her own. This was what people did. They rested and watched horizons and weren't panicked for a moment. This was how other people lived and she would have a piece.

She changed into the dress with the pale roses and spun on the polished floor. The dress would flare and return so gently. Flare and return. The afternoon came and the lake turned orange, pink and a perfect pale rose. Insects filled the air.

May woke to the sunset and stood from her chair on the deck. She had been dreaming of movies. The mudslide scene from *Romancing the Stone*. She'd loved that movie at the time, then later read about it. An article in a magazine. A woman wrote the movie but May couldn't remember her name. This woman was working as a waitress and Michael Douglas walked in for lunch. She seized her moment and pitched her script right there and he got it made. He bought her a Porsche after *Romancing* was a big hit and a few weeks later she's in the Porsche with her boyfriend. He's driving at 80 miles an hour, spins out and hits a pole. He made it, she died. Diane. Her name had been

Diane. Tiny flying creatures flickered and disappeared. It was night. A dragonfly landed on the wooden railing with its wings outstretched, catching whatever fell from the moon. May would drink a little more wine, eat bread and butter, and later find the blankets of her grandmother's bed.

The apple crate of books was at the front door when she went out to sweep. They were a day ahead of schedule. Casey had it as being the last day of the month and the books came usually on the first. The husband rarely made these kinds of mistakes. He had a calendar, she presumed, so perhaps he cared less about abiding by it. She would check again, though, to be sure. Check the codes she drew in her cookbook for the months, days and dates. The marks she kept hidden within the index of recipes. She would check to be sure but for now chalk it up as one of his errors. His luxury of knowing.

She carried the box into the kitchen and spread the books across the table. *In Praise of Folly. Starry Messenger.* She was delivered a selection each month and learned that she was expected to return the box to the doorstep with an equal number of books to be removed. *Lives of the English Poets. A Modest Proposal.* The husband seemed to not keep a strict count, though, as she had begun to hold back one more book than she returned and this hadn't been remarked on. So she had built up a small library. *The Wealth of Nations. Samson Agonistes.* She kept them about the house behind the unquestioned items: the stacked linen, the vegetables, the drums of oil. *The Marriage of Heaven and Hell. The Way We Live Now.* She didn't keep the library hidden entirely because she feared it being discovered. It was kept obscured so it would not be taken as a slight. *Prometheus Bound. Sartoris.* The husband must have accepted this as there had never been a warning.

She wondered where they came from. The town had a store that sold books, but it only stocked new titles and not many at that. She noticed that she would never see a book written after 1936. Nothing after the year she was born. The books would be of a certain kind. They were instructional. When she read them she heard them spoken in the husband's voice. The voice he used when talking of the greatness that he was returning to the lake. The one used when he described how their marriage would be. How she could bring them happiness.

These books were lessons and so for some time she fought to silence them. They were taken in and then placed at the front step a month later unread. Time, though, had its effects. It brought need and it brought weariness. So one month arrived that saw her hand reach blindly into the box and return gripping *Paradise Lost*. Perhaps there could be another way. She could take these books and fight for them to find another voice. Maybe that of these dead authors. Maybe her own. She could deny their intention.

This day's box was half Dickens. She would attempt to read them and see what sound they made. *Bleak House*. She had heard of it. She was never a good reader but maybe this could change. She could never seem to find the meanings the teachers intended. Maybe she could replace the voice of the husband and this would come to some good. There would be some hidden place of her mind. Maybe that one she still reserved for the sensation of love.

Chapter Nine

The 1956 Chevrolet Bel Air neared the bend of the street above the lake. May knew it was a 1956 Chevrolet Bel Air because Jean had announced it, heralded it, in the way of someone who knew and cared about these things: *1956 Chevrolet Bel Air*, then a series of numbers and animals and letters. V-something. Something horsepower. May saw only a car that was laughably large and laughably red.

'I've had one of my ideas. Do you have plans?' Jean stood in May's doorway with the clear morning at her back. 'I know you don't. Let's get out of here. We'll take my truck. I'll drive and you just stare out the window and be my tourist. I know you've got your work to do and your agents to find and the paperwork, but it can wait a day, right? Let me take you for a Sunday drive. Like you said, there is so much time.'

The grey of Jean's hair accepted the day's yellow. She smiled kindly and May thought of a dandelion ball, delicate and pleading to be blown back among the stems of the field. She asked Jean if her pale rose dress was pretty. If it was silly.

'Yes, both, perfectly.'

The car roared and spat and Jean seemed pleased by it so May nodded and patted the bare metal of the dash. A man was walking on the roadside; waves were exchanged and the man ducked his head to take a better look at May.

'You're the matter of the moment.' Jean brought the car back up to speed around the long bend. 'I've had half the town at my door. Muckrakers. Listen, if any of them find you, whatever they say, you just smile and tell them to go fuck themselves, okay? Don't listen to any of their bullshit.'

'What would they say?'

'Just ignore it. They're all caught up with themselves.'

They curved for miles and crossed train tracks and found industrial buildings to their left, empty fields of mowed grass to the right. From the other direction came only semitrailers and pick-ups. It combined to a pervasive smell of vanilla. Shop-brand ice cream. They went by a gasworks and water flashed into view through pine trees.

'I'll be tour guide,' Jean said with her hands high on the huge steering wheel. 'Welcome to the Missouri River. Iowa's that side, Nebraska this. Makes the east of the state. Missouri, Iowa, South Dakota. People might think the river's Big Muddy but no-one here will call it that. I will not give you the lie of Big Muddy.'

Between them on the leather seat was a paper bag of sandwiches and biscuits beside an old camping thermos. Jean then produced a worn book and put it into May's lap.

'See what Goyle has to say. I was thinking he could call the shots, if that's fine with you. What does he say on the river? Index is at the back.'

Its cover was cracked and thin and May carefully riffled the stained pages while Jean made encouraging gestures. The book's paper was like onion skin. May went to the index and ran a finger down.

Massacre Canyon

Meadville (ghost town)

Midway Pony Express Station

Minden pageant

Missouri River

'What am I looking for?'

'Whatever Goyle has to tell us.'

May turned to page 202.

The Missouri. The longest river in North America, it begins in the Rocky Mountains and meanders for 2,341 miles before quitting into the Mississippi above St. Louis. Depending on your feeling it goes by the names Big Muddy, Big River, Dark River, Emasulia sipiwi, Eomitai, Katapan Mene Shoska, Le Riviere des Missouri, Mini Sose, Missoury River, Ni-sho-dse, Niuctaci, Nudarcha, Rio Misuri, Riviere de Pekitanoni, Riviere de Saint Philippe, Le Missouri, Le Riviere des Osages, Missures Flu, Miz-zou-rye River, River of the West, Wide Missouri, Yellow River, and, the most appropriate, Old Misery. Call it what you like. If it corrects you, please do drop me a line.

'The only man I'll ever trust,' Jean said.

The book's cover was too damaged to decipher but May turned to the first page and found its title: *An Incomplete Roadways Guide to Nebraska* by William Goyle.

'We could hit the rock formations, but I was hoping you wouldn't be interested,' Jean said. 'Goyle goes east to west, mostly, but I've never really got my head around it. Loveland is on page nineteen. If you land us within a dozen pages of that we'll have a destination. Unless you'd prefer the rocks.'

Jean's knuckles were white as the car shook endlessly and seemed like an animal priming to buck them. They drove on by the sheds and piping. The green. The black-blue of the river which appeared in the breaks in life. Old Misery.

Page 49.

'Weeping Water,' May said and scratched her nail down the paper. *A quiet, quiet town.*

Home to the stream the Omaha and Otoe people first called Ni-gahoe, meaning 'rustling water.' French traders got it wrong and heard it as Ni-hoage, which they decided was 'weeping water.' It then became lore that the Omaha and Otoe once met at this place, at war, and all the warriors were slain. The wives and children of the dead discovered the massacre. They sat and wept and from their tears was born the creek that flows still. The story seems to have come about from the Frenchmen to give a story to their mistake, but it is poetic enough and fitting, and though not true is real, and so worth remembering. The town hosts a museum, the opening hours of which—in my experience—are as shrouded in mystery as the oldest of legends.

'Junction with S-14J. Three miles east: Weeping Water. Does that mean anything?'

Wind squealed through the car's broken seals and Old Misery kept to their left, mowed grass to their right. May thought of what was behind this trip for Jean. Maybe it was only what she'd said. A tourist jaunt and her chance to play host. May had agreed to it immediately, though, and so she could ask as easily what its point was for herself. It all seemed a little convenient.

A little invention. They drove on and found each other with glances. They smiled.

May looked out into the faded yellow and caught herself looking for familiar sights. She was trying to recognise something in the grasses and glints of water. It made no sense but this was the sensation. Of trying to trigger the memories of her grandmother. The woman had never spoken of the place in life so May wondered what she could hope to get from the woman in death.

They drove through the centre of Omaha and while it was green in parts it was still a city and so to May carried that creeping oppression of business and money. She wanted nothing to do with it and her shoulders only softened when the surroundings of buildings thinned as they went south on the 75. *South on the 75* because Jean had said so. Jean could let nothing pass without announcing it, narrating, and it was comforting.

'How's your mother?' Jean asked. 'Little Rosie.'

There was an awkwardness to the woman that May hadn't seen before.

'Little Rosie? She'd like that.'

May lessened her grip on the door's handle and stared out the window like Jean had wanted. Told her what she knew of Little Rosie.

South on the 75.

⌇

May imagined she loved her mother. With nothing to compare it to, she settled on the idea that it was love. And the feeling, whatever it rightly was, had expanded with the years. Expanded against her mother's increasing distance and tally of things unsaid. Rosie. She became Rosie as May became older and used to the ways of her own marriage and then motherhood. Rosie, the woman whose tiredness had merged with an ever-stiffer demeanour. Rosie fretted more but spoke less. May's father leaving had taken the worst of the warring from the house but other strains had come to fill the space. Rosie's cleaning jobs took their toll on her wrists and lower back, and May would rub creams into the points of her mother's bones and felt the skin grow looser. When Francis came Rosie shifted her worry to the boy and he obliged with his infant aggression and failure to sleep. Rosie would worry and the child would bite and smash. May would linger on the memories of when she was a child and when she imagined Rosie's character seemed closer to the surface. She dreamed of her mother once being angrier and able to laugh.

May's father's absence became the absence of Rosie as she worked her jobs. Days, weekends, nights. May would wait up and have food ready on a cling-filmed plate in the fridge for Rosie's return. When she heard her mother's key in the door she would run to the kitchen and set the dinner turning in the microwave. They would sit without speaking and watch the late news or the movie that began after midnight. When Rosie was done eating, the daughter would be sent to bed. There was school to think of and she would be shattered. They would kiss in the hall. Lip to cheek. The kissing ended with the passing years but May's love grew. This feeling she decided was love for this woman who became Rosie. Rosie with the sore back and the lips that found no reason to curl into a smile or pucker for that kiss. May wondered sometimes if the feeling she held was in fact pity but she could always in the end reassure herself it was love.

Leavenworth.

Columbus Park.

'This is the Ford Birthsite,' Jean said. 'Gerald, not Henry. Shortest presidency, not counting those who kicked the can in office. Took the place of Nixon, lost to Carter. What a sandwich. They say he was a klutz, but he seemed a straight-up guy. He did pardon Nixon, though. Gutless. Could have been good, maybe, but there was no chance after Nixon. Lived just about forever. Outlived them all.'

Bellevue.

La Platte.

—

They crossed the water and May could smell the salt and marsh. The rivers here went places, going and coming, and she thought of paddle steamers and Mark Twain. She'd never read a word of Twain but she had an image of him. That was the Mississippi, though, she was almost sure. Her rivers on the Sunshine Coast went nowhere no matter how fast they ran. Twain had his rafts and paddle steamers. That was May's image. White water over smooth rocks.

They drank from the thermos and then came a sign, WELCOME TO WEEPING WATER, and a run of churches, a petrol station and a sudden suburb of picture book houses. Stars and Stripes fluttering. They wound down their windows and May let the hot metal of the door frame scorch her arm.

They parked in front of a white-brick church with a digital billboard on its front lawn. In piercing LED red against black: EMBRACING AS IS. They bought coffees and the woman serving just loved that accent. Olivia Newton-John. That Steve Irwin. Oh, it was still so sad. They walked a little then sat with their coffees beneath a wooden gazebo in a park where flags rippled on bunting. Jean's hands could never be still and May figured they were an ex-smoker's. All of May's class in school had smoked. Her grandmother, mother and Patrick, too. She found packets and lighters in Francis's room that he made no attempt to hide. While still in school May had determined that not smoking when it seemed so necessary would be her only way to rebel and the position had stuck.

Jean was making circles with her fingers on the wooden table. 'Shall we find this creek, then, for Goyle's sake?'

They went down the slope of the main street and at the hardware store Jean approached the man setting up ladders. He said the water was almost within sight. Just turn at the end of the street and they couldn't miss it but they had to promise not to be disappointed. It was a beautiful town and a beautiful day and there was so much else to see.

They walked and the shops petered out and became unmarked sheds. Then silver silos, three or four storeys high. The sealed road cracked and went missing as they crossed train tracks and the heat continued to rise.

They heard an echoing *tap, tap* coming from somewhere below. Beside the train lines were the faint markings of a basketball court with rusted poles and backboards and a girl who May thought looked maybe eight was standing alone. She bounced her ball twice more then put it on her hip. She raised her free hand to wave and the women returned it. This seemed enough for the girl and she started taking shots. The loud shuddering of the ball bashing around inside the hoop.

They came to a short bridge that was all worn paint on steel. There was water below but it seemed shallow and was a chocolate-milk brown. May leaned over the railing, letting her arms dangle. She watched a leaf blow from the bank into the water and slowly make its way to their bridge and under.

'Can't stop Little Muddy.'

A truck passed and May clung to the steel against the shaking. Her mind was hardwired to the vibration of her phone and she found herself reaching for it.

'Hello there.' It was the girl from the basketball court, standing right behind them with her ball.

'Morning,' Jean said.

'I saw you talking to Mr Russ at the store. Figured you were visitors.'

'That's right. Just a pair of tourists, I'm afraid.'

'Don't be afraid. We want visitors. Everyone in town goes on about it. My mom's a teacher and my dad isn't working right now but they're both always on about it. The town needs custom or it'll die. That's my dad. You came for the creek?'

The girl's limbs were thin like grass stalks and her coiled black hair sprung from the back of her denim cap. Her body was young but her face carried the sneer of more years' knowing. May thought she was magnificent.

'You know how Weeping Water got its name? That's what people always want to know.' The girl switched her basketball to the other hip. 'There was a big battle here. The men died. The women cried so much it made the creek. The water wails too. Pastor told me. When the water runs you can hear the women.'

A pick-up rumbled behind them and the girl shouted hello to the driver. Joe Cocker was belting out from the open windows. The three of them then turned to look down into the stagnation.

⌒

The night before May was to marry Patrick, she was in the kitchen with Rosie, sorting the drinks. They had got in the slabs Patrick had asked for, and some wine. Four good bottles of sparkling that Rosie paid for, for the toasts. It was late and they were spreading the tinnies evenly across the plastic tubs ready for the morning, when someone would be getting ice.

Rosie began to cry. It had started without warning. She was wiping the kitchen counter then let out a horrible sound. An intake of breath that was a sob against a scream.

'Mum?'

'I'm sorry.'

'Mum?'

Rosie recovered herself and pushed away May's consoling hand. She laughed lightly at herself.

'I'm sorry, May. Jesus, where did that come from? I was thinking of your father, the silly bastard. Still makes me shudder. And his mother. You should have seen them.'

This was the story of Rosie's wedding. *You should have seen them.* The story of that day which Rosie would tell over the years and it was a warning. May rubbed the woman's shoulder and Rosie apologised again. The story went that at the reception after the ceremony Rosie had watched her husband slow-dancing with his mother and that they had been holding each other too closely. It was a lovers' embrace. The song had been 'You Are So Beautiful' and as the couple slowly turned the mother, now mother-in-law, had looked over the man's shoulder at her and Rosie would always remember the look as a hateful, jealous one. The mother was taking this one last dance. One final opportunity to spite the union and remind Rosie of how far from worthy she was of her most perfect son.

This moment in the kitchen was when, if they were different people, May and Rosie would have come together. When they would have talked truthfully of marriage and husbands and how things fail. They would have talked of May's father and the wrongs he committed and his absence from the memory of their family. They would have talked of Rosie's regrets. How she wished she'd done more to keep May from harm and hardship. The blame and who it belonged to. How Rosie had always worked, and worked so hard, and this was the way she'd cared for her family. May would have asked about her father and then her grandfather and Rosie would answer with everything she knew. Something about things repeating. They would have talked about the marriage May would be making the next day and how it was never too late. Never. That a person could always change their mind, even after they'd said yes. Especially after they'd said yes. They would have talked of these things if they were other people. If they'd had the bond that mothers and daughters had on television. If they'd kept the small, secret things of each other.

May had never spoken to Rosie about Patrick and the way he hurt her. About this terror that stole her oxygen. There were the bruises, of course, and the red and puffy cheeks and the shot nerves, but May would never speak of it because that was not what she had with Rosie. It had gone on for so long and what could Rosie say that would fix any of it, anyway? Rosie knew, of course she must have known, but there was nothing to be gained from turning it into words. Surely nothing.

So they cleaned the kitchen and talked about the beer and wine. The sparkling and whether it would be enough to go around. About the ice that was coming in the morning.

⌁

'If the creek gets flowing again someday, you'll be able to hear it,' the girl said. 'All those women crying. Come back and visit then. Pastor says the creek's going to run again. He also says that no matter where you run to, God and his love will hunt you down. That's the thing he says most. That and the creek's going to run. So you'll have to come back. Bye, then.'

The girl returned along the road. When she reached the far edge of the basketball court she sent up a wild hook shot that made the distance but kept low and ricocheted off the front rim. The ball rolled off into the dust and the girl ran after it. May and Jean stayed on the bridge, both looking down at the slow, dark flow.

'I wish this town had a better story for that kid,' Jean said. 'She seemed like a bright one. She gets the glory of men killing each other and women wailing into eternity.' A blush arrived on Jean's face in her irritation.

'Maybe she'll get other stories,' May said.

'I guess she will. I hope so. She might have a parent with something to say. What do I know about it, though? I know it's not that easy. Maybe that's unfair.'

'Blaming the parents?'

'Yeah, but I'm a teacher. I've made a career of blaming the parents.'

'Sounds right to me. We're all to blame for each other.'

Jean smiled at this and raised a hand in apology. 'Like I said, what do I know about it?'

They left the bridge and headed up the rise into town. Heat radiated from the road as loose dirt became bitumen.

LOVELAND, FEBRUARY 1957

It was after pushing a tray of vegetables into the heat of the oven and closing the door that Casey was reminded of Phil. It was so wrong of the memory to materialise then. So morbid.

Phil was in truth Philippa. Lover of horses. This was what the girl was always said her name meant, though Casey always called her Phil. This was her pet name and she would never say it when Phil's mother could hear. The mother would hate for her charming, tiny girl to be given the name of a boy.

Casey and Phil were best friends when they were nine. The pair of charming, tiny girls their mothers designed. They were this age when Phil died and so this was the age Casey would always remember them being. A truck had clipped the girl as she rode on her bike. The basic equation of her death. The thing a parent will worry over but never think would come true. Casey hadn't been with her that day and so could only imagine how the scene had played out. Phil on the decline of the hill they would freewheel down. Hugging the edge of the road as the truck stormed by with all its noise and width. Then the girl gone. Casey could never picture it.

The oven door closing had brought the thought of Phil because the only memory that Casey could keep clear was that of the girl's coffin disappearing on rollers behind a velvet curtain at the funeral service. Casey learned later that the girl had been cremated and she was certain that behind that velvet curtain was the open mouth of the furnace. The coffin was pushed back on those smooth metal rollers and Casey could remember the flash of heat on her cheeks as the curtain parted and exposed the flames. Later she would know this couldn't have been the case but the memory was so clear and true.

Casey's parents had never spoken of the dead girl again. Hadn't spoken of her at the time. Casey could remember dressing in her church clothes and being taken silently to the service. Nobody spoke in Casey's memory. There was just the sound of the coffin on rollers and then the gentle woof of the furnace coming open.

As Casey grew older the silence around Phil made her wonder if the girl was just some childhood invention. The death of a best friend would be something that would surely be spoken of. A parent would offer solace and protection. That there was none of this must mean that Phil was someone a child had summoned into existence. Yet there was this clear recollection of the furnace. The heat on her face.

Casey moved outside from the kitchen and stood watching the lake. The vegetables would take some time and she still had the ham to carve. She imagined what she could of Phil and thought it so sad that the memory that persisted of this friendship was the burning of a coffin. The heat on her face that couldn't have been. If she could summon the existence of this then there was nothing she couldn't make true by her imagination.

Casey waited for her vegetables to roast and watched the glare of the water. She summoned a friendship like the times she had forgotten with Phil. Summoned the escape that came with this. It must all be unreal but she wanted her friend back all the same. The lover of horses.

Chapter Ten

Jean directed the car out of town.

May had them on page 50 of Goyle's.

'Louisville.'

She read aloud and looked again into the tall grass, then the open shell of a rusted farm building and looked for what the grandmother had seen. Stories rolled into stories. Maybe Casey had known none of this or maybe the woman had walked across the crests of the hills and this had been the place she felt most at home. May continued to look, failed to see, and put her arm again against the door's heat.

The grandmother, Casey.

The woman was quiet and still and physically strong until her forearms gave in. She had been a seamstress all her working life and May's persisting picture of her was with her head bowed, fabric taut across her lap. Around her would always be neat, high towers of trousers, shirts and uniforms. Rolls of material. Thread and needles at her feet in plastic ice-cream buckets and the sewing machines set along the wall. This was in the back room at May's mother's house. Though the grandmother had worked and lived in this house for years, it was always clear it was Rosie's house. The grandmother had moved in to help after a few years of May and Rosie trying on their own. Rosie had finally allowed it and the grandmother had given relief where she was able, all the while working, keeping taut, ruining her arms for the repair of these dresses.

The grandmother had occupied herself every last day to ensure stomachs were fed and the house was kept, and when her arms had eventually become useless she had sat in the same room, the same chair, waiting for the next show to begin on the television and for the pain of her body to end. May knew nothing of this woman except her sacrifice and the pain she was repaid with. The shirts and fabric and uniforms. The material would be kept taut in her lap and the towers around her would never grow short and there would be always that *chugga-chugga* of the sewing machines.

Later, the thin whispering of the television and the popping of medication foil. When the grandmother died May was relieved. She would never tell anyone this—not that anyone would ask—but her feeling at the woman's death was relief. That the woman's pain and waiting was over. The mystery too. This silent, unknowable presence in May's life that she no longer had to wonder at. And besides, the grandmother wasn't lost because May's mother was as good as her mirror. Mystery remained with her and so May would go on wondering. This was the chain and May was simply the next. They had each just shuffled along one place. You sacrifice and work and grow quiet and eventually you become entirely still.

In the distance was a grey dome and silos as tall as city buildings. Jean said it was the cement works. She was driving at a crawl, passing banks, insurance brokers, a dentist. All dark and shut. They pulled over and parked in front of the Cornhusker Country Music Theater, which was abandoned behind faded wooden shingles.

They walked by the City Hall and its sign. LEDs scrolling TRASH SERVICE FRIDAY. Jean started half-skipping to the shopfront of Mrs G's Dairy Crème where a long, pastel pink ice-cream cone hung from wire. When May caught up Jean was reading a note in the window. *Sorry, we are closed for medical reasons until further notice.* A bouquet of flowers lay on its side on the windowsill. A man in overalls approached them, rubbing his palm against his stubble and sucking on the unlit stub of a cigarette.

'Closed,' he said. 'Mrs G's dead. Happened last night. People have been pulling up and reading the sign all morning and I keep tellin' them she's dead. Intersection.' He brought his hands together in a slap. 'The other driver ran.'

'Jesus, I'm sorry,' Jean said.

'Didn't know her. Heard about the crash, though. Heard she was dead.'

A couple with a child had stepped past them to read the note and May took Jean's arm and carried on down the street. The man was talking to the couple, bringing his hands together, slap.

'What a piece of shit,' Jean said. 'Am I out of line? That shithead. He didn't know her. He's taking pleasure in it.'

They got sandwiches and drinks from a diner. They'd seen an arrow for parkland back at the highway. Jean was still denouncing the man as a piece of shit when May read a store sign: LOUISVILLE LIQUORS. HANDROLLED CIGARS. She listened to Jean's hot blood. The fury at injustice.

Patrick had smoked cigars on the night of his thirtieth birthday. He'd arrived back at the apartment with his brother from their night out and laughed on their balcony inside a stinking cloud. The men had sat with a bottle of spirits between them, puffing and taking shots, and when May stepped out to try to quieten them Patrick had blown smoke into her face and asked her when exactly she'd forgotten how to have fun. She could smell it now. That choking bitterness.

'I'll just be a minute,' May said.

She told the man inside the shop that she wanted two cigars and for him to choose. Yes, that sounded fine. And she wanted bourbon, too. She'd never had it. She wanted the bottle of Horse Soldier that was on the shelf behind him. *Straight Bourbon Whiskey*, it read.

The man said it was good. The label said it was forged in fire. The cigars were rolled in brown paper.

They sat on the grass at the river's edge with their backs against trees. Thick parkland lay behind them and a narrow road. May brushed away a beetle from the toe of her shoe while plumes of white smoke dissipated over the flowing water. There was the sound of the highway's road bridge and a distant camper's radio. The high buzz of flying insects. Platte River. May felt the firmness of the cigar against her lips. She read from Goyle.

> Considering its two main tributaries—the north and south—
> the Platte River runs for near enough to a thousand miles.
> It begins with snow melting in the eastern Rockies and
> these molecules in time find themselves washed into the
> Gulf of Mexico by way of the Missouri and the Mississippi.
> The passage of the Platte comes angling through Colorado,

Wyoming, and Nebraska and so drains the best part of the Great Plains. As such it's damn thirsty for most of its length and though a mile wide is only six inches deep. Pig-mud brown. The 49ers complained that it was too thick to drink, too thin to plow.

The people living by it make use of what it offers. The Oto and Pawnee built towns and planted crops by its shores and lived very well by the thousands. The Spanish and French who came later would kill and fight over a claim of it until it was bundled up in the Louisiana Purchase. The Platte was the spine of the Oregon and Mormon trails, the Pony Express, the Union Pacific's Overland, and the Lincoln Highway.

In 1859, the first irrigation ditch was built along the Platte and this was the true beginning of the river's end. Wetlands were drained away to become farmland of typically outrageous human proportion. The Platte is now famed as the great American waterway most close to death. If you're a creature that swims, flies, breathes, or paddles then I offer my apologies and condolences.

Curls of smoke came from Jean's nose as she raised her cigar between two fingers.

'Terrible, aren't they?'

They laughed and coughed and agreed that they could stub the things out.

'Do you know Mark Twain?' May kept watching the river. 'He's the Mississippi, right? I keep thinking of him. I don't know why—I've never read a word.'

'The Platte ends up in the Mississippi, so maybe you're making the connection cosmically.' Jean cast a spell with her fingers.

Within the warmth and the shade and the buzz of the gnats May could have slept so easily. They had both drunk from the bourbon bottle and it was pulling May into a trance. If she closed her eyes the Platte might rise. Time would reverse and repair and those drains and dams would have never been made.

'The Gulf, the coast,' May said. 'If I closed my eyes just for a minute, could you tell me about it? Anywhere. Anything.'

May waited for Jean's voice and felt the warmth and dream coming over her. The river would spill across the grass and reach up the trees. They would join with the logs and rubbish and float east or south or whatever the direction. They would disperse to water and in time evaporate, rise and be turned to rain. Forever broken and repaired.

'New Year's Day, 2000,' Jean started. 'Do you remember the fuss about Y2K? I had a friend who taught computer science and she would not let up on the Millennium Bug. It was going to be the end. Nuclear power plants. The banks. Planes would fall from the sky. This friend, Lou, had a place at Pensacola and I visited for the week after Christmas. So it was a week of Lou and her Bug and it was going to be the end.

'Lou's place was on the beach. A shack but still the most perfect place. She took me around and all anyone would talk about was Apple Sam and his firework. He was a big man, they kept saying. The king of fruit and vegetables. He'd been telling the town for months that he was going to shoot the world's biggest firework into the sky at the stroke of midnight. So Apple Sam was taking a boat out in front of Santa Rosa Island and we had the best seats in the house. It was a beautiful, clear night and the beach was packed. Everyone was waiting for midnight and the world's biggest firework. Five and a half feet wide, Apple Sam said. He had this fishing boat kitted out with a great cannon. Lou kept saying everything was going down anyway, so why not with a bang?

'We waited all night on the beach and it was beautiful but goddamn freezing, so we drank Lou's wine and the thing is, it never happened. We'd figured the firework would tell us when it was midnight and then I checked my watch and it was five past. No firework and no mushroom clouds on the horizon. We checked the newspapers after and it turned out Apple Sam's banger never caught alight. The world's biggest firework shot up all right, went on its happy little arc unlit and dropped into the gulf with a silent little splash. That's it, May. That's my story.'

'Perfection.' May opened her eyes.

Jean made May promise that she would be the next one to tell a story. That May would drive and Jean would close her eyes and only listen. They washed their hands in the river and made their way back to the car. May wondered what her story could be. She could think of nothing at all.

A birth.

A marriage.

Nothing at all.

～

On the day of their wedding Patrick had twice gone to the toilet to cry. That's what he said. What he told May as they stood together and waited for the celebrant to finish her speech on the sharing of joy, new discoveries, and of the couple being not perfect but perfect for each other. Patrick had whispered in May's ear that he'd been in tears after breakfast and again just minutes before the ceremony. He'd asked if his face was puffy and if she could tell. The crying had been over his worry that May wouldn't pay him enough attention and that he'd be ignored amid the commotion and stress of the day.

He'd apologised and asked again if she could tell. She couldn't. When he cried, which he did often, his cheeks would be a bright pink and the little pouches under his eyes would plump up. His face now was unblemished and calm. His crying would always be accompanied by apologies, which came after she'd been hurt. That's how it was framed. Never that he'd hurt her. Always that she'd been hurt. He would apologise and be so ashamed. The crying would follow and she would hand him tissues and wait for it to finish.

The celebrant spoke and Patrick continued to whisper apologies in May's ear and asked again if she could see the trace of tears on his face.

There had been no clean moment of becoming engaged to this man. He had certainly never dropped to one knee and produced a ring. It was something that had occurred around her. The slow, invisible creep of circumstances. She would marry this man on the cracked pavers out the back of her mother's house in the same way disasters would take over the television news. As the royal family's expansions and contractions would fill the magazines. Lines would be etched on all of their faces, drawing the story of natural decline.

May's mother had read aloud the poem that the celebrant had suggested. The Keats thing. Then followed the proclamations and vows. May thought in that moment of running. Of actually running from the courtyard into her mother's house, down the hall and out into the street. That same idea would drift into her mind when things were not at their worst. In the hardest times it couldn't be contemplated, but in the moments of relative peace it would appear like a silent vision from a film. She imagined that others would think it was the obvious solution. You would run from a charging animal. Run from a building on fire. So run.

May knew, though, that it was closer to the sensation of standing in the road with a car speeding at you. She knew what it was to freeze in fear. To have the will to move but have your feet fail to respond. The car kept coming and she stared into the eyes of the man behind the wheel. Her body refused to move and she could only wait.

The wedding had played out and May smiled to the appropriate degree and assured this man who was now her husband. Kissed him and told him not to worry, that nobody could tell. He looked away to the small circle of guests. Their immediate families, some cousins. She looked at the shape he made in his suit and spoke quietly into his ear. He would never stop reminding her of this wedding day and the tears she had reduced him to. Her wedding dress easily covered the fresh bruise on her hip and the older ones on her upper arms. She reassured him. Spoke so only he could hear.

～

Goyle was directing them to Blackbird Hill but it was at least two hours away and they agreed this was too far and that it was time to find their way home to Loveland, a drive of sixty miles. They would settle for Goyle's account of the hill.

Blackbird Hill is the place of one of Nebraska's most retold ghost stories. It is said that 200 years ago, or thereabouts, a young man and woman from the east coast were in love and engaged to marry. The man set sail for what was to be a year of adventure, to return with the couple's money made. The year passed, then another, then several more, and he never returned. The woman gave him up for dead and married—here's the rub, of course—the dead man's brother. The newlyweds moved west and made a home atop Blackbird Hill.

Some years went and they were quite nearly happy. The woman was surprised then, one cloudless morning, to see her long-dead fiancé walking up the hill to her homestead. He was a little surprised himself. He told her his tale. Of his ship having been wrecked and his scramble to survive. Of his destitution and years-long quest to return. Upon at last making it back to America, he found his mother dead and his brother married and gone west. He joined a wagon train for California, searching all the way. Reaching the far sea, he abandoned his search and, heartbroken, began his wandering back home and, in time, set to following the curves of the Missouri. That very morning he had found himself meeting a hill upon which he followed a path to the homestead atop. He was going to ask for milk and bread but instead had found his lost love.

The woman, overcome, repledged her love and told our tired traveler to wait until nightfall; when her husband returned she would tell him of her wish to be free. Our man waited in the trees by the river and at sunset watched his brother walk up the hill's path. Inside, the husband begged his wife to stay. She refused and he grew angry. He attacked her with his hunting knife. She ran outside, bleeding, and the husband followed, gathering her up and carrying her to the steep cliff over the river. Deciding everything was lost, he jumped, taking them both down to their deaths in the Missouri. Our traveler arrived at the summit just in time to hear his love's bloodcurdling (and it is always described as bloodcurdling) scream.

From all this, several legends arose. That the ghost of the woman wanders the hillside still. That if you were to gather (as many reportedly do) on the hill at sunset on the seventh of October (the anniversary of the murder, it was decided) you would be treated to the sound of the poor woman's bloodcurdling scream, echoing down from that tragic moment. That to this day nothing will grow on the hill but for the bloodgrass that clings to the cliff above the deathful waters.

It is a harrowing story and a good legend and, as with most legends and all the best stories, not a bit of it is true.

Jean pulled the car over on a straight, quiet stretch and asked if May could manage the final spell of driving. May said that was more than fine—though she struggled with the vibration and keeping the thing straight, certain she would inadvertently steer them into the wrong lane—and she preferred to be at the wheel. She wished she'd offered sooner.

Jean closed Goyle and his endless tales. May could still think of no story of her own to relate.

That wedding.

That child.

Nothing at all.

⌒

Francis's birth had been an indefinite event. May had until then imagined that life came into being in an unmistakable moment. The child would emerge from that room of liquid to a world of air and she would become a mother by her part in that conversion. Women on television screamed like lions and accepted the proof of their work on their chests.

A week after his due date Francis had still shown no sign of wanting to join the air realm. May had by then scratched the skin of her back and arms into expanses of permanent graze. Her bedsheets were stained with the spots and streaks of her blood. She had told her obstetrician that the itching was unbearable and that she had read up on it and wondered about this condition called cholestasis. The doctor had reminded May that she was having a baby and some discomfort was to be expected.

When Francis was a week late a doctor at the hospital had examined May and told her that they would induce immediately. Her obvious condition—the disorder of her liver—meant a serious increase in risk for the infant. Slow heart rate. Lack of oxygen. Fetal distress. May had called Patrick and asked him to bring in the suitcase she had packed and ready. He arrived a few hours later with a paper bag of burgers.

For the next three days they would wait to be taken down to the birthing rooms. More immediate cases had wandered in. A woman with twins off the street. It wouldn't be long.

When at last they were taken in to the operating room May could think only of the skin of her back and arms. The itching. The unendurable itching. When they cut her open and lifted Francis out May was shaking from the epidural and felt nothing but coldness. She shivered terribly. She remembered only that the baby's testicles were flaming red and wondered if that was normal. Patrick had gone and stood by the child as it was rubbed with towels and inspected. They had lowered the screaming child into her arms but she had soon asked for it to be taken away. She was so cold. She worried she might drop him with her shaking. Later, Patrick would tell her that he couldn't understand how she had not felt that mother's feeling. He would remind her always that she had ruined the child from the start.

Francis came to her in pieces, over days and then years.

She would never fully shift those early sensations, that Francis arrived alongside only relief and fear. The fear would never leave her, of having to face the child and see it learn the life it had been given. The scratching had ended and left only faint scars.

May had always been able to keep anger at bay. This was one of her great, old tricks. But it was a trick that she seemed unable to access now, as she sped across the shimmering, yellow plain. Maybe she had left it behind, and it couldn't find her this far from home. Whatever, May was angry. Angry that her stories were of these two men. The husband and the son. That she talked and thought and imagined herself only in relation to these others. Her story was only and always about them. Them.

The anger could be fleeting, so for the moment May revelled in it. Swam in the poison. These people with their stories. Even the story of Loveland, which should be her family's, belonged to these others. These Nebraskans.

Jean was sleeping. Her bonnet of grey hair was dark with sweat at the roots. May pulled over at the sight of something from a bent dream. She clapped her hands together and flung her door open. It was a tent at the side of the highway flanked by an inflatable eagle two storeys high and wearing a jacket of Stars and Stripes. A banner was roped to the tent: FIREWORKS! BUY 1 GET 3 FREE! She cast Jean's spell back at her through the windscreen glass. Another cosmic connection. Another daydream. May walked into the tent amid the stink of burnt gears and petrol and gunpowder.

—

They drove into Loveland and a sun shower fell without warning, spotting the glass, and May said she remembered her grandmother calling it a fox's wedding. That it was the sky celebrating the animals' union. Jean said she'd been taught it was the devil and his wife fighting and these were her tears. The women turned to each other, laughing in despair.

LOVELAND, AUGUST 1957

The knock on the door was not the husband's. He always knocked but only as a prologue to the door bursting open. His knock was a taunt. This, though, was three quick raps, a pause, and then a heavy fourth. It was a warning or a request, and in response to either Casey's heartbeat grew loud. It would be okay. It would be someone from the electricity company. Someone from the council or a roadworker with tools coming to give notice of some works. They had come before. Casey went to the door and turned its handle before anxiety could cripple her muscles. It would be a salesman.

It was a woman, tipping forward as if on the verge of falling. She was holding the front of her dress up with both hands together at its middle.

'Eggs,' the woman said, looking down into her pouch.

Casey stood straight with her hand still at the door; the eggs began to unsettle and the woman laughed in panic. Casey put her hands out instinctively and together they stabilised the clutch. The woman continued to laugh between apologies and thanks, and Casey directed her inside to the kitchen table, where they released the eggs gently onto the wooden surface. One rolled close to the edge and the woman lunged, caught it and squealed at her success.

'Jesus,' the woman said. 'Sorry. Another of my disasters.'

She was young. A girl, and younger than Casey certainly, but there was something in her that spoke immediately of someone older and sure. A woman, regardless of her age, and Casey caught herself staring.

'Eggs, I was saying, to state the obvious.' The woman put a hand to her hip. 'I'm Jean. I hope you're expecting me. I only just arrived and I went up to the house, up on the hill, but I couldn't find your husband. Mr Love. You're Mrs Love? Don't tell me I've messed it up. I only found some man in the kitchen and he didn't seem at all pleased to see me and he sent me down here to you. Said you'd asked for eggs and he'd just got hold of them. I asked for a basket but he wasn't at all pleased to see me. Have I messed it up?'

'I'm Mrs Love—Casey—and no. I mean yes, thank you.'

'I'm sorry to just bowl in like this. I'm nervous as hell, if I'm being honest. I talk a lot when I'm nervous. And curse.

I'm sorry, you must think I'm a terror. I'm Jean. Did I say that already? I think I didn't. I couldn't find Mr Love and they'd told me to report to him the second I arrived. Oh, I am sorry, am I a terror?'

There was nothing of the middle in this woman's voice. It was from the east, Casey was sure, and in that moment it was a striking joy. It was a blessing to hear this strange woman's words and to recognise something other than Nebraska and its utter middleness.

'Thank you for the eggs,' Casey said.

'You're welcome, though I was just doing what the man with the stiff neck told me. Oh, that's something from my mother. The stiff neck. Must have slept on his pillow funny. I hope I'm not offending you. I don't know his name. He wouldn't tell me, though I said mine enough. Just between you and me and the chickens, I think I might keep clear of him if I'm able. His knees were green, so maybe he works in the gardens? They did tell you I was coming? I hope I haven't messed this up already. They told me to report to Mr Love but I figure I'll be working for you just the same. With your young one on the way. They didn't tell me much, if I'm being honest. Just that I'm to be your maid and right hand until the baby is born and then whatever the hell you might be needing once it's here.

'Oh jeez, I'm sorry. I just cannot shut the hell up. I haven't got much in the way of skills. I'm not sure what they told you; I hope they didn't make any promises. I'll work hard for you,

Mrs Love—Casey—I'll do that. I promise. And I *can* make a dress. Anything to do with a needle and thread and cloth and a machine. That's my thing, I suppose, if I have one. One day I'd like to be starting a business making dresses, fixing dresses, whatever in the way of dresses. When I get my clams in order. If I ever do. But don't get me wrong, I'm not looking to run away. I'm here to work for you. You and the baby. You and Mr Love. I'll work hard. You think I can get a glass of water?'

Casey stared into this creature's glowing centre. The husband had always observed that Casey's features left her permanently a child, and yet here was this girl, younger but so obviously a woman. Casey stared into this vessel of amber light. She would get Jean her glass of water and have her stay for a cup of tea. Casey wondered what trouble might be in store, with Jean as her right hand. Whatever, she was worth any risk and punishment. In that moment Casey wanted only to be in the presence of this flash of existence. This woman.

Chapter Eleven

Back at the boathouse, May wanted to ask Jean in but she seemed tired from their day and May had to remind herself that Jean was seventy-five. *I find people wonder, so best just to say it.* Maybe it was rude to consider this. Condescending. Maybe seventy-five wasn't all that old anymore or never was. Jean seemed proof of one or the other. May got out of the car and waved goodbye and went in to the boathouse.

There was nothing peculiar to this act of returning. No unfamiliar scent. It was like returning to a house of her own. She used the toilet, washed her arms and face. A small mirror hung on the wall and May thought she looked sad. Sadder than she felt, anyway. She went to the kitchen, fixed some food and took it back to the table, where she'd left the fireworks and bourbon. May peered into the box of sticks and rockets. She didn't know why she had bought them. Why she had felt that ludicrous eagle so compelling. Fireworks were boring things. So many times she had waited in the dark until some scheduled minute with her head craning back so she could watch an empty sky fill with light then smoke then emptiness again. It was always over so quickly and left nothing but frayed nerves. But that roadside tent with its Stars and Stripes and promises.

She took cheese and bourbon to the verandah and felt comfort at seeing her lake. Her foul water shining brighter than the sun. She reclined in her chair, put her feet up and drank the bourbon from her plastic mug. The first mouthful took her head off but the rest less and less.

She must have been woken by the voice of the young man because as she realised he was standing in front of her in the entrance to the house she felt no surprise. May calmly scanned her memory. In the kitchen there were tins of food. They could work. One of their edges struck against a man's temple. The knife from the hunting shop was too far away in the bedroom. The wooden chopping board was close and would have a useful weight.

'Sorry to disturb. I could see you through the windows. I'm Red.' He smiled and it was a beautiful smile and she knew everything about him.

'I'm May.' She shook his outstretched hand. 'You seem to be in my house.'

'Forgive me.' He put his hand to his heart and, again, the smile. 'I ran into Jean back up the street. She said you were in and I've been meaning to say welcome. My parents too. The Goldings? I'm not sure if Jean mentioned us yet? We're just down from her. Last house on the street. Last before yours. We used to be the last folk before the lake, but now that you're here I guess that's you.' He laughed, only to show his perfect teeth. 'If you're staying.'

He was young but muscular. The face, though, was a child's. A little boy surrounded by this worked flesh of a man.

'This place is yours then?' He walked across the verandah with his hand still at his heart. 'We always wondered. The general opinion was that there was no family left to speak of, but Jean would never talk on it and so some had their suspicions. It's a suspicious little town. My father, for one. Hal. My mother's Alice. I'm not sure if Jean mentioned us yet? The Goldings. Do you mind?'

He pointed to his feet and their intrusion. The smile.

'I do mind a little, Red.'

She had settled on the boy being harmless but wanted to stall his little performance all the same. She looked away and went inside. She poured bourbon and juice into her mug and went and stood where the sun caught her face.

'None for me,' he said. 'Hal will kill me if he smells liquor on my breath.'

'I didn't offer.'

He leaned into the hot railing, matching May's pose. They watched the water and its perfect flatness.

'It must be strange to be back,' Red said.

'It's my first time.'

'For your family, I mean. The Loves are back. It's strange. Jean never talked on it, like I said. I guess it's right to be suspicious sometimes.' He raised a hand needlessly above his eyes. 'This place must have been something, back in the day. Shame it's all gone. Not worth a thing now. Nothing compared to what it used to be, is it? No offence.'

Confidence was twisted so neatly into the fibres of this one. This kid and his teeth. Preening his feathers.

'None taken,' she said.

'The real Loveland. There's a big framed photo of it in my father's study. You should come see it. Loveland when it was just a name for the tourists. Something silly. The rich folk playing. You'll see in the photograph. It was built up along the water. All around here and over the way on the bend. The grand hotel. The promenade. People always talk of the promenade. I'm not exactly sure what they mean. Dance hall. Amusement arcade. A damn Ferris wheel. They say it was something. Let off fireworks over the lake to see out the week. Always sounded pretty lousy to me, but I guess times were just more dull back then.'

May looked at the bare earth to the waterline. The scrubby grass and the line of distant trees. There were no signs of this old Loveland. No remains. Nothing but blushing water and rubbish.

'Rich folks' playground.' Red showed his palms. 'That's how it's always said. Since 1877. When the river flooded and gave Judah Love a lake in the middle of his stake. We get all that in elementary school. We'd put on little plays. You'll have to see this photograph of my father's. The place kept up until the war, when I guess folks didn't have money. Sat quiet for years until Moses sent it up in smoke.'

She didn't know what he meant by this, but wasn't prepared to ask. He wanted it so badly. May wondered if this kid had dreams of being an actor. He would be the type devouring fried chicken in a commercial.

'Moses was my grandfather.' She drank from her bourbon. 'But I'm not a Love. I'm just here for the house.'

A little of the child wiped clean from Red's face as his expression turned serious.

'You know about him then,' he said. 'Burned the place to the ground. Cut his own throat. It's quite something, if you think of it. Loveland stood for generations then Moses brings it down in one night.'

She would give this kid nothing of what he wanted. The little showman. It must have been the drink that then sent a brief chill through her. To her fingertips and down the back of her legs. The boy's act was cute enough but it had grown old.

'It was nice to meet you, Red.'

His hand outstretched again and asking for hers. The smile. The grip held too long.

'The thing is, May, I wanted to say my welcome on behalf of my family because my parents have been talking of you. Like I said, it's a suspicious little town, and when we heard a Love was back in the boathouse, well, some of the people nearby got worried. It's the claim, May. Hal and Alice got worried about the class action and I wanted to offer my welcome before my parents or any of the others got their chance. They've got their little minds buzzing. Their cogs spinning, you see. Suspicions.'

'I'm a little tired, Red.'

'There's not a place within miles that can sell. It's the poison, May. That's what the claim's about. My family, all the families, in court for years fighting the state for compensation. So I'm just trying to keep things civil because they're worried, Hal and Alice. Heard you might want to sell and that set them worrying. Might hurt the claim. Hurt the families. So this is a friendly welcome. That's all. The friendly welcome before anyone rolls down here all fretting and heavy.'

The chill again. To her fingertips and to her heels. She would not give in to this kid actor or these old ways of feeling. She had been out into the lake and she had known Big Nothing. She was changed. She must be.

'Like I said, Red. I'm tired.'

He nodded, put his hand to his heart again and went back out through the house. She could hear his boots falling away down the stairs. Then him scraping and kicking the hardened dirt up to the road. It was the way he walked that she finally recognised. Beyond the confidence and looks. Red walked like her husband.

May returned to her seat and refused the feeling in her gut. The nerves. Instead she put her feet up, looked out at her lake, and drank.

May was startled by what her body remembered as thunder but which couldn't have been. There were no clouds. No storm. She had been unable to rest since the boy's visit. He had tried to steal something from her, or have it leave with him at least. What she carried in her of Big Nothing. This thunderclap had brought her attention to the day ending, the missing sun, and she made the decision to go under the house and pull the dinghy out into the water. She would not let this be taken from her. This understanding.

She managed it easier than the first time. There was no elegance but likewise no flailing as she tucked the bourbon bottle into the space under the seat. Her stomach had turned and she was done drinking but she liked its colour and the feel of having it with her. Its weight and slosh. She rowed and the muscles of her back brought a welcome ache and in time the boat reached the lake's centre. That smell again of sweet bodies. The feeling again of being drawn into a sink's plughole. She was made of particles, as was the lake, and so they followed a series of rules and actions and found themselves in some configuration. There was nothing special to this. To anything.

Her nose and cheeks were hot. When Francis was a toddler she had worried too much about him getting burned by the sun. Playtime in the park began with fighting over the lotion and him swatting away her greasy hands. She would force it onto him and the stuff would get in his eyes and he would cry and so she would have to rub at him with wipes and it was always such a scene. The sun was the thing to be feared but in the end it was her greasy hands that he ran from. She worried about those early things. Sleep, food, his runny nose. They sent her home from the maternity ward with a colour chart to match against what she found in his nappy. Green streaks meant mucus. Grey meant a problem with the baby's liver. Bright green meant too much foremilk. Black meant bleeding in the digestive tract. Colour meant everything and always danger. Big Nothing. The lake was now its pale yellow-green like a broad palm leaf held up against the sun and May lay back and let the tips of one hand's fingers dip into the water. She hummed her song without fear of consequence.

She willed it to come, Big Nothing, and so it did.

—

First a silence and then her body being gripped and taken into the sky with crushing reassurance. The pain that she welcomed and the smell so sick and sugary that May gagged. The rings of unseen muscle around her body propelling out the contents of her lungs. That honeyed air. In time her head became free enough to move and to see the lake frozen to a smooth crust before countless droplets, synchronised, broke the surface in every direction. It seemed like something from a machine, but then May watched the soft lime-green water became only gore. She had seen the colours of spilling blood before. It was so familiar. The sky switched to night and May was again seeing things in their true form. This was everything bare and it took no mathematics or code.

May understood.

Humans walked into the vision. The sky filled with these characters. When May was small, this was how things seemed at the movies. The seats and popcorn and her parents melted away to leave just the reality of the screen. Now she watched the people, at first naked then dressed in animal skins. These became togas and tunics. Forward to another place in their history, dancing in fine clothes on the polished wooden floor of a ballroom. Forward and the world was underwater and these people were once again naked and drowning in the waves. This was how it was always going to end and yet these people carried on. They made families. They continued to dance. It amounted to nothing but they continued.

Then, her son.

Filling the screen was her boy and in just seconds she watched him become a man. At speed she could see his ageing as a series of failures. Francis's skin becoming grey to match his hair. His back losing its shape. He was so quickly an old man and then a dying one and then gone. May could briefly smell his decay. That curl of fetid air from a corpse before it's drawn back into the dirt. Then just the sweetness.

Loss.

The first time Big Nothing had left with May the lingering sensation of freedom. Its visions had taken her pain. She had seen that all things came to nothing and this was a liberation.

But now she experienced what was lost.

In her heart, she felt it.

All of a person would be absent in the end. These lives and memories. They were real. Real enough to be missed. We matter. We matter and it would all be lost. Her son would age, become old, and it would mean something for him to be gone.

The sky became darkness again. There were no pleasant mirages of dividing cells or volcanoes. Just the fading memory of that rotting body. The ones we love are turned to meat and even the memory of that will go in the end.

May fell from the sky.

With something unbearable in her chest, she fell.

In darkness.

No starlight.

Only loss.

A wind rose and May was just a tired creature again, floating
at the centre of the lake. A person alone in a boat at the end of
a Nebraskan Sunday. She felt nauseous and caught sight of the
bourbon at her feet. It had no more romance to offer.

She understood now that all that had ever lived was significant.
And it would be lost.

She pulled at the oars and found herself weak. One of the
blades skimmed above the surface and the nerves in her back
twisted painfully. The boat turned slowly about and, looking
ahead to the shore, to her boathouse those couple of hundred
metres ahead, she saw a boy dragging some animal. It was Red.
That boy too much like a man. He let go of the creature and
stood at the base of the stairs. Struggling, the animal came up
from its knees. A calf. It made no sound.

The boat continued its slow turning and the boy climbed
the stairs. He was looking through the windows. The curtains
were pulled back and so he would be able to see into every
part of the boathouse. May watched him move back down to
the calf, which was writhing on the ground. It must have been
tied. Gagged. Red took it by the front legs and dragged it to
the stairs. The boy looked around again, steadying, then took a

knife from his jeans. Even with the distance, the movement of the water, May knew it could be nothing but a knife. She saw its shape and the way he held it high above the animal in the way butchers raised their blades above a carcass.

The boy brought the knife down, split the calf open at the neck and blood gushed. May could not see it but the blood must have come. Red held the animal by its ears and waited. The life pumping warm down the bleached wood. When it was done, the body drained, the boy let the calf fall and walked away from the house. He seemed to wipe his hands on his thighs as he took the rise to the road. The boy moved out of sight and the boat continued its gentle spin.

LOVELAND, SEPTEMBER 1957

She walked across the grass of the hill that led to the big house. This was all wrong, Casey knew. Certainly not permitted. How the husband would react was untested and it was only now, walking between the outcrops of dark flowers and nearing the open front door, that fear made itself known. It squeezed and her lungs struggled to retain air. This was wrong, but she had made a promise to Jean.

They had occupied that morning together as they now so often did. Jean had knocked early with two mugs of coffee and the story of her previous night's telephone call with her mother. Of Jean's fruitless attempts to be forgiven for having left home. Jean was a grown woman now and independent. She had resolved to make her way in the world and that from here on in her mother might have to make do with letters. *Lord forgive*, Jean had exclaimed in that voice which was either a squawk or a screech, Casey could never decide which.

Casey had in return directed Jean to her secret library. She could return the last and choose another, as she always did. Jean had taken to books in the way the husband must have hoped Casey would. She devoured them and seemed to retain some of their meaning. Jean said that she had always been curious but her father had discouraged her reading. It was idle and unattractive. She had seen the spine of *Paradise Lost* and convinced Casey to part with it.

Casey worked on a shortcrust pastry and a filling for pie, and once it was in the oven they cleared the kitchen table and moved to Jean's instruction on hems. This latest dress was the first Casey would make all by herself. She followed Jean's words and watched the woman's steady hands. The dress would be finished that day after the pie was set by the window to cool.

Jean then invited Casey to come to the big house for dinner, as she had done so many times before. It was perhaps the sense of futility with which the invitation was made that compelled Casey to accept for the first time. The husband was still away. Yes. She would come to dinner. Of course she would. It was a normal enough thing. Casey asked only if the meal could be early. She would need to return to the boathouse by sunset. Jean didn't question this.

So Casey now stepped between the wildflowers and went in through the open doorway of the big house with her stomach acid splashing up into the base of her throat. This was wrong. It was not too late to return home.

Jean came from behind and linked her arm through Casey's. She kissed Casey's cheek and pulled her close, then led her through the kitchen and then the dining room to the table set on the wide verandah. A family was introduced. The gardener, Henry, and his wife, Zoey. Then two cousins. A daughter and son, both in their thirties and with children of their own. They were nameless. The children ran and played and made only happy noises.

Jean sat Casey beside her at the long table. The gardener was cool at first and seemed put out, but Casey's silence seemed to appease him and he later came from the kitchen with cold bottles of beer, the first of which he placed on the tablecloth in front of her. Jean drank and introduced her guest by standing and speaking her name to the centre of the commotion. Zoey made a gesture of welcome with a salad server. One of the children appeared to Casey's side and asked in the smallest voice if he could brush her hair. Casey smiled and declined and the child took no offence and ran back inside with the tight curls of his own hair pulsing at each leap. Jean continued to talk and laugh crudely. She held court. The children played and food was served. Casey listened and learned that there had been only one booking for the hotel in the last two weeks and they had cancelled in the end. The other staff had been sent away and so Henry had brought in his nearby relatives to make some dent in the wasting stores of fresh food.

It was the serving of bread that brought on Casey's collapse. Zoey was standing above her, slicing the loaf. She had asked if Casey wanted two slices or three and then stood applying thick coatings of butter from a ceramic bowl. Casey waited as a child would and this had begun her fall. She was so close to happiness and so afraid. Jean patted her shoulder and waved the others away. The sky was beginning to darken. The child with the hairbrush returned and asked Casey why she was sad.

'Leave her, poppet,' Jean said.

Casey smiled at the boy, who could have been only four. 'I'm happy. I'm very happy.'

'No,' the boy said. 'You're sad.'

'Yes, you're right.' Casey laughed and wiped her face. 'Yes, I'm sad.'

She stood and refused another beer. She apologised and thanked them for the food.

'Stay,' Jean said, still holding her by the fingers.

'I'm sorry.'

Casey slid from Jean's grasp and moved back through the dining room and along the corridors of the big house. She escaped through the front door and hastened across the grass. She felt the earth harden beneath the balls of her feet. This was wrong. Those streaks of wildflowers grabbed at her ankles. The sun was still just above the horizon so she would be home in time to at least honour that rule: to always be in the house with the darkness. But she had spent time with the gardener and his family and this must surely be a breach.

She reached the stairs at the side of the boathouse at a run and the husband called out her name from the water's edge. He was cooling his feet in the lake as he often did after a long journey. She had done wrong and rules had been broken. The husband called again, this time raising a hand. She had not heard his voice for a week. The previous Sunday he had spoken to her briefly while making repairs to the decking. His voice then had been flat and he had spoken to her shoes. Now he spoke in a more familiar way. She had never truly placed his accent.

He smiled. 'Wait.' He walked over to her.

She could not speak. The terror in her chest.

'You were running. Are you okay?'

She nodded.

He appeared younger than the image she maintained in her mind. The voice was softer. It was the smile.

'Yes, I'm okay,' she said and looked over his shoulder to the big house. A grey line of smoke issued from one of its chimneys.

'Good,' he said. 'I want to be sure.'

He took a step forward so the tips of his toes met hers. He put his hand out, took Casey's and pushed his fingertips into the soft centre of her palm. She smelled the toasted earth and then the beer on her own breath. His face came in close, awkwardly, like a schoolboy.

'You have all you need,' he said.

This sat lost between a question and statement. Understanding washed over her. An instant containing full knowledge of her world and its shape.

The husband truly imagined he loved her.

Truly.

And so he could be overcome.

She put her hand to the baby inside her. This thing she could barely bring herself to believe was true. This beginning of a person she was so fearful for.

But this husband. She understood now.

He could be overcome.

'Yes,' she said and returned a fraction of his hand's pressure, just enough to register, and watched the smoke of the big house continue into the colour of night.

Chapter Twelve

'Ma'am, you need to take a seat.'

May's fists were on the counter and she brought them together, interlocking the knuckles. She had always pushed this down. Always taken a seat.

'No.' The pain of her wedding ring against the bone of her finger became too much. 'You need to tell me what you are going to do about this. You need to get off your arse and do your goddamn job.'

'Sit down now or I will take you in.'

'Take me in? Oh, this is perfect. This is beautiful. Okay, you take me in. For being loud. For not sitting down. Beautiful. While there's a fucking psychopath walking around your town. Okay, you take me in.'

May had brought the boat in beneath the house then approached the outside staircase with the calf lying dead in its pool of blood. She had leaped over it and gone upstairs, found her keys, phone and wallet. Outside she stepped again over the poor, bound body and ran up to her car. It was only when she reached the town centre that she realised she'd being driving on the wrong side of the road. The side of her instinct. A truck's silhouette coming directly at her, all headlights, blasting its horn. She had yanked the steering wheel, skidded off the road, and the truck driver had stopped and walked over. He had asked what was wrong with her and told her she was crazy. Eventually he gave her directions to the police station, two streets over. She was crazy.

The tyres of her car had screeched against the concrete of the station's car park and inside she had demanded help. The officer at the counter had not listened to her words: boy, knife, blood. He had raised his hands and told her to calm down and this was now only about May and her refusals.

'Frank, it's okay.' Another officer had appeared behind the station counter. She had put her hand on the man's shoulder and managed him back into his chair. 'I'll get this.'

'Take a seat, ma'am,' Frank had said again to May before resuming his own, his arms folded, looking away.

'What can we do for you?' The other officer had exited through a door at the side and stood next to May. 'Let's sit.'

'I don't want to sit.'

'That's fine,' the woman said. 'But if it's okay by you I'm going to take a load off; it's been a hell of a day.' She backed herself into the last plastic chair in a row against the wall.

May rubbed her palms together. She wanted to punch a hole through something's centre. To have the foundations of the world tremble at her violence. She sat. The sound of lights buzzing and clicking. Air conditioning.

'I'm Officer Carter. What's your name?'

'May. I already told your—'

'Hello, May. I'm going to help you. Now, what's happened?'

'I've already told your friend.' She looked at Frank, who gave an unpleasant smile. 'A boy called Red brought a live calf to my house and cut its throat open on my doorstep.'

'A calf?'

'Yes, a calf. A cow. A little cow.'

'I want to help you, okay? You say his name was Red.'

'Red Golding, and he is a smug little shit and is walking around your dogshit town with a knife, cutting throats, and I thought you might have some thoughts about that, being the police and all.'

Officer Carter looked briefly back at Frank. 'May, why would Red do something like that?'

'How the hell should I know? He's a deranged motherfucker. Why are you not doing anything? Why are you sitting here, doing nothing? Jesus Christ.'

May put her head in her hands. Fuck them, one and all. It added up to nothing in the end and so they may as well all get fucked now. Husbands, sons. Teenage boys with confidence they haven't earned. Grandfathers and deaths and inheritances being burned to the ground. The world could burn. Fuck the police. Fuck this cheap, vomit-green carpet.

Her eyes settled on the chaos of dots and swirls below her. The floor's pattern was like the ones in most public places. The patterns she and her mother were employed to clean. Patterns that understood the world would only turn foul in the end and so didn't bother to fight back. She looked at her shoes whose soles and toecaps were stained with red splatters and saw that the officer was now staring at the shoes too. Staring down at the calf's blood.

'May, can you take me there?'

As they passed the counter May turned her face away. The man would get none of her anger or victory. Not even a roll of her eyes. Fuck Frank.

Outside, she went for her rental but the officer insisted on taking her squad car.

'It's the boathouse,' May said. 'The lake.'

'What were you doing there?'

'Living.' May sighed too loudly. This woman was trying to help. It was Frank who had done her wrong. Her husband. The arrangement of life. This woman was trying to help. 'I was there because it's my house. It's mine now.'

The main street was still except for activity at the entrance of a bar. The Grill Club. A man pushed open its door as they drove by and May had a glimpse of its unnatural red interior.

'I didn't know anyone was living at the boathouse, that's all.' The officer adjusted her mirror and then the seatback. 'It's been empty a long time.'

They passed houses where the shape of families moved in the pleasant squares of windows and May's breathing slowed.

'Your name is Officer Carter?'

'That's right.'

'Am I allowed to know your first name? If there's a rule, I get it. I'd just like to know your first name, if that's okay. I know Frank's but I'd rather know yours.'

'I'm Cath.'

'Hello, Cath.'

'Hello, May. I'm a little confused by all this.'

'I'm not sure I can help with that.'

The calf was gone. Cath directed the beam of her flashlight around the staircase again. The wood was damp with water.

'Why would I make this up?'

'I never said that, May. I'm just trying to figure this out.'

'He stood right here and cut the thing's neck. There was blood, right here. He's come back and washed it away. You can see that. Cath, please. Why would I make this up?'

The sandy ground at the base of the stairs was dark and wet. May scooped up a handful and brought it into the light.

'Look, it's pink. This is blood. Cath, please.'

'I'm going to need you to go inside, okay? You go in the house and sit tight.'

'What are you going to do?'

'I'll go talk to Red.'

'Talk. Jesus.'

'Go in the house, lock the door and sit tight. Let me figure this out.'

'Lock the door? Why am I the one being locked up? The kid is a fucking killer. What are you doing?'

'My job.'

May tapped the toe of her shoe against the wet timber. Her eyes were adjusting to the low moonlight. Nothing would come of this. It may as well have never happened. Perhaps it never had.

'I'll be back, May. Lock the door. Sit tight.'

May made herself some food. Cheese, margarine, bread. The night was still warm but she pulled the doors to the verandah closed against the insects. They were hovering at the entrance like uninvited vampires. She sat at the table and pushed around the bourbon bottle. No television. She missed it. What did people do without television? How had Casey and Moses dealt with their nights? She thought of her grandmother at this table, sewing or mending some garment. May had never threaded a needle in her life. Never knitted. Maybe Casey had sat here and written poetry or recorded the day's events in her journal. May was picturing Casey as some Jane Austen character from the movies but the woman had been in the house in the fifties. May knew nothing of that time, nothing of her grandmother.

The vision of the calf returned and the boy using his violence for a neat purpose. A demonstration of how easily it comes. Like that needed proving. May pushed around her bottle and watched its brown settle.

When Cath returned her expression confirmed what May had expected.

She pulled a chair up to the table. 'I talked to Red's parents. I talked to Red, too, and he says he knows nothing about it.' Cath's attention went briefly to the bourbon. 'Says he came down to say welcome and that was all.'

'That's fine,' May said. 'You know what? I don't care. What else would he say? If you can do something like that, then lying about it's nothing.'

Cath was scanning the room. 'There's not much I can do from here. I want to be honest with you, May. The parents weren't happy, I'll tell you that.'

'They shouldn't be.'

'At the accusation, May. They were stirred up. I spent a long while talking them down. They wanted to come down here but I told them to sit tight, just like I told you. Okay? I told them they're to stay away and I'd advise you to steer clear.'

'I don't even know them, Cath. Or this kid. He turned up, delivered something close enough to a threat, then killed a cow on my doorstep. That's messed up, right? I'm assuming this isn't something regular around here. Or am I missing some subtlety? Fine, I'll look after myself. Fuck that kid. I won't going looking for him, but if he shows up here again I'll look after myself, I can promise you.'

Cath was tapping her index finger against the table. A fast heartbeat. May recognised the tempo.

'This is your place, then?' The officer looked around the walls, the light fixtures. 'It's nice. I'd always wondered. I knew Jean was keeping it up but I wondered.'

'You know Jean?'

'This is Loveland. I knew that she was keeping the place up but I never knew why.'

'It was my grandmother's. She died.'

'I'm sorry.'

'It's fine. Everything's fucking fine.'

Cath started again with her finger and May noticed her tired, kind eyes. She seemed like a good person. One who tried. May felt a tug in her chest.

'Off the record, May, that kid's a piece of work. He was excited when I asked him about all this, I swear. His blood got pumping. And the parents are no better. Best to keep clear. Their name's been in Loveland a long time and they think that comes with something. I want you to know I did my best but there's not much more I can do now.'

The evening would burn itself out and May would sleep, she supposed, and the first day of the working week would follow. She should be finding a real estate agent and maybe a lawyer. There would be applications, contracts. Patrick's voice in her ear to get this sorted. Her son refusing to speak to her. The sick water and generations of silence. Money, its lack. Her mother. The fucking heat of this place and the insect vampires.

'I'm angry,' May said.

Cath gave a creaking smile.

'That's all.' May rubbed at her sore eyes. 'I just wanted to say that out loud. I know it won't change anything to say it but here we are, I've done it. It's sitting in here. Right in my chest. And I'm not going to do anything about it. Not a thing.'

They stood at the door to May's car. Through the police station's glass doors they could see the brightly lit counter was unattended. Frank would be in back. May's rage had cooled but her thoughts still arrived easily at *fuck Frank*.

'I'm sorry, Cath.'

'Don't be.'

'Well, thank you, then,' May said. 'I'll say thank you.'

She got into her car and her back ached like she'd been swimming. The chemistry of her brain polluting her muscles.

Cath knocked on the car window and May found the button to lower it.

'Take this,' Cath said. 'It's my card. I've put my number on the back, my civilian number, though I'm not supposed to. If there's any trouble, you let me know, okay? I believe you, you know. In case I didn't say. About the kid and what he did. I believe you.'

'Thank you.' May turned the card over and saw Cath's neat handwriting.

'Don't thank me—it's my job. Any trouble, you call, okay? You don't hesitate.'

LOVELAND, MARCH 1958

The baby came.

In the weeks leading up to the birth, Moses had become all of Casey's world. He had decided her weariness had become too much and so put her to bed. He had insisted and grew heated when she asked to step outside for sunshine or to stretch her aching legs. She was allowed in the end to walk within the house. To step out on the verandah but no more. Jean and the other staff had been instructed to keep away, and so Casey had only Moses until the evening came to call for the doctor.

The labour had been much worse than she'd imagined. She had expected pain, welcomed it even, but it was beyond what she thought possible. Casey had screamed. Roared. She couldn't stop sobbing and calling for relief that wouldn't come. Moses had told the doctor that he would be waiting up at the big house and that he should be found when it was all over. He held his hand to Casey's sweating forehead before walking wordlessly from their bedroom.

The agony went through the night. The doctor had seemed kind but he could bring Casey no mercy. He held her hand, brought her water, gave directions. Daylight had filled the room as the baby finally broke free and joined Casey in her cries. The doctor cleaned and wrapped the child and brought it to its mother's chest. The sight of the baby was the only part of this that had held true to Casey's dreams. The beauty and perfection of the tiny girl. Casey stroked her and kissed her face and hands. They both continued to weep.

Moses appeared at the bedside and asked the doctor whether it had played out as it was supposed to. He asked if his son was healthy and showing the right signs. Moses had never talked directly of his hope for a boy. He had spoken of it as something that was without question. His preparations and plans were for this imminent son.

'Meet our daughter,' Casey said. 'Come.'

There was something in her exhaustion that meant she had no fear left. Moses must come and kiss their girl. He had hesitated at Casey's command but no reaction came to his face. Not disappointment, not anger. Just a pause and then he walked to their side and brought his hand to the baby's head. They remained like this and eventually the doctor spoke and described what they should expect from the next few days. He would be back to check the bleeding and that the baby was feeding.

When the doctor left Casey spoke from within her delirium of courage. 'I want to call her Rosie. She's so precious. We'll call her Rosie.'

His hand didn't lift from the baby's brow. He told Casey that she could do whatever she wanted to. The child was hers and hers alone.

Chapter Thirteen

Next morning Loveland was once again alive and framed within the window of the diner's booth. Dogs being walked. Humans greeting one another. Shop signs being turned to OPEN. The pick-ups driving along the main street had lost their peculiarity to May and they seemed now a more reasonable proportion. This was a large and insistent world, after all.

Coffee arrived with her toast, the eggs to follow. The caffeine's promise hit on contact with her throat and May was powerful with hunger. She turned her phone on and found her son's number. She called him because that would be a regular thing to do: a mother calling her son.

'Francis?'

She could hear his breathing.

'Francis, it's me.'

'I know. Your name comes up.'

'What name do you have me under? No, don't tell me. Where are you?'

'My room.'

'What about school? What's the time?'

'I don't know the time. Mum, why are you calling?'

She heard only his breathing again, and then the rustle of junk food.

'I'm just calling. I'm on the other side of the world so I'm calling my son.'

'Well, that's great. As long as it makes you feel better. I'm happy for you.'

'Francis.'

'Am I wrong? I want you to really think about it. Are you calling because you want to know how I'm going or because you want to make yourself feel better? I'm too old for this. I can see through it. This self-serving bullshit. We can see through it.'

'You and your father.'

'That's right. Me and the person who's here.'

'I didn't want to leave.'

'Really? Because you did. And people do exactly what they want. Anyway, fuck it. I don't care. We're here, you're not. I'm too old for these tricks. I'm seeing things clearly now. I have to go.'

When Francis was small, May would steer the moments with Patrick into another room. If there was a solid wall between her husband's shouting and her son's little eardrums then she was doing her best. Keeping him cushioned. When he was older she would send the boy out or be sure to have Patrick's screaming done early, usually in the car. But she knew Francis heard and she knew he saw. Now his transformation into his father seemed complete. They weren't just a pair, but the same. She had protected him from nothing and she was tired of doing her best.

May held her phone out with her arm straight. She faced its screen. The seconds of the call ticking over. Francis and his breathing. She screamed. Not a cry or a shout. A deep and real scream. She thought of Blackbird Hill and the woman dying. Murdered and falling from the cliff edge with that scream that was always bloodcurdling.

If it all meant nothing and it would all be lost, then there could be no harm to fighting and screaming. She had done her best and it had brought her to this, so she would scream because it was her instinct. Francis's name lingered on the screen for a few seconds more, she heard his breathing, and then the call ended silently.

The waitress arrived with the eggs.

'I'm sorry, Gloria.'

'Why's that, May?'

'The screaming.'

'Oh, never mind. Better an empty house than an ill tenant. My grandma used to say that when she passed wind. Now, who's making you scream, May? Mother, lover or kin?'

'If you don't mind me asking, how old are you, Gloria?'

'I don't mind.' She folded her order book and slid it into her trouser pocket. 'I'm twenty-one. Twenty-two in December.'

'I have to apologise. I thought you were a teenager. I don't think I ever said it but I thought it every time. I'm sorry.'

'If I could stay a teenager forever I'd take that in a second. I'm feeling ancient. I can't believe I'm twenty-one. I know I shouldn't say that, I know it's nothing, but I feel it. Would you do it again? Be twenty-one, I mean. If you could.'

'In a heartbeat.'

'Huh. I hoped so. Here's your boy.'

Tate was coming through the diner's front door, unsettling its chimes. May called him over. She told him to sit and said that she would be buying him the breakfast of his life. He should order everything he had ever wanted because, afterwards, there was so much work to do.

All the things she should be doing. The settling. The moving forward. Tate stepped out from the boathouse's bathroom and May had to bite hard on her knuckle.

'Oh, that is delightful.'

'Laugh it up, May. This is on your dime.'

He squeaked with each footfall. They had bought the fishing waders together at Sargents but it was still a treat to see Tate emerge dressed in shining khaki from plastic boot tips to the top of his suspender straps. With his slender frame he looked like a chicken wing dropped into a rubber glove. May took her turn to dress in her waders and Tate took his turn to mock. They squeaked out to the verandah, where they had laid out everything they had bought that morning. Arm-length rubber gloves, face masks, waste bags, long-handled tongs, shovels. Two rubbish spikes that Tate had built from broom handles and long screws. All they needed for May's futile mutiny.

She had checked with Tate's mother. First that she could again hire the son for the day, and second that she would agree to him coming into the lake if May arranged for the appropriate gear. Tate's mother had welcomed it all. The lake had been this way for years and they had always been assured that unless you drank a gallon of it the greatest risk was only its stink. Tate had been maddening lately, *maddening*, so May would be doing her a favour by taking him off her hands.

So they would clear the waste from the boathouse. The chip bags and burgers wrappers. The wet boards. The nests of antique fishing line and rusted tackle. The shopping bags and cigarette butts in the reeds. The broken glass in the banks and the mess of time and its world. It would continue pressing in—the refuse, the world, time—but for a piece of a day they would hold it back and this would be May's anger turned solid. She considered everything that she should be attending to and instead she would make her house sit pretty. They began their work.

It was mid-morning and unfiltered daylight shone from all directions with the sky cloudless and the water still. The shore was glistening where the sun bounced back from tiny freckles of minerals, and dried sludge made worms across the ground against the lighter sands beneath.

May started with her spike, patrolling the sides of the house and spreading out in a slow spiral. She filled a bag before completing her first orbit. The pole was a hunting spear in her hand and sinking it into a flattened beer can felt enough like piercing the flesh of some fast-moving quarry. Cigarette packets. A baby's red shoe. A decaying book without its cover that turned out to be *The Great Gatsby*. She'd been set that one in school and never read it. Its last page showed itself now and it was just some jumble of letters trying to emerge out of a hopeless stain. May read what words she could—*the green light, the orgastic future*—could make no sense of it, and it went in the bag with the rest.

Tate had started with the plywood sheets he had pulled free from the windows. He piled them in the area of scabby grass up near the road that they had designated as the dumping ground. After, he waded into the water up to his knees and said he would move towards the house in low, slow sweeps. May had wanted him on dry land but he had been keen for the lake. He tied two plastic bags together and hung them over his shoulders so he could deposit what he found as he went.

'Look—rope,' he called out, pleased, just a few steps in. 'I'm going to follow it.'

He gathered it, coiling it into loops, and May stopped and watched as the water ran from his pink-gloved arms. Yellow drops like a melting icy pole. Maybe the rope led to the lake's plug and Tate would pull it clear and all this would drain away.

'What's on the end?'

'More!' He kept on spooling, hunched and peering down. 'More rope, May. Just more.'

They kept on and built a pyramid of rubbish at the bank by the road. After the obvious things at the surface they found that layers of deeper, older litter would be exposed with just the toe of their rubber boots or by scraping with the point of their poles. Tate grew more methodical and intent with his sweeps, circling ever closer to the house. May flittered more, heading into the shade on the roadside and then wandering out into the shallows. She watched Tate pursue his prey. The tension, the execution, the release. He was a good, spirited boy. He should be out burning at some interest of his own instead of this, but then what was *this*, after all? What point was she proving? He was getting paid, though, and he seemed happy with it. He was getting paid, so that wiped sentiment clean. That's how the world had built itself. Everything was wiped clean.

It was hot inside the sticky layers of the wading pants and moisture was pooling inside their gloves. Tate would pull his away and let the sweat and lake water run free. She fetched them glasses of water and brought one of her new towels down to the grass by their rubbish mountain. They made groaning noises as they flung down their tools and gloves and sat. They drank and wiped their mouths and ran the towel across their faces. Resting back with their elbows against the earth they looked out and Tate gave a series of satisfied sighs.

'I hate this,' he said. 'Happens every time. Whenever I do a job of work it feels exactly as good as my mother always tells me it will. Unbelievable. Don't you tell her.' He was smiling, glowing. He exhaled more fully than he needed to. 'A good day's work feels good. It's true and I hate it.'

'I've been working since I was sixteen,' May said without taking her eyes from the lake. 'Cleaning up after people every day of my life and, you know, it's never felt good. It never did and it only got worse. I envy you, Tate. Working just drives me deeper into the ground. You're a better person than me. You must be.'

She wished she hadn't spoken. Rained on his parade. It *was* a trick, though. Work had never left her renewed. She felt sunburned and tired and the skin at her ankles was raw. Work had always left her tired and diminished. A trick. This redemption it promised. A bone dogs throw to themselves.

'This is looking much better,' she said. 'You did a great job, Tate, and you can't stop me telling that to your mother.'

The house looked inviting and younger. Closer to how it must have been. May thought of the lake cleansing itself and rising again. She imagined the shape of her son. She thought of the pale ring of calf blood on the ground around the steps.

'Do you know a boy around here called Red?'

'Yeah,' Tate said. 'Yeah, I know Red.'

'He's a friend of yours?'

Tate laughed.

'But you know him?'

'Well enough. He was supposed to be going away on some football scholarship. That's what he told everyone. But he's still here, like the rest of us. They're just up the street. The Goldings.'

'I've only met Red.'

'Stay away from them, that's my advice. Not that you asked for it. I mean, I'm just a dumb kid who gets his kicks from working hard, so what do I know?'

This sweet, spirited boy. He smiled and she was released.

Tate had protested at being taken back to his mother's store, but in the end fell silent. May had thanked him and said goodbye and he had only said *yeah* and left her car without looking back. This is what we do. We fall short.

May was back in the house and had just finished cleaning the kitchen counter when the pulsing came of someone calling her phone. It showed her husband's name. He rarely called, only sent his little texts. She picked the thing up and answered because he would be expecting her to avoid him. It could make no difference.

'Patrick.'

For five minutes and thirty-five seconds this would be her entire contribution. The time of the call announced itself in the screen's pixels. What remained was only his voice. Patrick's words that became only static. He was so angry. So disappointed. She had abandoned him. Abandoned their son. His words were the usual ones and she had heard them so often that they lost any meaning. He was no more. Big Nothing took over her body and she was at once all loss. All anger.

His furious mutter went on as she held the phone with her arm outstretched and screamed. The same scream she had delivered to her son. Her final scream. The husband went quiet and May brought the phone to her ear. She spoke slowly, clearly.

'Patrick, I need you to listen to me. I need you to understand what is happening here. I am leaving you. Listen to my voice. *I am leaving you.*'

There was so much more to say but none of it could find its way to her tongue. She had said the thing. The true thing she feared above anything else. Other words would only be explanation and he didn't deserve them.

She was leaving him.

Had left him.

And now he knew.

She ended the call and the screen went dull. She put the phone down on the counter. She stood for some time without moving and watched the device. It buzzed and flashed with the husband's calls. She would never answer them. Never again. Then the messages came—one after the other, his words typed and boxed on her screen. This was a moment she had imagined so many times and his words were exactly as she expected.

She knew the flashing and buzzing would continue, so she left her phone and walked out onto the verandah. Her arms were trembling but she had anticipated that. Heat was spreading through her body and in time it would overwhelm her blood and bones. Her rubber wading trousers were drying, draped over the railing. She had thought her work finished but with this change there was nothing to do but dress again in her uniform and see to the impossible fixing of the lake and its house.

She would vomit. It was brewing already in her burning guts. May would dress again and go into the water to find the waste and debris of the centuries. There would be another baby shoe somewhere. A library of unread books. The shaking would worsen and the anger and fear would intertwine and find new ways to escape. May would scream again and search for the rope that led to the lake's plug and maybe she could finally realise an act of destruction that matched her need.

—

Jean was crouched, sitting on the heels of her flat shoes at the lake's edge. The water was halfway up May's shins as she stood ten metres out and leaned against her rubbish pole while the boy, Red, was running his fingers through his hair. He stood among the clumps of pale grass. He had called out and waved as if spotting friends across a crowded bar and May had frozen to the spot. Jean had arrived just a minute earlier, having brought over a gift of a salad and a promise that she wouldn't stay because she knew May had so much to organise. Jean could help, though, but only if May wanted. They had been talking when Red appeared with his swept-back hair and smile.

'No.' May said this without thinking and at a volume that could only just reach Jean.

Red continued his approach, raising his hands and laying on a familiar expression. He stopped beside Jean, who rose to her feet.

'No,' May said, still in a whisper. 'No.'

Jean, looking from May to Red, seemed at last to understand.

'Ladies,' Red said.

Jean took steps towards the boy. 'What is this?'

'This?' Red asked. 'They call this a hello, I'm sure. I'm May's new friend.'

Jean was standing close to him now and had raised her hand so her palm was in line with his chest. 'That's enough.'

'Enough? I'm only here to help. There seems to have been a little case of mistaken identity, hasn't there, May? I got a visit from Officer Carter last night and she was flustered over something.'

Jean glanced back at May then pointed a finger at Red. 'Kid, you need to leave. Right? Whatever this is.'

'This is exactly what I'm talking about.' His smile brightened. 'Y'all are flustered over something but I don't know what. My parents were not impressed, though. But I'll tell you what I told them, May, and what I told the officer: I don't have a clue, not even the tiniest clue, what you've got yourself all hot over down here.'

'Leave,' Jean said.

'I welcomed my new neighbour to town, and the next thing I know I have the police at my door.'

May became aware of the pole in her hand. She felt the smooth grain of its wood against her skin and the resistance of the long metal screw at its end as it dug hard into the mud of the lake bed.

'Leave,' Jean said. 'We're not having a conversation. You're leaving.'

He raised his shoulders in a shrug, kept his gaze on May, blew out his cheeks and exhaled in exaggeration. *Crazy.*

'I guess I'll be on my way.' He motioned to Jean. 'Nice-looking salad you brought. I'm guessing a lunch invitation is out of the question?'

Jean only continued to stare. He retreated slowly up the shore.

'I'll leave you ladies to this little drama of yours. Nice seeing you both. Jean, I'm glad I caught you, actually. My parents were talking about you. I had no idea you went so far back with the Love family. You and Moses, huh? I had no idea. Never knew you went that far back. It was so long ago, though, I wouldn't worry about it. I'm sure all is forgiven. It was so long ago.'

He made the area of firmer grass, still smiling, and brought up his hand and rubbed it against his throat. He turned and moved off up the hill. May watched the silhouette that could have been that of her husband, her son.

Jean waded out into the shallow water to where May stood. When she spoke it was in a soft monotone.

'May, what's happened?'

'It doesn't matter.' May moved a little now. Brought down her shoulders. 'The more I think on it, the less it matters. Like it never happened at all.'

'Should I call the police?'

'No.'

'Anyone?'

'No.'

The early afternoon had brought a sheet of low, dark clouds and the water had taken on an opalescent sheen. May imagined the promise of rain. She pulled her spike free from the mud but neither woman moved to leave the water.

'Your grandfather,' Jean said. 'I don't know where to start, May. Jesus, this is the wrong time. I want to tell you but that's just about me, isn't it? Selfish. We just want to get things off our chests.'

'Tell me,' May said. 'It won't matter, I promise you.'

Jean began to speak and brought her hand to rest on May's shoulder. May would listen, with her heart still thumping and the heat and nausea. Her fear's familiar passage.

Jean had been sixteen when she came to work for Moses. She was working for May's grandmother too, but it was Moses she answered to. She didn't know what she should say. Didn't know what mattered.

'None of it matters,' May said.

'I was sixteen and he was already forty. Married to your grandmother. And I promise you, I was just a kid. I didn't know a thing except that Casey was my friend and I loved her and that I'd fallen into a situation with Moses. I don't know what to call it, May. I was sixteen and he was a man and I fell under something. It wasn't love but he called it that.'

'Yes.'

'I loved your grandmother. She had my love. She was the closest person to my heart in the whole world. Closer than a sister. After everything that happened I only thought of Casey. I never made it up to her, though. I tried, but I never did.'

Everything that happened.

May watched something in Jean show through to the surface. The raked embers of a fire.

⌒

May was sixteen. She walked into the house looking for her mother but Rosie had been called in to work, so it was just May's grandmother at home, drying dishes in her slow way.

There had been an argument between May and her friend. Something over a promise to cover for each other's lies and one or both of them failing. May would go to her mother with these things because she could rely on the response. The half-listening. The chance to turn it into a fight that satisfied.

'When is she going to be home?'

'Late,' her grandmother said.

May stamped around the kitchen and searched aimlessly through the fridge. Pushed a mug into the sink. She knew already how this would play out with the friend and that there was no real loss in it. She was a child like the rest and May had grown used to how they acted but there was still this unspent energy in her. Why was she the one left to dispense with it? She pictured the friend somewhere telling her version of it. Lying and gaining sympathy and then laughing and planning their weekend.

The grandmother was now washing the mug May had pushed into the suds. This woman who seemed only a visitor. A figure who hovered and did the washing-up and everything was stillness and apology. Always apology. May stepped forward, took the mug from her grandmother's hands and threw it at the floor between their feet. It smashed with a better sound than May had even hoped for.

Within the fright of that noise, for that moment between the mug's detonation and the grandmother recovering her composure, May saw the living animal. A flash of colour in her eyes. There was a woman beneath the mute trappings and for that second May was in her company.

The grandmother mumbled something and then went under the sink for the dustpan and brush. She got on one knee and pushed the pieces of the broken mug across the lino. May stood over her and, unable to summon anything else to say, told the grandmother that she was pathetic. That she hated her. The grandmother didn't pause and didn't look up.

May knew.

She was looking down at her future self. That was all. This was the grandmother, her mother, her. This was their lot: to work and grow silent and eventually still. May drew in a breath to scream but abandoned it. There was no point. This was their lot. The grandmother apologised and continued to sweep up the mess.

The wind breathed across the water and the sunlight was weak. Jean's expression turned to something near relief.

May was scared: this was the truest word for it, no matter how childish. She saw the face of her husband reflected across the lake. His terrible, beautiful face made into water. Water that was sick with floating corpses. So many bodies, facedown and bloated with gas. The scent of it came on the wind and May retched.

The water, though, would soon become a great wave. It would rise to sweep her off the sand, turn her over and drive her into the lake's bed. The wave was rising to snap her neck and crush her bones.

'My turn for a story,' May said. 'My husband. *The husband.* Jean, I haven't told you about him because I can't bear to hear it. I don't tell anyone, in the end. It's not much more complicated than that. I just can't bear what the words would sound like.'

'You can try, if you like. I won't mind how it sounds.'

'I'm so scared,' May said.

'Yes.'

'He hurts me, Jean. I'm so scared. Every single day. I think he could kill me. I think he will. I don't know how else to say it. Am I making sense? I'm so scared I can't breathe.'

'Sweet girl.'

'I told him that I'm leaving him. He sent messages. I'm so scared, Jean. The husband. He's coming.'

LOVELAND, MARCH 1958

Casey walked along the sandy ground ten paces from the last stair and turned to admire the gentle wall of green and purple that the whole side of the boathouse had become. The plant she had rescued from the gardener's weeding had taken immediately in her wooden box. After a month she had transplanted it into a space she cleared in the ground by the roadside. It had spread fast and wide and she had been returning to it several times a day to give it water and remove any spent leaves. The gardener had said it was Prairie Smoke and that he thought it an awful trouble and had put his gloves around it several times to tear it free but Casey had teased him away each time. They had grown warmer towards each other and sometimes spoke now about the coming season and the progress on the buildings. The hope that guests would surely follow.

The Prairie Smoke had reached both corners of the wall by early winter. It died back to a brown and seemingly dead scaffold, and Casey worried over it, but after the first week of warmth it was green and twisting with new growth. She cared for this creature of proud, bee-calling flowers that flailed like whiskers and she thought of her recent reading of *Candide* and its conclusion of work being life's answer. Of nurturing the garden. She felt briefly in the presence of those people of the past and far away. Others who had wondered and worried and toiled. In this she felt her fear lessen.

She was responsible for this living thing, so she watered and she tended. Its life and death would recur and recur. Spring, winter. Winter, spring. Each year that passed would bring the worry, and each year the shock again of life.

In her arms the baby cried.

Chapter Fourteen

It was again a morning, again a working day, so May had at last come to town with the intention of walking into the office of the first real estate agent she could find. There would be one on the main street. This was what Karl had told her to do before she left Australia. Find a realtor, he had said. Give them my card, explain. Get the rock rolling.

At the edge of the town centre she followed the footpath into a square of neat park. A statue of a man looked skywards. He had an eagle perched on his raised forearm. Wooden benches bore plaques of dedication to loved, missed and dead residents of Loveland. Behind a row of trees was a small library and to the side of that a building of ochre bricks with *City Hall* stamped above its doors. As she walked by, May stopped at a community noticeboard attached to the exterior.

MASS CASUALTY TRAINING
LOVELAND FIRE AND RESCUE WILL BE CONDUCTING
MASS CASUALTY DISASTER TRIAGE TRAINING.
THIS TRAINING WILL BE STAGED AT THE LOVELAND
ELEMENTARY SCHOOL. WE WILL HAVE EMERGENCY
VEHICLES RESPONDING TO DESIGNATED
MOCK INJURIES LOCATED THROUGHOUT
LOVELAND THAT EVENING. THANK YOU!!

FIREWORKS AND CAR SHOW
MARK YOUR CALENDAR FOR JUNE 9TH!
14TH AND WILLOW DRIVE.
INFLATABLES, DJ, PONY RIDES, PHOTO
BOOTH, DUNK TANK, BEER GARDEN, FREE
HOTDOGS, FIREWORKS AT DUSK.

A stone sculpture rested on a pedestal inside a fence of hedges. It was about two metres wide and looked like granite in the shape of a painkiller tablet. On its front, under clear plastic, was an information panel and a faded photograph of a dozen people in that same spot on some day past, standing awkwardly, smiling hard.

This time capsule was sealed by Doreen Bowery, Clerk for the City of Loveland, on 16 March 2009. The City of Loveland was incorporated in 1930 and this capsule is to be left in peace until its reopening on 16 March 2080, on the occasion of the sesquicentennial of the city. We enshrine these humble tokens to celebrate our accomplishments, to remember our past, and to share our hope for the future of the citizens of Loveland, Nebraska.

A woman walked out through the building's automatic doors and May recognised her immediately from the photograph by her wide show of teeth.

'You're interested in our time capsule.' She pushed a pamphlet into May's hands. 'People are always a little shy to ask, so this here is a complete inventory of all the items sealed away until the sesquicentennial. There's a little something from every corner of Loveland. I'm crossing my fingers I'm there to see everyone's faces come 2080. That'll be something, won't it? I'm crossing my fingers. You never know. You're just visiting for the day?'

'Thank you.' May looked at the pamphlet and shook it encouragingly. 'Yes, just visiting.'

'Oh, that accent. Now tell me, is that Australia? Wait, is your name May—is that it? May? And you're down at the old boathouse?'

'Yes. Yes, I'm sorry, I need to get going. Thank you, though. For this.'

'Welcome to Loveland, May. It's really something to have a member of the Love family back home. You promise me you'll come say hello and I'll fill you in on everything going on in town. We are alive and well and there's a lot going on, and I want you to hear all about it, May.'

May murmured a vague promise to call in on the woman, enough to see her appeased, then she made her way back to the main street and entered the first realtor's office she saw. She gave them Karl's business card, explained, got the rock rolling. She was ushered into the back office and asked to wait just a moment. As she waited May read her pamphlet.

Minutes from the first city council meeting—7 July 1930.

$1 bill, quarter, dime, nickel, penny.

JC Penney catalog from Spring & Summer 2009.

Sponge Bob Square Pants whoopee cushion.

Holy Bible.

Envelope with a "forever" stamp.

This obsession with time's passing, it relied on it meaning something. That things could be changed. But what if it was all just this concrete slab, unalterable? It was all there, trapped in stone. Whatever she would pass on to her son, her older self, the queue of dead relatives. We're born with the legacy we'll leave. It's in the slab.

The realtor returned, all smiles. There were some forms, papers. It would be just a moment.

She told the realtor it was no trouble, there was no rush.

—

May slept deeply that night without dreaming and it was only the ascending chirps of her phone that drew her into the next day. It was Jean, restored to her full-blown pluck. Another road trip, if May wasn't sick of her. This time with Goyle left silent in the glove box. Jean said her family farm awaited. West a ways.

May gave it no thought. Yes, of course. She was so drained. Depleted. They could all have whatever they wanted.

Jean would be straight over.

With the phone still in her hand, a call came from the realtor. They spoke quickly, warmly, efficiently. Her name was Justine. Or Jane. There was much to do and she was the one to do it. She said she had spoken to May's attorney and it took May a little time to twig that she meant Karl. Justine or Jane and May's attorney had worked through the logistics. The realtor talked on as May walked barefoot through the living room, out through the glass doors to the verandah's railing. She leaned against it and daylight stung her shoulders and the rough skin of her neck.

'May, this is a curly one, but I've never backed down from a challenge. Now I need to know: how motivated are you? We can make it work, but it's going to take a pile of motivation. A big old truckload. I need to know, are you a motivated seller? And do you trust me? Trust and motivation, that's what we need. Do you trust me, May?'

'I trust you.'

'Are you motivated, May?'

'Honestly, I could not be any more motivated.'

'Oh, May, clients like you are why I get up in the morning. I want to get moving on this. I've got Karl working on some paperwork but don't you worry about that even a little bit. I'd like to drive down this morning and get myself familiar with the place. I'm going to bring down my little truck of miracles. Ferns, May. I will let you in on my secret. Nothing sells a house like a fern. We need the house to live. *Live*. So, your place at, say, ten?'

The sun was already too much. The lake was radiating heat like a hearth stone.

'Ten is perfect,' May said. 'I won't be here, but I'll leave the key out for you. I trust you.'

They were driving west. Jean said it would be a good few hours and they should settle in. She had brought a cooler of decent food and drink this time, and it sat between them making pearls of condensation.

The swoop of dark clouds began an hour into the journey. They were heading into the stomach of the bad weather Jean had forecast. May felt so heavy. She could summon no will. It seemed it had always been an illusion. Spots of rain appeared on the windshield and Jean raised the idea of them staying the night out at the farm. It belonged to her brother. There was plenty of space and it would be no bother. He would welcome the company. It was still a good few hours off, though. They should settle in.

May had been asleep and woke up to realise Jean was speaking. She was talking as if answering rolling questions. Nervous, talking about the Plains.

'Out west. That famed flatness. The emptiness. All that sentiment and poetry. But it's the pothole towns of Nebraska that deserve the fascination. The dogshit towns. You stand there in the hit zone and you're really standing at the edge of an eternal nothing. There's your poetry. Eternity needs people for scale. The Plains are pretty in parts. And that's something. The sunflowers, for one. There's this story. The Mormons were being driven out of Missouri and so they followed the sun and headed out to Utah. It was deadly and slow and tricky and so they spread sunflower seeds whenever they found a better way through. Here's the part people love: the next year, when the families followed in their wagon trains, they just followed the blessed sunflower trail. Great pie dishes of yellow on the end of sky-high stalks leading the way from misery to the chosen city. People love that. Love it to death. Now, here's the thing. I've checked that story out, done the reading, and I know if the story is true or not. I know. But the question is: do you want to know one way or the other? Does it matter if a story's true so long as it's pretty?'

—

The clouds now covered the sky and had a strange, dimpled pattern that May had never seen before. Sagging hills in uniform rows. They were giving up their rain and against the noise of the engine, the road, the falling sea, the wipers, Jean was still speaking, a tone of defeat in her voice now.

'May, I'm going to confess: I've brought you out here for a reason. You must have guessed already. I want to tell you what happened. I'm sorry. This is so selfish. It's all about me. Unburdening.'

May would allow it all to come. She knew so little about this woman and nothing about this man, her grandfather. It was so long ago and in a place just as distant. It could make no difference. May saw Patrick, his face looming above them in the purpling clouds. Her fear was like electrocution. Instant. Ancient. They could all have whatever they wanted.

⌒

Jean had come to work for the Love family through a connection of her father's. She had turned sixteen and finished her schooling, and Moses Love and his young wife were in need of help. There was a baby on the way. Jean's father had made a lot of his daughter's strong mind and back. Her obliging ways. She was sent for and was given a room in the big house. This was in the summer of 1957.

Moses was calm and exacting with his instructions. There were a scattering of others employed with the maintenance of the buildings and rooms. Moses explained that Loveland was to be returned to its former glory. The people would come. They would come with the fine weather.

Casey was quiet and uneasy, but in time Jean was able to bring her out. They became like sisters. Though younger, Jean had been raised on the land and with some freedom and so took to tutoring on worldliness. In exchange Jean learned a measure of Casey's softness. It was a love and it tethered them.

'The business with Moses began in the week after Christmas. He just came into my room, my bed, early one morning, didn't say a word. It happened too quickly. Everything.'

Later she learned the year of Moses's birth and figured out that he had on that morning been seven months into his forty-second year. She was sixteen. Sixteen and forty-two.

Jean continued to dream and to hold Casey's hand and receive early morning visits from Moses. Every day, Jean would run down the hill to the boathouse. The big house was so cold and empty and smelled of mould. Jean had noticed Casey taking a boat out onto the lake since the last of the winter ice had broken up. She would row out into the centre and sometimes stay for an hour or more. Jean had asked to join her but Casey had insisted on going alone. It was her time to consider things, she always said, but Jean worried about her. Casey would return from the lake troubled.

The baby was born, Rosie, and with her the start of the last trouble. It came quickly in the end. The other workers had left with the start of summer. There was no money left. Nothing of the great Love family. The visitors would not return. None of the grandeur. It happened quickly in the end. On the last morning that he visited Jean, Moses had been all fire. Everything was lost and gone and he said he was going to tell Casey of these mornings in Jean's bed. He left in a wild fit and Jean, ashamed, fled to the nearby forest of pines. She only returned at the smell of smoke. To the sight of the great buildings and structures ablaze. All that Moses had resurrected. The big house, the amusements, the boardwalk, the pier. Flames and towers of black smoke.

At the boathouse she had found Casey with Rosie in her arms and Moses at the water's edge with his shirt blackened and torn open. He waited for Jean to approach before making their confession to Casey. Telling her of their crime. Moses was looking directly into Jean's eyes as he brought the knife to his throat. It came so quickly.

⌒

'Your grandmother left with Rosie. Packed two cases and went to stay with an aunt. Then Australia in the end. She sent me letters. I'd write to her but there was nothing left. No sister.'

The burned boards and foundations of the lake's structures were cleared and most of the land taken by the banks and government. The debts were cleared or forgiven, as far as Jean could figure. The boathouse, though, and its patch of shore, were kept in Casey's name. Jean made sure of this, as she would go on to ensure that the house remained standing. That cocoon. The years would pass. There would be those few distant letters. Then May and the news of Casey's passing. Death. Call it death.

May woke at the rumblings of the gravel road to the farm. May had expected something old and sick with charm, but the family house looked recent and was made of functional red brick. The sky was dark and the rain was pelting down as they scurried from the car to the covered porch.

'Jean.'

'Brother.'

The pair held each other in a long, deep hug before all three went inside as Jean made the introductions and the brother made offers of coffee and a meal. The brother went to work in the kitchen, sending the women out to the back deck. His name so far had been Scott, Scotty, Bruv, Scooter. He seemed a similar age to Jean but the years had slowed him more obviously. He walked with a stiffness. His lips were thin and disappeared with his smile.

'I shouldn't ask again,' Jean said as her brother went inside, 'but Patrick. What can I do? What do you need?'

They were sitting at a table set back from where the deck's roof opened to the pulsing rainfall. Ahead was unending farmland. Fields of perfect green stripes without animals or machines. Lightning sparked on the near horizon. Empty order consumed by storm.

'Nothing,' May said.

'We can stop him. You need to tell me how.'

'There's nothing to tell. I'm supposed to be selling the house and so I will. There's nothing else to do.'

The brother returned with a tray of mugs. Thunder. Jean took May's hand.

The siblings fell into their routines and May submerged herself in the sound of it. Their stories retold for so many years. They each told the parts they had taken possession of. The coffee eventually became wine and the stories became older, more intimate ones of their families and the farm. As the storm drew closer Scott answered Jean's question on the prospects for the season. The tasks that were normally performed in June would this year wait until July or even August. The wet spring. He described to May the procedures of seed corn: males and females, tassels, the three rows cut back and the fourth row standing tall.

The feeling of her husband's presence would become strong to May in the moments between stories. The wave, rising, coming to its greatest height. Scraping cloud. Throwing everything else into its shadow. It was coming.

If she were to surrender she might be spared. It might not be too late. She thought of Francis. Where her son was in this. In truth he was a stranger. He had fought so hard to remain unknown. She could surrender but she knew the wave would still come.

Jean would not let her hand go.

Scooter had become Scott and said the storm was a decent one and that they should stay the night. There was plenty of room. There was the football on television.

They drank more wine. The siblings teased each other about the horror of their old age and which of them would be the first to give in and retire. It all fell within May's ears. Scott's love had died a decade earlier. Christopher. The beautiful Christopher. They went quiet at his name. The short illness. Scott became Scooter and smiled and showed a thumbs-down and announced what pathetic, hopeless specimens they had become. There were bags of chips in the pantry. May watched the sky. Storm chasers were passing through the town, Scooter had heard from the neighbour, in the hope of a tornado.

⌇

May stood watching her grandmother in the kitchen, the relent-less yellow of the sky behind. The grandmother was facing the small rectangle of window, washing the dishes as she always did.

She had cancer.

May had just been taken aside and told by her mother. It was cancer, definitely, and it was in a kidney. That might be the last of it or it might be the first. There would be surgery and likely much more. Yes, it was certain. All of it, yes.

So May stood watching her grandmother in the kitchen and watching the arch of her shoulders and those hands going under the suds. May could think of nothing to say or do because for that she would need to know a little of this woman. Of what happened inside and how she might be helped. This visitor.

May was angry and she knew this was the wrong feeling. Not angry at the kidney or fate but at this woman who had now lost any chance to be known. These were the wrong thoughts and yet here they were. It would make no difference, though, as there would be no shouting from May and no welcome flash of fire in the grandmother's eyes. There would be no apologies. It would remain only as thought.

She should have stepped forward and put her arms around the woman. Held her and supported her weight and maybe said something about love. Found some movement and words. But May stood and said nothing. Did nothing but watch the woman wash the dishes in her endless way. Watched the shape of her grandmother's back and those hands going under the suds again.

～

It was in fact two storms, Scooter said, that had combined. They amassed in the distance of the fields as a long, cheerless shelf with the afternoon sun catching its lower edge. The colours were ones May hadn't seen before. This cloud was living. Lightning fell and the rain became so heavy that Jean and her brother had to shout to be heard. The air had turned warm against the downpour and May stood with her arms out over the wooden railing and the drops hit with reassuring jolts.

Tap.

Tap.

Babies want those gentle shocks to their backs. Takes them back to their days before time.

May noticed an insect pressed into the meeting of the railing and a vertical post of the deck. She leaned in close to it and held a fingernail over its back. Her impulse was to stroke its wings. It was sheltering from the storm just the same as the humans, and May wondered if this should be some moment of revelation. Of understanding that these creatures and she were of the same type, subject to the same concerns. Having duty to each other. She let the tip of her finger connect with its wings. It didn't seek connection, though. It only pressed itself deeper into its joint. This thing wasn't loving. It wasn't built with that need. It had concerns but humans weren't one of them. It would see her species die without a twitch of recognition.

We put ourselves at the centre of everything. Humans imagine themselves there but maybe it's empty. Maybe there is no centre at all.

'I'm going out,' May said and pointed to the fields.

Jean winced. 'Out where?'

'Will that be okay, Scott? If I go take a look? I don't want to step anywhere I shouldn't.'

'I think you should stay here in the dry, but look, it's fine by me,' he said.

'A coat,' Jean said, seeing May already moving to the steps. 'Scotty, a jacket?'

She caught up as May took her first steps on the dark soil of the field. The rows of corn stood in perfect parallel and May cut a crooked line through them. Jean forced a plastic raincoat on her, even doing up its buttons, and as she did she told May that it would be okay. She would be safe. May realised only then that she was crying and she wondered when it had begun.

'We'll go to the police.' Jean put her hands on May's cheeks. 'We'll get help.'

'It doesn't matter what we do.'

May turned away and went into the stalks and leaves. She ran with her hands held out so her fingers brushed against these orderly things. Perfect, parallel. She ran and something was overtaking her heart. That expression, *blood ran cold*, had always been just one of those lines. Something from the television. Now, though, the blood stung inside her like it was truly near freezing. Tiny teeth of ice.

The mud and pools of water was up to her ankles. Jean was left behind. That gentle, hurting woman. May thought of her own grandmother, standing in the lake's shallows and watching her husband slit his own throat. What was the blood of one human against all that water and what difference could it make? Her grandmother, then, looking to poor Jean at the shore. Young, scared Jean. May looked out through Casey's eyes. Went within that moment of her grandmother's and the fear she must have felt. The searing, complete anger.

May became alone.

The storm had stretched beyond the limits of a mere human's view and so it disappeared. The crying wouldn't stop but that was only her body. Just the faulty meat. In that moment, May had gone to a place only of her mind and it had spilled open, fully, at last.

The tune of Big Nothing was all that remained.

May's body was gripped and lifted from the ground. She rose like she had above her lake. She rose into the sky and its storm and she lost all control. All pain. The wind blew through her body and made Big Nothing's melody on its way to the core of the twister. That's what the brother had called it. A twister like the ones in films. It was only a question of where it would touch down and what it would tear apart. Here she was at its middle.

May turned and turned at the centre of everything and could no longer hear or see or feel.

The naked truth of things.

LOVELAND, APRIL 1958

Jean was working at her embroidery but more often looking across the kitchen table to watch Casey's progress with her lace. Casey had struggled the last time but was moving smoothly now. A slow assuredness had come to her dressmaking and she had started to drink the beers that Jean would bring with each visit. This afternoon they had both just started on their second bottles.

'Keep it taut,' Jean said.

'I'm keeping it taut.'

They both watched closely the securing of the final loop of thread.

Jean reached over and took the dress. 'Getting there,' she said.

Casey furrowed her brow comically and took a long drink.

'Keep it taut next time,' Jean said. 'Still, you're getting there.'

Elvis came on the radio. Jean couldn't bear the silence in the boathouse and after weeks of campaigning Casey had agreed to let her bring over the small radio from the big house, though only after the husband had left for the day. That had been a month previously and now Casey had grown enough in bravery to allow the volume to creep above the knob's first notch. 'Wear My Ring Around Your Neck' filled the room. It carried itself boldly out through the open door and windows. The husband must have heard it by now. He would be listening. Casey admired her own work with the lace.

'So, I have news,' Jean said. 'Well, maybe some news. Maybe-news.'

Casey continued examining the lace, afraid at the interruption.

'I'm going to the city,' Jean said, letting her excitement spill. 'Maybe. New York. Probably. When the money's through. My cousin Getty, the one I told you about; money from her grandfather's will. And it was quite a bit, Getty says. Not a fortune but more than she thought. I never met the grandfather so I've decided to not feel bad about it in the slightest. He had a will and plenty of nickel and it's just trickling down. So Getty's getting the place in New York we've been talking about. I can't believe it's really happening! It really might. I know I shouldn't be so happy, but it's what we've wanted for so long. Casey, tell me you're not angry. It's what we've talked about all this time. The city, Casey. Tell me you're not angry.'

Casey continued to pat at the lace hem. If she didn't look up, this might not be occurring. Jean might change her mind. They might both forget.

'Casey? Did you hear?'

'Yes.'

Elvis went on and a dragonfly landed at the window. Casey hadn't heard Elvis for so long. His voice seemed absurd.

'That's it?' Jean clapped her hands together. 'I thought you might be happy. Excited, maybe. The city! I know this means I'll be leaving, but who says it has to mean I'm leaving you? Who says I would ever want to? The city, Casey! It's a big place. It's what we've talked about. This could mean whatever we want it to. You don't have anything to say?'

'Let's see if the money comes through.'

'Jesus. New York. Casey, New York. Come with me. Do I have to say it so straight? You and Rosie. Come work with me. Getty and me and the business. Getty is better than anyone at the numbers and she says she'll figure it out. We can almost afford to pay ourselves. This is it, doll. Think of it. We get a tiny place. The shop out the front and we live in the back with the cockroaches. You cook, I boss you around. Rosie can run free in the streets.' Jean turned at this to the baby sleeping noisily in her cot. 'Don't say you're staying.'

'Of course I'm staying.'

'You're kidding me.'

'I'm happy for you, Jean. You deserve this.' Casey put down the lace. 'I'm not angry.'

Jean seemed to swallow a scream and directed her unspent energy at the bowl of apples. They scattered.

'I deserve this? What about you?'

'It's not my money.'

'Money, Jesus. I want you to join me and have a life. What's stopping you? I don't understand why you're here and I've never pressed you on it. Never. I leave you be.' She growled and clenched her fists. 'I thought we were friends.'

'We are friends.'

'Then tell me why you won't come. Why you don't deserve a life.'

Casey began to cry and this surprised her before it did Jean. She hadn't cried in so long. Her first months in the house she had shed what she thought was her lifetime's supply of tears. Those had been months of impossible aching. She had wanted death entirely but kept herself alive for this absurd hope that seemed built into her heart. She couldn't bear to know she had left this world before its last chance had been spent. Then Jean arrived with her unstoppable insistence. It was returning Casey to a land of pain. Hope was pain.

Jean steadied herself and let out slow breaths. She moved to Casey's side of the table. Took her hand and kissed it.

'I know this is hard for you,' Jean said. 'I don't understand but I want to. You think you can't leave this place. I'm not saying I understand, but there are things we can do. Come with me.'

'No.'

'You can't stay here.' Jean shook her head and kicked at one of the apples she had spilled. 'I know it's your husband. I know you don't want me to mention him, but Casey, you're dying. I know you think you're trapped. Come with me. You and Rosie deserve a life. It won't happen here.'

Casey had been only half listening, and then not at all. A wind had found its way in from the windows of the deck and something of it had taken her attention. It seemed almost like a tune being sung in her ear. The melody was gone the moment she tried to recognise it but its work had been done. She thought of her life, her child, and the lake. The arrangement of things and how they must change was suddenly so obvious.

Clarity came to Casey as if it were the simplest of things and her tears stopped. She breathed deeply and for the first time in so long felt the oxygen reaching her lungs' depths. She exhaled. In that simple animal's breath she had arrived at a decision. She would act.

'You need to leave,' she said to Jean, bringing their gazes together. She spoke slowly, making each word certain. 'I'm happy that your cousin will have her money and I think you're right to leave. You need to go. I'm not angry and I wish you well. You need to leave.'

After a brief silence a series of noises occurred. Noises tied to the actions of this woman, Jean. Casey turned her head away to the windows. Jean must have left the house eventually, as there was no more noise or movement other than the light breeze against the curtains. Some minutes passed. Casey stood and cleaned herself of thread and flour, fixed her hair and left the house. She would walk purposefully and directly but without any suggestion of undue haste.

This was how a prey was stalked.

Across the grass she walked steadily until she reached the beginning of the pier. He was repairing its boards. The ones soft and claimed by age and water. She knocked on a length of timber. She knocked again. Not urgently but with a firm repetition. The husband stopped and stood with his hammer halfway through its blow. She had made her choice. She kept her shaking hands deep in her dress pockets.

'Come to the house for a drink,' she said.

His brow reacted but the man said nothing. He looked at his hammer and then, quite obviously, down to the curve of her hip.

'Come to the house for a drink,' she said again, more forcefully. To her face she summoned every faint memory she held of what her mother had called sweetness. Mother had wanted a girl with sweetness.

She must be patient.

Patient and then she would act.

She turned on the heel of her flat shoes and walked back towards her house and its open door. She heard at first only her footfalls and the insects, but then the counter rhythm of the husband's boots against the baked earth, following.

Chapter Fifteen

Days passed and May took to rising early, showering, dressing and moving to the boathouse deck. None of the west's storms came within influence of Loveland and ahead was just unblemished blue above gold. Only insects and the waft of heat smudging the boundary. After buttered bread and instant coffee she would walk into town. If she crossed someone's path, as she did increasingly when she was close to the town's centre, she would launch pre-emptively with a slight smile and give her *hello* and be sure to keep up her walking pace. She wouldn't hide and she wouldn't lay herself open. She would go about her day and exist in the ordinariness of it all.

What Big Nothing had shown her was too much. Too much for a lowly human to bear. The truth was unchangeable: the end was coming and there was nothing to do but wait. Maybe feel the sun's heat against a mere human's skin. Smell the air. It was carrying the scent of salt and dust and flowers.

At the diner she responded to Gloria's smiles and questions. May took her coffee and slice of pie and was left to look out the tall windows. She observed the busy, moving days of this town that bore her family name. Trucks. Dogs walking behind. The tipping of hats' peaks.

She went again to see the time capsule. The statues in the street. The old bank with its history engraved into a tarnished plaque. At the second-hand store she bought the first book she saw from the bargain table on the footpath. *The Heart is a Lonely Hunter*, one dollar. She took to reading it in the diner.

'Carson McCullers,' Gloria said. 'Who's he?'

May said that she wasn't sure and went back to reading.

The next day Gloria asked if it was any good. May said that she wasn't sure.

A child. A skinny, freckled thing that the librarians would greet with welcoming smiles and by leaning over their counters. May would nod in reply as this was something she saw the adults do. This was the Cotton Tree public library, where she would come after school, getting off the school bus at the stop near the roundabout and the surf shops. This was in those few years before her grandmother had moved in with them, when May and her mother had made a go of things as a pair.

The library closed at 5.30 p.m. and so May's mother would do her best to get there by then to take May home. Ima was the librarian who took the most interest in the child. Asked her about her day at school and if she needed a drink of water. Later, Ima would stand in the car park with May after the library had closed, waiting until Rosie arrived, full of apologies. Ima would only nod in that adult way and say nothing.

So this library was May's. For those two hours each day it was her domain. She knew each of its corridors. She read the magazines and found the cartoons in the newspapers. Finished the jigsaw puzzles and played the board games against herself. Ima would take her to the books and May would look but never read. It was too hard and slow and belonged to others. The mothers and daughters that May watched as they laughed and squealed with pleasure at these things. They could keep it. The kids clutching the books to their chests. This wasn't for May. The books here, in their shelves, made walls and streets. This little girl's territory.

She lingered in the aisles for adults, where she would walk with her arms outstretched and run her fingers along the books' spines. She liked the structure of it. The knowable streets. The words might be fine and they were there for whoever might care but that wasn't her. She was there because it was quiet and safe and she knew its limits and dangers. Sometimes she would watch the others with their precious books, sometimes wonder, but May knew her place and it was standing in the car park and waiting for her mother, who would surely come.

⌇

It was a Friday, early morning, and May was stretched flat on the deck of the boathouse, one paragraph into the third chapter of her book, when the Goldings came to the door. The couple stood with shoulders touching, identical in height, perfect smiles.

'Alice, Alice Golding.'

'Hal, Hal Golding.'

The woman held out a large bottle, one hand around its neck and her other cradling its weight. 'This is for you, May. Champagne,' she said. 'You don't have to drink it now, unless you'd like.'

Hal laughed in a false way and Alice kept the bottle aloft, her smile widening, waiting until May accepted it and set it on the table.

'That's the real thing,' Hal said, looking around the house as he spoke. 'I don't want you to think you've got a pair of cheapskates on your hands. Billecart-Salmon, 2006. The Cuvée Louis.'

'This is Hal's department. I just drink the stuff. I'm sure you're the same, May.'

'The 2006. It's been sitting there, staring up at me. Begging. And today I just thought, what the fuck.'

'Hal.'

'It's the 2006. It elicits a passion in me. A special gift for our special new neighbour. A housewarming. Welcome, May. Welcome to Loveland.'

'Give her a chance to breathe, Hal.'

'I'm a victim of enthusiasm, what can I say.'

'And we just wanted to give you a little something after the misunderstanding the other day.' Alice was standing close to May, her voice softened and familiar. 'Whatever all that business was with our Red. Whatever started that confusion. We just wanted to say it's water under the bridge.'

May latched her thumbs into the belt loops of her dress. These two seemed not much older than her but their voices carried that vibration of authority. Of employers. Hal's hair was grey and proud in a quiff. Alice's was lush, brunette, shining.

'Yes.' May pointed for them to sit.

'Terrific,' Alice said as they took their places. 'Oh, that's terrific. It means a lot to have things cleared up. I just cannot stand to have things a mess, if you know what I mean. Just cannot abide a misunderstanding.'

Hal was examining the room. Looking up at the fittings. Craning his neck to the view of the water.

'Welcome, May,' he said and drummed his fists into the table. 'Officially and well overdue. Welcome.'

'I was going to apologise for us turning up at your door at this hour but I see you're an early bird too,' Alice said as she ran her long fingernails through her hair. Gold rings with jewels at her knuckles. 'I was going to apologise, but here we are. We've been meaning to come down and then there was the misunderstanding with Red and, well, anyway. Water under the bridge.'

May smiled enough for Alice to be satisfied then asked if either would like coffee. It would have to be instant. Alice waved the offer away and Hal started again on the champagne. He asked about May's refrigerator and when it might be coming. When all her things would be coming. The move and when it would be made official. That he hadn't known for sure that the boathouse was still in family hands but that he'd figured. It would be something great for the town to have someone back in the boathouse and a Love no less. Although, of course, there was no escaping the trouble of the lake.

'Criminal,' Hal said and was quickly on the edge of anger.

'Hal.'

'Alice, it is. Criminal,' he said. 'It's not mismanagement, it's a crime. It gets me heated up. It's a crime, May, what's happened here. And that the action is still bouncing between courts after all these goddamn years. It's one crime on top of another.'

Alice dabbed at the corner of her lips, then an eye. 'May, you'll have to excuse my Hal. It's a little much at this hour of the day, isn't it? Try being married to it.' She leaned in. 'But you know about that. I see your ring.'

May realised she was smiling. These awful people. They would be so wounded to learn how common they seemed to her. She had met them so many times before. May turned her wedding ring. She would tell these people whatever it was they wanted to hear. A version of honesty might work best. It might speed them to whatever this conversation was heading towards.

'Yes,' May said.

'And your husband's coming soon, I suppose.'

Honesty.

'Yes,' May said.

'Just the two of you?'

'I have a son. Francis. He's seventeen.'

'How nice.' Alice was drawing in Hal, who was still inspecting the room. 'Our Red is nineteen. He'll be pleased. Not many his age around. They get away, don't they? At that age.'

May looked between the couple's tanned, groomed faces. She wondered if one of them lived in fear of the other. Maybe both. A marriage might work best if each half was the other's nightmare. Orbits tight and locked. May would give them whatever they wanted. She willed them to arrive at their point and looked to Hal, offering blankness as an invitation.

'I want minds to be put at rest.' He licked his lips like a cartoon animal. 'How much do you know about the action, May? While I think of it, I need to take down your phone number, in case anything comes up. Anything important. Don't let me forget. The action. We weren't sure about your family and the house. I guessed, though. I figured.'

Whatever he wanted.

'I don't know a thing, Hal.'

~

In 1970, the city authorities commissioned the first water-quality testing of the lake. There had been reports of algal blooms, high acidity, discolouration and the presence of unidentified toxins throughout the 1960s, since the body of water had fallen into disuse. The town children would be warned off swimming when the shades of yellow and green failed to retreat as they once did. The city would put up signs. The crawdads were smaller each year and came in smaller numbers. Locals wouldn't set their traps.

The blame fell on the old Loveland lead works. On illegal dumping. On the unavoidable cycles of a static body of water. On mismanagement of the Missouri up and down its length, interfering with groundwater and replenishment. On flooding. On the absence of flooding. Some said the trouble had only started with the Loveland fire.

The city continued with their testing and their signs. It went on year after year, and the blame continued to travel in circles, as did the election and dismissal of governments and officials and agreements. The cause and the blame would never be settled. The homes near the lake had stayed within their family lines since the time of the lake's glory. As the town slowed and fell, the homes remained in order. The families kept them, painted them, trimmed their lawns. The houses took on the imagined value that drained from the water.

The class action was filed in 1998, with Hal Golding named plaintiff on behalf of the affected residents of Loveland. The lake had been mismanaged: egregiously, knowingly, negligently. The lake's demise had substantially, entirely, depleted the value of the surrounding properties. Those well-kept, trimmed, painted house of the Loveland families.

Over the subsequent years the target of the suit became as much a point for clarification as its claims. Whether it be the city, the state, the river and park authorities, or environmental protection agencies. Whether it be those local or those upriver. Those contemporary or those of the past.

The class action went on.

The signs would be planted and fall.

The lake cycled through its colours.

⌒

'May, we need to know your intentions here.' Hal pressed a finger against the table. 'I'll be blunt, because you understand that we are deep in this. We need to know your plans. To know they are in line with those of the town. It's your family's town so I know you'll want to stay in line.'

May expected another of Alice's calming gestures, another *Hal*, but Alice only looked on and continued to straighten her already mechanically straight fringe.

'Intentions?'

'The house,' Hal said. 'The family house, May. We just need to know that you're not making moves to sell up. That you're going to hold on until after the action settles. Maybe you're even planning to settle here with your husband. Your boy. That would be fine. We can make it work. We just need to know you're not going to sell, May. That could hurt the claim. Hurt us.'

She went to answer, twice. Wondered if there was a point to speaking at all. The conclusion might come faster if she just let them tell their stories. It was becoming warm. May looked out to the lake and saw the horsehair clouds. She would need to change her dress before the real heat of the day was upon them. There was something synthetic in the dress and it scratched at her neck.

'More than hurt,' Alice said. 'That would completely fuck us. Fuck us, May. It is exactly the kind of thing the state's going to dig their teeth into. Anything to keep the action going. Anything to weaken it. Our whole case is built on us being unable to sell. Who's going to buy a house next to this toxic fucking dump? That's the whole basis of our claim for compensation. So if you sell, if you get out, that could fuck us, May. Fuck us all.'

The tan of Alice's face had reddened. Her teeth showed, wide and white.

'You can't think only of yourself,' Hal said. 'You're worrying a lot of people in this town. I will tell you that for free. They are worried and I want to put their minds to rest. We just want to be able to sleep at night. So you tell me, May. Put my mind to rest.'

May's attention had drifted down to the label of the champagne bottle. It was in French. When she was younger she had imagined drinking something like this at her wedding. Then drinking it for her thirtieth birthday. Then her fortieth. She wondered if it was sweet. She couldn't tell these people what they wanted to hear. They would just have to wait and see. The end was coming and they could only wait.

'Thank you for the wine,' she said. 'You need to leave.'

May smiled, stood and walked to the door. She looked outside, serenely, without speaking or meeting the Goldings' eyes. There were some noises of objection but eventually May heard the scraping of the wooden chairs against the floor and then Hal and Alice were walking past. Hal was saying more about his needs. More about what she couldn't give him. Up on the edge of the street was a car with the Goldings' boy sitting in the back seat. He was smirking, holding a palm up against the window glass.

'I had him wait,' Alice said. She had her fingers on the skin of May's shoulder. 'He wanted to come in, after that business of the other day, but I had him wait. He's always been my little pit bull, which I know a mother shouldn't say. People see the way he is and think he's going to bite. Leads to these misunderstandings. Loyal creatures, pit bulls. I know why people get scared. So I told him, May. I told him, *You stay in the car this time, my little pit bull. Just this one time.*'

Later, May went to town, but when she reached the diner she couldn't bring herself to speak. She left and bought some drinks and bags of chips from a vending machine at the petrol station.

Back at the house, she couldn't settle, so she took her book to the lake. She walked around to the eastern side. The ground grew steeper until it became like a short cliff and blocked the hot wind which had been rising steadily. The sky blue church was somewhere above her. She took off her shoes and left them on a square of sun-baked clay. When she stepped onto the stones of the old promenade she felt a swing come into her stride. It must have been something to arrive here in the lake's good days. Children must have run ahead at the sight of the pier. The children would have known only comfort, so no doubt they complained the same as all children. Those with nothing are supposed to be grateful for it not being worse. These rich, moaning kids. May could hear their tempers.

There was something to the atmosphere that felt like an ending. It was the final Sunday of a school holiday as a child. The air was just as warm and the world was a dream but she knew she would soon be waking. The wave had reached its highest point and all that was left was for it to crash. She walked along the cooked ground and at the bend May sat on the low stone wall and started again on reading her book but its letters wouldn't settle.

She saw Patrick as soon as the boathouse was in view. He was still far away and May had to squint to pull her husband into focus but his silhouette was undeniable. The shape she had found so beautiful at seventeen. The figure of a swooping bird. She watched him walk up the stairs and stand at the door of the house. Lean against the frame.

He waited and she continued walking towards him.

She wasn't conscious of any panic, though she knew this was wrong of her. Some message had failed to fire in her system. There was no adrenaline or shortened breath. At any moment she could run up the hill and escape to the road as he wouldn't have seen her yet. But she walked on. The wave would crash over her and nothing would be escaped by running.

He saw her as she reached the softer ground of the shore.

The rubbish from her day of clearing was still in two high mounds on the grass and as she passed them she dropped her book in with the rubble. The story had run out and she was no wiser.

Patrick stood with his arms crossed. Neither spoke. Usually she would always be the one to break but now she could think of nothing to say. There was nothing that seemed enough. She walked towards the front door and so ended up at his feet.

'What did you just throw?'

'A book,' she said.

'What book?'

She could smell his breath. His mouth was just above her cheek and the warmth of his stale coffee and unbrushed teeth fell across her face. She opened the door and stepped inside. Her hand ran up the doorframe and the other went on her hip. She was blocking his way in. She wasn't answering and this left him confused. She had always answered. Always filled the spaces.

Eventually he smiled and nodded. 'So, you're leaving me?'

May remained in her position. She wouldn't respond and she wouldn't smile. It wasn't defiance, though, and she hadn't discovered some streak of bravery. May realised that she had lost control of her actions. This was a body finally, entirely overtaken by fear. Instinct was compelling her to stand guard over the house and bringing no words to her lips.

'You think you're leaving me?' he asked.

When she continued to stand and say nothing and wear no expression he stamped hard on the wooden deck. His face was red and he bit on his bottom lip. It was exactly the vision of their son's tantrums. The toddler realising the limits of his power. The husband began to shout and rant, and as he did May stood perfectly still and watched his spitting and his feet pounding against the timber. He described what would and would not be happening. The house would be sold. It would all be settled. She would not waste a second more of his time and she was coming home with him. She was not leaving. Not their family or their home. She was not leaving him.

The longer she remained motionless and silent, the more he became the opposite. The impotent fury of a boy.

Why had she not settled things?

How much did she think her family could take?

She had hurt them so much already.

Why would she say she was leaving?

It seemed a reflex to be standing, barring the doorway. This was her family's house and they weren't a family any longer. She didn't want him inside.

He was so tired of what she was putting them through.

Did she even remember her son?

He was her husband. Had she forgotten?

Later she would wonder if it had been her face that had let slip. She didn't speak and was sure her hands hadn't budged, but the corner of her lips might have shifted just a little. It wasn't a smile but that's how he read it, and that was all he needed. The lips had let slip.

He punched the doorframe to the side of her face like the men did on television. Like he had done so many times to their doors, walls, refrigerators at home. Still so unoriginal after all this time. The timber doorframe offered more resistance than its faded paint promised, though, so when he reached the next part of the performance, of showing her what she had brought him to, there was a deep, bleeding gash across his knuckles. He pushed it at her face.

Another instinct came and it was something old and deeply rooted. May reached out her hand to tend to his injury. When Francis would come to her screaming and bleeding she would lift him from the ground and try to pass the peace of her heart to his. She had taken her husband's hand in hers as blood began to run down to his elbow. He pushed it at her and she felt the wetness on her face.

They stood in this pose for long enough that the wind could travel from the lake to meet them. It was hot and full with its stench and May felt it against the blood. It made a whistle between them and this seemed to be what made Patrick break away.

He shouted again and showed his wound. He stamped on the ground. He spat. Against this she still filled the doorway and this seemed to be a barrier he couldn't process. He looked at his dripping hand and she recognised embarrassment in him. This was what made him leave. The child's embarrassment. He spat again, to claim the moment, but he left. Down the stairs and away to the hill and the street. He had a car, a blue rental, and she watched him spin its wheels and eventually drive out of sight and hearing.

She stayed filling the doorway, already feeling her arms shaking. Registering the thumping of her heart and knowing that she was going to be sick.

May was spinning Officer Carter's business card by its corners. *Any trouble, you let me know.* She had called the number and then heard her own voice break at the first word, *Cath*. She'd then apologised; it should be *Officer Carter*. She was sorry, for the name, for calling at all. Cath had told her none of that mattered and just wanted to know what the trouble was. Whether May was hurt. If anyone was hurt. Then she said that she was on her way and May was to lock the door and sit tight.

Cath finished her questions and asked May if she could make them coffee. May apologised, said that the officer must have work to do, and Cath just asked again if May wanted coffee. May nodded. She was crying but again it must have been just some mechanism of her body as she wasn't feeling a thing.

They sat with their mugs. May's tears stopped and she straightened a little in her chair.

'I'll do what I can, but it won't be enough,' Cath said. 'I need you to know that. And you have no idea where he might be staying? Okay. I'll put the word out and I'll keep as close as I can, but that won't be enough. This is bullshit, I know, but you should think about leaving. I know you shouldn't have to. You could find a room in town. Or there's a motel on the highway. You shouldn't have to, May, it's bullshit, but I don't know what else to say. You have to leave. This place won't keep him out if he wants to get in.'

May smiled. 'I'm sorry. I want to do the right thing. I can't, though. I'm staying. I know I shouldn't, but I'm staying right here. I'm so sorry.'

LOVELAND, MAY 1958

The husband sat opposite at the kitchen table, looking tired from his day. A kind of nervousness had come to his movements.

'Chicken and leek pie,' Casey said and attempted again to measure the man.

He nodded and picked at his thumbnails. She busied herself with the serving of food and the wiping of surfaces, careful to avoid his gaze. His nerves required care. Perhaps this was what happened in a union. Perhaps this was what marriage entailed and so was the surest sign yet of her future. She had stopped speaking her daily truths for they were in the end untrue. This was how things would be. She had chosen to embrace a life and so this was how things must be.

'Do I have something else?' he asked, pushing away the beer she had brought to him.

'Wine.' She placed their cutlery on the table. 'I'll pour us wine.'

'Just me. You have your beer.'

They ate without speaking. The radio played Satie and this seemed to be angering the husband so Casey lowered the volume. Turning it off would be too much a demonstration. She drank her bottle quickly and started on another. He reached for his wine on three occasions but failed to bring it to his lips. This was a life, Casey thought. The pain was an ancient iron scalding the muscles of her heart. She brought out tinned fruit and a tub of vanilla ice cream that she had carried back from town wrapped in towels. They ate and she looked out onto the lake.

'There's been news,' he said. 'From my network.'

'Oh yes?'

They remained out of each other's vision. He spoke into his glass.

'News,' he said. 'Things may change. It's too complicated for you to understand. There have been some difficulties and it's hard to know how things will change.'

'You can tell me.' She covered her lips with the beer bottle.

'No.'

'Not the news. You have an important position and of course I wouldn't ask you to tell me everything. But I want you to know that you can tell me how it affects you, if that's what you'd like. You can tell me how you are feeling because that is important to me. But it's up to you. Your position is the difficult one. But if you tell me your troubles it would ease my heart because we are connected. I want you to know that. We are the same.'

Satie's just-audible tinkling returned and the husband filled his cheeks with wine. He swallowed, then seemed to ease.

'There have been some problems with my negotiations,' he said. 'Things may be coming to an end. My networks and finances. There will be some stoppages.'

'I understand.'

'Work may have to end. The staff. I can't be sure of their wages. They'll leave, I suppose.'

'It's okay—' She hesitated briefly but recovered herself. 'It's okay to be scared. If you are. I understand. Whatever this news is. However difficult. We will deal with it.'

They drank.

'Together.' He spoke this word weakly.

'Of course,' Casey said with her eyes still on the starless lake.

'There will be change.'

'Things happen,' she said and put her hand out on the table. 'Things change. That's a good thing. We'll make the change together and we'll make it one to our liking. This is our life and we can make it how we please. Together. You have nothing to fear.'

'Yes.'

'We have our perfect life and you have your important position. If something is coming then we must protect ourselves.

You've worked too hard. You have a position of such importance. We owe it to you and everything you've achieved. If change is inevitable then we must act. We will leave.'

'Leave.'

'If change is coming then we will leave.'

'No.'

Casey fought the quiver of her lip. 'We could go to the city. San Francisco, New York. Make a new start somewhere.'

He turned to look at her directly and she could see his thoughts realigning and certainty returning.

'We're not leaving,' he said.

'But if the money is gone. If the work here is ending.'

'We're not leaving. You are never leaving.'

He broke his wineglass at the stem. He did it so calmly Casey only noticed after the wine began to spill from the table edge. Later that night he would break the rest. Everything from the kitchen smashed in a great show.

'This is the family home,' he said. 'We stay no matter what. You are a part of this family, do you understand? You will not destroy my family. We are the Love family and so we stay in Loveland. You need to stop questioning this.'

The pathetic thing the husband must see before him. So weak and easy. Weak because she knew so well the certainty of his power.

'You'll be buried in Loveland,' he said. 'Your baby too.'

The pathetic thing Casey saw before her. The husband. So weak. Weak because he trusted so much in the certainty of his power. She commanded her lips to be still. She looked out to her lake and the insects rose in their universal noise. The sound of them screaming to mate and hunt and die.

Chapter Sixteen

Tate was drumming with two straws against the table of a booth when May walked into the diner. She ordered him a burger and vanilla milkshake, made him eat. It was late morning and May checked her phone to be sure. Thursday. Tate was in a playful mood and so she smiled and encouraged it. She had arranged with his mother to hire Tate for the day but now work on the house was childish and it would be wrong to have the boy there when Patrick could return at any moment. So they went to the supermarket and she had Tate carry and fill a handbasket. He wondered what was next on their list and when May said it was only the shopping he said that she could have done this herself. She nodded, shrugged.

The realtor called and left a message as May drove back towards the main street. She called each morning and the message was always the same. Checking in. They were on the case. It was a curly one, that's for sure, but they were the ones they liked best.

May pulled over in sight of the general store. She felt so heavy suddenly. Her attention and energy was being siphoned into the atmosphere. Tate put his feet up on the dash and May found herself answering his questions without hesitation or lies. No, she wasn't fine. Generally and specifically, no, not fine. She had a teenage boy, had she told him that? Of course. A son and a husband and the husband was here. His name was Patrick and he'd punched the doorframe. You could see his blood where the paint had broken off. Yes, she'd been to the police.

Tate was too young for this. It was unfair. She came to from her half-sleep. It was unfair; none of this trouble should be his. He should be playing computer games. Fretting over his hair, his complexion. She apologised and said she was tired.

'May, this is horseshit. I can help. We have to stop him. I'll get my gun.'

'You aren't serious.'

'I haven't got it yet, but Ricky owes me. He's fixing me up.'

'The creep at the camping shop?'

'If this guy's coming for you.'

'What do you want with a gun?'

'Jesus, I don't know. The same reason as anyone. To deal with whatever needs dealing with. This fucking place.'

He was too young.

It was unfair.

'You're seventeen.'

'That's not an excuse, May. Not like it was before. I'm stuck here doing nothing and it's not okay.' His hands were rubbing across his chest.

'You can leave.'

'Where to? Are you at all aware of what's going on out there? It's on fire, May. It's coming down.'

None of this should be his.

'I'm just going to say again that you're only seventeen.'

'Seventeen's not what it used to be.'

They fell quiet and Tate looked embarrassed by the drama. This sweet boy with so much on his mind. The real danger of the world had reached him already. These kids had no chance of holding on to that adolescent stage of ignorance and this was their great loss. Tate, her son, all of them. She wished they could be fools. She should comfort him but she knew nothing that would console him and be true. He was still young and bright, so one day he would arrive at a better answer than hers anyway.

'I'm in no position to give you advice,' May said. 'And you haven't asked for any. But I'm going to suggest that you don't buy a gun. Will you let me get away with this one bit of guidance? From one hopeless loser to another. Don't get a gun.'

He squirmed, trying to hold in a smile.

'Maybe I'll get religion,' Tate said. 'My mother always asks me how I expect to get by without it.'

'Get by? There's no chance of you getting by, kid. You're done for. Kaput.'

He rolled his eyes but a smile followed. The one her son used to have but had lost. The one rare and real.

Of the two moons, the one in the surface of the lake was the more convincing. It flickered, just slightly, and against the water's chemistry was a pale blue like the ones in photographs. The moon in the sky was too small and stationary. May squeezed Jean's hand. It had been the stroke of midnight when they had left the woman's house and begun the walk down the centre of the road. The wine and then the chime of Jean's mantel clock. Jean had begun to sing about going walking after midnight and though May didn't know the tune she held her to it. The night was hot and the world was a body's temperature. The thick air, her friend's hand, and surely the lake too. May imagined a swan dive off a plank like those frolicking women in the newsreels.

Earlier, Jean had made them dinner at her house. The half-thawed steaks. The California bear red wine. May told her flatly about Patrick's arrival and Jean had turned frantic about calling the police. May said there was nothing to be done. She should turn the meat while May made the salad. Jean said that May had to come stay with her, to be safe, and May only said again about the meat. All night Jean would become agitated and May would thank her, stroke her arm, tell her that there was nothing to be done. Jean said they should try the police again. May had made the right noises and poured more wine and asked if they could play more of the music from that first night. May asked for the Elvis.

Walking along the road, after midnight, Jean had begun to cry when they came in sight of the sky blue church. They were on the eastern crest, where the ground was hard like tiles, and when the stone of the promenade began they followed the drop of the hill. A narrow track drew a line through the grass and Jean continued to cry without making a sound. May wouldn't interrupt. She knew how easily the relief of it could be spoiled. She held the woman's hand and helped her down the slope.

May carried the fireworks and matches. As they had neared the lake the idea of her roadside rockets remaining unlaunched in their box seemed unbearable. Jean was against them stopping at the boathouse but May promised they would check from afar before approaching. Look through the windows to be sure that Patrick hadn't turned up. Jean eventually settled and said she knew how to launch the fireworks and told May to bring an empty wine bottle. So Jean was carrying the bottle and stood it beside her as they reached the low wall by the water's edge. They sat and Jean talked about how things were when she'd first arrived. She pointed across the way to the boathouse and to the places where the other buildings had stood. The boardwalk. The

Ferris wheel. It had all been cleared away after the fire. You wouldn't guess there had been anything here. Certainly nothing grand. Nothing to remember.

⌒

The big house with its two great storeys of ashen stone veneer. The empty pier. The grounded sailboats. The Ferris wheel that she'd never seen turn. Moses would walk with his pinkies hooked behind his back and talk of the way it had been in his father's time and how it would be again. The good families would return. He would make a wide swirling gesture around the lake and talk of the plughole pulling the money from their pockets. The money would pour in, and when it amounted to a hoard of sufficient size he would be cutting loose and running. He had been to war and so he was owed. Owed everything. And he was a Love and that name used to mean something. He was the last rung of this family ladder and so he was owed. This nothing town. Moses hated the place. Hated the lake and its people and the tiny thoughts of Nebraska. He would bring back the family glory only so he could escape it. Hated its smallness. Flatness. He wanted to find a city that would understand his destiny and offer it to him. Their destiny, because he would take Jean with him. All these things he said.

⌒

'Every Sunday. It was before my time but they would end each week with their fireworks,' Jean said. 'In the heyday. Every Sunday was New Year's Eve. The guests would gather on the shore and drink their cocktails and watch the display over the water. Sick, really, but it must have been something.'

She took the wine bottle and pushed its base into place in the soft earth. May watched and the scene seemed too bright to be natural. The moon was too powerful. She handed Jean the rocket and matches and the woman smiled with her cheeks still showing traces of tears. Jean went down on one knee and moved as if there were nothing new to this. There was no hesitancy. She held up a match.

'Shall we?'

May brought her fingers up to her ears. The firework was joined to a thin wooden stick which Jean had lowered into the bottle. The rocket was leaning towards the water as its fuse caught alight. It spat out golden sparks and hissed. Jean let out a squeal and stepped back to May's side. They were children, covering their faces and laughing with excitement. The rocket suddenly fired and launched into the sky with a piercing whistle. The pair flinched and laughed and May just caught sight of the smoke trail before the firework exploded high above the lake.

A boom that was felt in the heart and then a shower of green embers. It was a small thing in the end and brief. The shock of it was so much more than the sound and vision. May continued to laugh at how young she felt. Jean had her arms around her.

They stood giggling and slowly regaining their calm. The air smelled of burnt powder and the flower of smoke dispersed against the moonlight and the water.

'I was a kid,' Jean said. 'I can't even put myself there now. It was so long ago. I just have this memory like something I was told. It's just a story to me now, you know? I can't get into that place again.' She straightened and pushed the hair from her eyes.

'I was pregnant. He was so angry at first, but later said he would take care of things. Told me he would keep us safe and I was so scared. I was so young and with a baby coming. Hell. And Casey had turned against me. She just flicked a switch one day. I loved her though. I knew that at least. I could never make it right with her. It was my fault.

'Moses. Jesus, just saying his name. He never thought for a second he was in danger. That he could lose. Casey was looking him right in the eyes as he died and I swear, I don't think it even crossed his mind then.'

The boathouse was just a box in the distance. May had left the lights on inside. She thought of her husband, somewhere, pacing. He would be back and soon. There had been no messages from him and no calls. What was building in him couldn't stand. When exactly he would arrive was just detail. Her body was cold as she thought of her son, a world away and staring without expression into a screen.

'I just found them like that,' Jean said. 'The two of them in the shallows and everything on fire. It's just a story to me now, but I'm in it every single day. I was so young. Jesus. We were children.'

May couldn't picture her grandmother young. Casey had been always an old lady, and then dead, and now this image of her in another life. It had nothing to do with May and she held no claim.

'The baby,' May said. 'You had a child.'

'I lost her. That was after everything.'

'I'm sorry.'

'Jesus, I'm not owed a sorry. For a long time I thought it was the punishment I deserved. It was the universe making things square. I don't think that now. I don't. But still, I don't want a *sorry*. I could never repay your grandmother.'

May took the weight of the woman's arm.

'Thing is, you can never make things square,' Jean said. 'Don't you do it, May. Don't carry these things.'

Jean pulled May in and kissed her cheek. That temperature of a body.

May tried to picture Moses. The face of a man who never woke with fear. Never knew loss even when his eyes closed for the last time. A man falling back into the water with a pretty stream of red where his body had been. Casey and all her years in the back room at May's mother's house, sewing her clothes. Carrying this. Trying to make things square.

She would walk Jean home, put her to bed and refuse her arguments. May would return to her boathouse and see if her body would sleep.

The next morning May woke late and checked her phone. Three missed calls from an unknown number and a voice message.

'Hello there. May, this is Bill Miller. I'm representing Hal and Alice Golding, and I'm calling about this business with the action. It's just a formality. We need to get everything sorted and down on paper and the i's dotted and them t's crossed, as we're fond of saying. If you could visit my office we can get it sorted and cleared away and everyone can rest easy. Call me on this number and my secretary will make an appointment for you. You need to be able to rest easy, May. I'll see you soon. Bill Miller.'

Her eyes settled on the wall where light was bright against the painting of the desert. Its distant storm and dullness. May felt the linen of the bedsheet. Casey would have had no time for all this. She would have met the hot arm of Moses to her right, the leg of the baby's cot to her left.

The wave was coming. It had been set in motion long ago. May had been waiting all her life for the inevitable to happen. She had reached the end of waiting.

The wave was coming so she would swim out to meet it.

May stretched and realised she was smiling. The day bounced around the polished boards of her sweet home. Casey must have seen this light. Rosie too. Maybe in the moments before Moses woke and commanded the day. May felt the muscles of her arms and kept on smiling. It was, after all, another perfect day.

The Goldings' house was not as impressive as she remembered. Jean had pointed it out. Standing now on its doorstep, it seemed just a nice house with a neatly clipped lawn. It seemed beneath the couple who had sat at May's table. This must put acid in their guts each morning. This might be the start of the spite they reserved for each other. May saw the way they hated each other and how well they concealed it. With this, May was their master. The grass was a giveaway. It was too adored. May pressed the doorbell again and Hal answered.

'May, hello there. You've caught me out.' His posture fell into flirtation. 'I'm supposed to be working but I'm watching football. Alice is out, if you were after her.'

'No, you'll do. Either one of you is fine.'

'Well, what can I do for you? Probably best to speak to the lawyer. He'll have answers for you. Only, the football's on, like I said.'

'I'm here as a courtesy.' She had her hands deep in the pockets of her jeans. 'I thought I should tell you that I've given everything a lot of thought since your visit, and since I heard from the lawyer. It was kind of you both to let me know how things are, so I thought it fair I do the same. The thing is, Hal'—she stepped in close and gave her face its softest, sweetest incline—'the thing is I'm going to have to ask you and Alice not to come near me again. Not me, not my house.'

'May, you need to—'

'Here's the thing, Hal. Within my house, I am the law. I am the supreme being. That's starting to mean a lot to me. So, it's pretty simple. You keep away. You don't come see me. You don't come tell me your thoughts on what I should do with my house or my life or anything else that's mine. You can have your lawyer call me. Send me letters. I can't stop you there and that's your right. If your lawyer stays reasonable then I won't stop that. But you—you, Alice and your son—you need to stay away. And that's all.'

'Listen, May . . .'

'No, I don't think I will. The beauty of this, Hal, is that it does not matter what you think. It does not matter. It's just something that's happening to you. I'm here as a courtesy. I'll leave you to your sports.'

The son appeared in the doorway and May saw now how much he resembled the father. Distant, amused.

'Hey there, neighbour,' Red said, gripping a beer bottle by its neck.

'I'm glad you're here,' May said. 'Red, I have something to tell you. The burden shouldn't fall on your father to relay it. You don't come to my house and you don't come near me. If you see me walking, you cross the street. Does that make sense?'

The boy smiled hard.

'Red, that little something that took place on the steps of my house—the little misunderstanding? I swear to you now, on my life and yours, that I will do to you what you did to that animal. This is where you say that I'm crazy. Go right ahead. If there was no animal and no blood, then there's nothing to worry about, is there? But you listen to the very particular tone of my voice: if you come near me again, then you're the calf.'

'You're one crazy bitch.'

'Enjoy your game.'

She walked back down the path and saw that the lawn was truly exceptional. Not a weed, not a bug in sight. Not one ounce of love. As she got to the street she heard a voice shouting after her. There was no way to tell if it was the boy's or the man's. Just that same, familiar barking.

May answered her phone and walked out to the deck. It was her mother and Rosie began immediately. She was so upset. What she had to say mattered and was true and was so hard for her to say. Could May just let her say it, let her speak?

'I'm embarrassed, my May. I'm ashamed. I never told you all the hell with your grandmother because I thought it would die with her. We both did. She told me after the cancer. I still only know parts of it. I mean, this was my father. I thought it would die with her, but nothing dies, does it? You sell that miserable house and we'll start new. You and Francis need to be free of this. Please.

'I need to know you're safe. You call the police. Promise me. You get help. I've got Francis here with me and he'll be okay. But Patrick's going to hurt you. He's lost you and he knows it now. He's so angry. I'm ashamed, my May. He's hurt you for so long and I never stopped it.'

The rest was lost in tears and apologies.

May could think of nothing to say to her mother that was comforting and true, so she told her she was forgiven. That there was no need for forgiveness. They were both ashamed and she couldn't understand why. Shame. It was this strange force that acted always in the wrong direction.

He had hurt May for the first time, the flesh of her, after they'd been to see a movie. She was finished with school and had moved out of her mother's house. She and Patrick had been together for months and she remembered how happy she had been on the walk through the quiet shopping centre, just before midnight, back to the underground car park. It had been cold so she'd nestled in to him. So what if it would just be the two of them now? That was all they needed. This was how it would be.

Later, she could never remember what the movie had been or what exactly she'd said, but she remembered him pushing her straight on, hands at her shoulders, so that her back struck the edge of the open car door. She had been so shocked by it and stood unmoving by the door as the pain arrived fully. He hadn't paused but moved around to the driver's side of the car and sat behind the wheel, waiting. It hurt to bend but she slowly got in, they drove away and neither of them mentioned what he'd done. She wasn't scared at the time. It was something that failed to find the proper place in her mind. When Patrick turned on the radio and started talking about the movie and the early start he would have in the morning she really did begin to question if she'd imagined it. Her muscles began to throb. Her pulse and the ache down her spine. Her back would take so much of it in those first years. The table edges and doorframes and what-ever was behind her when he pushed. Her back became a wide, easy canvas and he'd leave marks that would shift over the days to come. Pink, blue, green and, at last, yellow.

More came, over time. Worse, beyond any hope she might have had that it was something mistaken or imagined. Being held down on the couch with his arms pushing into her chest and neck until she passed out. Her kidneys: fists, a knee. His weight on her against the mattress. The knife point brought to her throat. The marks on the flesh would heal. Time would pass. Fading pink, blue, green and, at last, yellow.

May stood on the deck for what she knew was the final time. It had all collapsed and broken down, the lines between things. Big Nothing. Now. The water and the sky, the past and the compartments of her mind. It was the relief of conclusion.

A feeling of calm arrived as she settled on the truth that Patrick had followed her to Loveland to end her life.

He had threatened it so often but now it was here. He had come with the strength in his arms to shape the world. His arms were stronger than hers, and this seemed enough for him to put himself at the centre of the universe. It was so primary and laughable. He outmatched her muscle and this was what made him a god. How could this pathetic disparity be behind it all? His arms, which she had thought so handsome when she was a girl. His worker's hands and callused palms.

What had been the start of his ways? He'd never had brutality to draw on. May had heard of that, of these things being passed between generations, but she knew Patrick had suffered no horror. His pains had been real but they were the regular kind. What was the source of it all? Something other than him to pin this on. She was searching for an excuse to hand to him. She did this, always, but what reason could be enough? He certainly wasn't aching over his reasons. She doubted he spent even a moment looking for the place in him where this was born. He seemed unaware of his crimes. Maybe they disguised themselves. Maybe Patrick couldn't know.

She was so tired of this.

Her mind finding a path, always, to his escape from himself. Something outside or in the past or promised for the future. Finding ways for Patrick.

So tired of even that word, *Patrick*.

It was the husband who had followed her and it was the husband who would never stop. She looked across the water to the line of gold and imagined Francis. He would remain Francis and never become *the son* because she would fight for him.

May was calm as she resolved to action.

No more names.

No more agreed-upon stories.

The husband would kill her.

—

A dragonfly hovered close to May's face and she didn't wave it away. She saw her grandmother in the shallows and in Casey's arms was her sleeping baby. An endless echo of women standing behind her. A great line of birth. Beneath the fabric of their dresses she saw their stripes.

LOVELAND, JUNE 1958

The first of the day's light was constructing the world but Casey had already washed and dressed as there was much to do. The house needed work and later she would shop at the market and then make the pastry.

Much to do.

Making and keeping things right was a task that was unending and it was a gift. A duty and, yes, a gift. She sniffed at the breeze and welcomed the aroma of grass. The aroma of a day's work. She took the lamp down from its place on her bedroom table. She'd filled it only the day before so it hung from her fingers with a good weight. Stepping outside, walking down the stairs, she examined the wall of Prairie Smoke. The flowers' stems were thick and thirsty. She unscrewed the cap from the lamp's reservoir and began to pour kerosene into the soil. She made sure to spread the stinking fluid all over so it would find its way to the roots and kill these unnecessary things. This weed.

She thought of Voltaire and his *Candide* that he must have thought so wonderful. In truth, *Candide*'s conclusion was none at all. That we're to work and cultivate our gardens. This will keep the evils away. Hide from the world and deal with the dirt and pests.

That is a retreat, Casey thought, and the luxury of a person with the burden of choice. Well then, Casey thought, let that burden be hers. She would have the problem of living. She continued with the kerosene and when the lamp was empty she replaced its cap and went back inside. She wanted to begin on the floors. The sun brought a message that the windows were clouded with dust. In her bedroom she saw the build-up on her painting of Australia. Its dullness. That place which she'd always thought might be at the end of her story. A place where a person could disappear. These had been the thoughts of a child and fool, because a person can disappear wherever they stand. Vanishing is something inside. The walls too seemed dirty now. She wouldn't allow her eyes to turn to the lake, its centre.

The intruding thoughts came. The ones determined to steer her away from her mission. They came, they came, they came and she fought them.

It was a perfect life.

Later, when the pastry was resting, she would take to the flowerheads with her scissors.

Chapter Seventeen

In the boat, she watched.

May checked the time and it was one minute until the sun was due to leave the sky. She'd looked up the schedule and found things weren't as straightforward as light and darkness. There were stages and degrees, each with their name and time-table. Daylight, Civil Twilight, Nautical Twilight, Astronomical Twilight, Night. She had watched the last of the disc go and the horizon was an overly sweet orange. Her mother had taught her this was dusk but from now on she would think of it as Civil Twilight. That time before the true night, when there was still enough daylight to work and to read. It was appropriate and she liked the meaningful sound of it.

Dragging the boat out from under the house she had known it was for the last time. She wondered if her grandmother had known on her final day. If she'd walked around the house touching doorframes and running her fingers along the wooden railing of the deck. Looking out to the clean, transparent water and the doomed structures. May had pulled the boat out, shoeless and not troubling to roll up her jeans. Whatever the lake was going to do to her had already been done. The oars found their cuffs. The ache and joy found the muscles of her back.

As she rowed to the deepest point she reached for her song and found none of its words where they should be. Her 'Ballad of Big Nothing'. May used to fear the loss of memories. A familiar catastrophe was the prospect of waking one morning to find that all the names for the world had leached from her mind in the night. The objects in the kitchen. The word for the person in the bathroom mirror. Now amnesia had come for her song but the absence brought no pain. The music had once been fused to the spine of her life and now it had fled and she felt not a bit of regret.

She rowed on tunelessly and called for the visions of the lake to awaken. She summoned them and laughed and thought of herself as a witch. The husband had called her that once, meaning to say *bitch* but losing the right curse in his excitement. She'd laughed at him and he spat in her face. What was a witch, though? Just someone who sees and accepts. The storm is coming with its noise and lightning, so call for the lightning to strike.

Stand straight and call for it and it will channel through you on its return to the ground. They will call you a witch because they can't see and accept. Can't see that we are the lightning. She pulled in the oars and raised her arms and laughed as she cast a spell on the dwindling sky. She summoned Big Nothing and what it had to show her of a broken heart.

A vision of her son.

She had tried to call Francis through the afternoon. The time in Australia made no difference. He had cut her off. She knew the motions he went through in lifting his phone, his heavy outward breath. The effort of having to extend and flick his thumb to erase her name. She projected the scene of this across the sky.

She would hold him in her mind. She would contain it, in full. The failings she had imagined of herself. Her failure to build the right world for him and the pain that was too great to stand. She had failed to protect and provide. The temporary arrangements and the name she would give this. Acceptance. She may worry and ache but she would accept the past of things. She would correct what she could and make enough peace with the rest.

Big Nothing came as she commanded.

It was all her doing so she made the world spin and the lake turn to gold. Above was the universe with no end and Francis's face miles wide and making a moon. His hair mixed with clouds in this Civil Twilight. She had wanted to speak to him only so that he would hear the calm of her voice. For that calm to be something he remembered, after, but he wouldn't answer and wouldn't return her messages. This wasn't how she wanted things but then her intentions had never run true. She laughed again. Mad people laughed. And witches. So her son would have no warning and this was just how it would be. She could only fail him after all. All we do is fail and that's a place to start. Francis with his eyes closed and the muscles of his face slackened into sleep.

May remained planted on the splintered wood of the boat's seat. She would not rise into the sky. There would be no strangulation and no pain. It was all at her command. The boat had swung and straightened to face the boathouse where the light from her lantern was enough for May to see in to its empty rooms. The gently pulsing glow cast out in diagonals to the earth around. She could see the outside staircase, the vacant stage of the deck, the shimmering place where the sand went beneath the lake.

The husband was coming.

She knew this because she had commanded it. Sent him a message, asking him to come to the house because she had something final to say to him. He would be close, striding through the dark fringes in that way of walking he finds in his anger.

—

He came just when and how May determined. The husband would have been staying at a place near town. The small motel near the highway. He would have received her message, dressed himself and finished drinking his rum, and aimed his rental car through the vacant Loveland streets. Over the crest, where the lake was in sight. This was how she'd imagined it. May watched her design materialise in the dusk of the boathouse light. He took the steps of the outside staircase two at a time. The husband's movement was exactly as she'd foretold.

Her message to him had been calm and truthful.

She'd asked for him to come to the house. There was something final she had to say. Calm and truthful and without provocation.

He had then sent three messages of his own.

> *Here's something final for you.*
>
> *You're dead.*
>
> *Bitch.*

May watched him now move to her front door and knock twice. She had wondered if she'd be able to hear from this distance but when the noise sounded, bone and skin on heavy wood, it was clear and close. That sharp *tap, tap*, bouncing across the few hundred metres of water between his knocking fist and her.

Francis, in the sky above, didn't wake.

The husband went to the windows and started calling May's name. He would do this for a while, his voice rising and falling as it locked into the rhythms of his frustration. She had seen this, heard this, so many times. She had seen it play out. May had determined how it would come to be and the husband would be so angry to discover how predictable he was.

On cue he tried the front door and found it unlocked. May knew the exact sequence of ugly expressions that must have fallen across his pretty face. And it was pretty. May had long since grown blind to it but she could remember how she had once desired it. He didn't hover at the entrance. The husband did what he was always going to do and she watched. He walked inside and went directly to the kitchen table where May had left the glass of water, the kerosene lamp burning, the flower upright in a teacup, and the letter.

Husband.

I have things to tell you and I've written them down so that they are clear and neither of us can be mistaken.

1. Our marriage has reached its end. I will be making whatever arrangements are necessary for a divorce.

2. You will not be receiving any of the proceeds of the sale of the house. It was left to my mother and what she chooses to do with

*it is no business of yours. I intend to obey her wishes and follow
her instructions.*

*3. I don't intend to have any further contact with you.
Any correspondence must be sent via my solicitor. You have
Karl's details.*

*4. As part of the divorce we will need to make custody
arrangements for Francis. I will be applying for whatever legal
orders are necessary to keep you away from me and our child.*

*5. If you attempt to hurt or threaten me, Francis or any member
of my family I will call the police immediately. I will not
hesitate. You will not hurt us again.*

Goodbye,
May

When he finished reading he sent the flower and cup flying
across the room. Threw the burning lamp against the wall. Then
the glass of water. She couldn't see this, but May imagined it
shattering and spraying across his shoes. This was how she'd
determined things. When she'd flattened out the letter, set
down the glass of water, lit the lamp and propped up the flower.

There'd been a cluster of the flowers growing on the bank
just where the lake started to bend and May had run out to them
in her bare feet. They were a gentle shape with purple whiskers
making a crown and she had pulled one away. It was soft and

heavy and May shortened the stem with her thumbnail until it would stay standing in the teacup. It was a beautiful, living thing and the closest she would allow herself to provoking the husband.

Over the years May would at times consider happiness. What it could look like. A silly moment of perfection that she could dream of but never experience. It was a rose garden as the sun went down. People would scoff at the cliché of roses but it was her fantasy and to May it was a faultless one. To stand alone and know love in the last moments of a day.

She had chosen the words of the letter with care. Every one of them needed to be true. True and calm, because of what would follow. The blame would not fall on her words. She would communicate her wishes coolly, and then the rest was his. The flower was all she would allow herself. Even in this world surely no blame could fall on a single flower.

Big Nothing continued with its vision and it was only of her boy.

Francis, sleeping and at peace.

There was no terror or strangulation or the pain of being brought into life. Just a picture of May's son sleeping. That sensation of love.

The water from the glass would have pooled at the husband's feet. The lamp and its kerosene had shattered and gushed and the flames immediately took hold of the curtains. From these they took to the timber. The old wood of the walls was dry and waiting and the flames would not miss their chance at life.

In the house, it began.

May started her actions after the husband's. These were his consequences. She took her phone from her jeans, found the number and spoke only the truth with no embellishment. There was a slight tremble to her voice that must have been the adrenaline. She was an animal and so her body would have its animal reactions. Even there, out of reach at the dark centre of the lake. For a moment her blood ran hotter than she could contain. Her chest and cheeks would be blotches of pink and her lungs were lost to the hot smoke of breathing. She steadied. Slowed her words and told only the truth of what she could see through the house windows.

The husband and flames were taking the place apart.

He was in the bedroom for a time and May could see a slivered view of the bed being upended and him throwing what he could through the doorway. He stepped out into the pulsing flamelight of the main room and ripped a dress apart. The fire was moving up the walls, lapping at the ceiling. Smoke was darkening the air and the man became a silhouette. The first window was smashed. It had been a silent performance until then. He'd thrown something through a glass pane. Surely one of her plates. He had broken so many plates. The sound was a pure one. Across the water bounced the soft tinkling of shards falling against the wooden deck. May had hung glass baubles from their Christmas tree one year and they had made the same sound as the husband crushed them. The lost window must now have achieved something for him as he then broke them all, more crockery sent through the centre of windows. But then he put his hands on the broom and this proved perfect. He held it as if he were a warrior thrusting a spear at an ancient enemy, with no idea how silly he looked. A grown man punching out windows with a straw broom. A man colluding with fire.

When all the glass in the house was shattered he stood, seeming to pant a little as he leaned against his broom. He was coughing against the smoke and flames were curling out of the empty window frames. It was taking so quickly and completely. He remained within it and made no move to escape. It took three attempts for him to break the broom over his knee. He went again to the kitchen and May saw he'd found her bourbon. The Horse Soldier. Surrounded by fire he became still, with the bottle upended, the neck fed into his mouth. It must be burning his throat. And the flames his body. He must feel it.

The sky filled with none of its clichés of a molten earth. Those cells splitting and approximating life. Only the face of

May's son. The boy slept through it all and May remained in her boat.

The sound of a fist pounding against the front door of the boathouse seemed to surprise the husband but not May. She had known it was coming; the pounding and the shouts were what May had determined. She had considered the time it would take to drive from the police station. Others would be drawn in time, to fight the fire.

May had known that the first would be Officer Carter. It was the face May had pictured. This woman who had been Cath but must now be Officer Carter. It was Officer Carter whom May had called and told of the husband arriving at the boathouse. Beginning to tear the place apart. The fire. It was Officer Carter she told because this was to be the cool, elementary truth. The husband was in May's house and he had lost control. She warned Officer Carter that the man was violent. He had hurt her before and he would try to hurt whoever came. Officer Carter would need to take care. May thought he was capable of killing. This was what she feared and why she had called.

May had then faltered and made the officer promise to be careful. To please promise. She stopped herself and took her breaths. The deep, counted breathing. This was to have nothing to do with friendship or the heart. This was a person in danger calling the police, truthful and cool.

—

The days before. May replaying and replaying what the officer had told her.

Don't thank me—it's my job.

But May knew what was coming. This was unfair. It wasn't right.

Any trouble, you call, okay?

All these years without asking for help and now all this on a stranger. This was why it was possible, though. The only way May could bring herself to ask, and why she would follow the officer's directions, after all this time.

You don't hesitate.

So May watched someone doing their job. Officer Carter approaching with her gun drawn. Another officer May didn't recognise behind her, gun low. The doorframe and the stair side of the house was taken by the fire and the pair couldn't make their way in. Officer Carter was shouting commands and the voice was clear and deep across the lake. The roof had ruptured and the flames reached into the night, lusting for oxygen. The sound of more glass breaking. Of timber crackling. Officer Carter was shouting for the husband to come out, to drop his knife.

May hadn't seen the husband find the knife but she knew it would be one of the ones with a serrated edge and wooden handle. She hadn't hidden them but neither had she laid them out. They were in the drawer where cutlery should be. He had been the one to take a knife. He had moved close to the doorway and shaken the thing at Officer Carter as if he meant to stick it in her.

Drop it.

He wouldn't.

Drop the knife.

He never would.

The husband stepped into sight again. A silhouette against the blaze. He was screaming something. Words mangling until they were just some creature's moan.

Through this the sky had returned to its blackness from the pale youth of Francis' face. It had become only a regular sky with its darkness and spots of stars. Big Nothing had burned itself out, unneeded. No more magic. There was only the empty night and the knowledge of her son, sleeping. The planet's satellite at peace.

Drop it. I will shoot. Drop it. I will shoot.

Before, May had stood at her kitchen table with her knife from Sargents across both palms. *Marbles Ideal, five-inch.* She had thought of placing it to the side of the letter to the husband. This would make things clear. *Blade's a razor, tip's good. Battlefield condition.* She would be putting this in his hand and things would be a little surer. But then she would carry too much. This all had to be on the husband. For her to move on, this had to be his doing. She was only speaking the truth. People were doing their jobs. *This one went to the beaches. A little damage near the throat.* He had hurt her enough already and she would not carry an ounce more of this than she had to.

So she had taken her knife out with her into the boat and, as Officer Carter issued her commands and warnings, May held it by its smooth handle then let it drop over the side into the water. It made no sound. Her eyes closed, May saw the knife fall into the hands of her grandmother. A youthful Casey, standing scared in the shallows, at her place in this orbit between them. Casey took the knife, May's courage, and put them to use. The courage which would find its way back in a lifetime.

Casey had been so sure of her failure; her failure to protect her family from the inheritance of this hurt. May recalled being a child with a tick burrowing into her scalp and her grandmother seizing the thing and pulling it clear. Straight out, never twist. Hair always came out with the creature and it always brought pain. The rubbing alcohol. *Brave girl.* Casey couldn't have seen how that courage and love would pass endlessly between them and spin this great circle of action. The rupture and repair.

May opened her eyes and was truthful and calm. The knife had left their hands and settled at the bottom of the lake.

—

Officer Carter would have fired. This was her job. May had imagined it would be four times. To be sure. Each shot would emerge from a halo. Cath and her gun, disappearing against the fire. When police fired it was always to be sure.

But the officer couldn't get close enough. They would have been gunshots sent without aim into a glowing tower of flame. The husband was inside somewhere, now beyond sight.

May knew him, though.

What angered him and what satisfied. She could see only smoke above the boathouse, the structure now transformed into a burning star. She closed her eyes and could then see him clearly. Putting himself at the centre even of this. He had dropped to his knees to make it a greater performance. He would never come out because that would be submitting. The husband would never loosen his control and so he was choosing the time and manner of his demise. The officers continued to shout and he would hear nothing. He would not submit. Not to them. Not to May. This was his victory. This was his consequence alone.

Time passed. It was only a matter of minutes but they were the minutes of an unchecked fire. Minutes that saw to the very end of things. Officer Carter returned to Cath. She had given up on the doorway to the house as it had ceased to even be. She holstered her gun. It was Cath again. The woman who had made May promise to not hesitate. The body of the husband would be losing its shape. May couldn't see what had become of it but it would be somewhere in the heart of the fire. Fuel. Some motion of blood. The orphaned muscles of a heart. Cath had been calling for the other officer to retreat. They were still stepping away from the heat to the lake's edge. She took her radio from her chest and spoke to whoever would be listening. There were sirens coming and soon the lights of the fire truck would be visible.

It had been determined.

The scene was now one great, unending flame and those who came would realise that nothing could be done. They would stand and watch the house burn through the last of itself until all that remained were marks. The square of its foundations. Everything solid would have turned to cinders in flight.

All that he had done.

No more names.

No more agreed-upon stories.

LOVELAND, JULY 1958

The message arrived from the bank early in the morning, as the mail always did. It was waiting silent in its envelope outside the door when Casey woke to feed Rosie. In the past it would have been brought down from the big house by one of the kitchen hands. Sometimes Henry the gardener. Now there was only Jean.

It was over. Just a few pages of text and their life was undone. It was addressed to the husband, of course, and opening it was a breach, but he was out working on the pier and anyway they were now beyond indiscretions. His voice came by reflex.

You'll be buried in Loveland.

Your baby too.

Casey had never been allowed close to the particulars of money lending but she knew enough to understand the implications of a notice of foreclosure. Attached to the formal document was a handwritten letter, more personal, from the manager of the bank. It spoke of the bank's long history with the Love family and the manager's reluctance and anguish at having to bring things to this conclusion. It spoke also of the extended periods of warning and notice and of the husband's failure to act in good faith. The tone sharpened into talk of collateral and the necessary and prompt sale of assets.

Casey realised she had been willing this. She had long since given up praying for a miracle and instead had summoned the inevitable. He would be out standing on the boards of the pier still. He began work with the daylight to escape the worst of the heat. The husband would return to the house at his usual time and he would find this letter on the table. Everything his family had made was destroyed in those few pages. She wondered if the bank manager had thought of her and the baby. If he'd even known of them. Regardless, he couldn't have known the great favour he was extending them in this calling of time.

She went to the bedroom and pulled the curtains open. The husband had restored the window and its frame to the wall, cemented them in.

The sun was still new.

She went to the front deck and opened the glass doors, putting her bare arm into the early hours and finding it warm, and she smelled something like smoke. Maybe some chemical the husband was painting onto the wood of the pier.

The baby cried from her cot. Sweet, unknowing Rosie. The bank manager couldn't have known what a gift he was giving. This perfect life. They would be happy.

She looked down at her lake and knew she would never take herself out on it again. Never grapple with the oars of her boat and row herself out into the lake's centre, asking for answers. No more daydreams and magic, she told herself. There was work to do.

Again she smelled smoke on the breeze.

Chapter Eighteen

May had thought of having a last meal. She could have gone to the diner. Jean and Tate both would have come and they might have had peaceful moments to remember each other by. In the end, though, May couldn't wait.

She had been surprised at how little time, how little administration, was required of her. May had brought the boat to the shore and made it to the heat of the fire before Cath saw her and called for her to wait. Demanded she step back. Within the smoke was a sharp, treacly smell and May decided it was from the flower she had left. She could imagine whatever she liked. She couldn't go any closer and didn't want to. The other officer, the man, led her to his patrol car. After a time he turned the heating up and drove her away.

May was at the station for two hours giving her statement. She spent the night at the motel near the highway and the next morning Cath came to her with a backpack in which were some of Cath's own clothes, some toiletries. May assumed she wouldn't be allowed to leave but Cath said there was no particular reason she couldn't. Although Cath would have preferred her to stay—there would be an investigation into the fire and questions from the coroner and procedures for the body, when the time came—she wouldn't stop her from going. Cath made her promise to see a counsellor when she got home and May said she would. It was the demand of someone doing their job and May would show her that respect. They hugged, both laughing a little at Cath's badges and devices between them, then May got into her rental car and drove away from Loveland towards the highway. Staying on the right, the right, the right. Heading south until she saw the planes taking off.

She could have been having pancakes with Tate, having Jean order more than just toast with her coffee, and it would have been something wholesome to see the two of them speaking. But May couldn't wait. She returned the car to the rental company and checked in for her flight; she had bought a ticket for the next available.

Tate and the troubles May could only guess at. This sweetest of boys who had already tangled himself so. Filled his pockets with some impossible heaviness. He hadn't lived enough to have earned it yet, surely. May wasn't certain what anchored him to Loveland so stubbornly but she felt a part of it. She ached for him.

Jean and the weight she carried for Casey. The obligation that had tied her to this town and its unsettled water. She'd given her life to a memory. There would be so many threads to untie and May was one of them.

She left letters for them both. Tate's slid under the door of the general store. Jean's in her mailbox. That would have to be the end and start of it.

She could have driven to the lake to see what remained by daylight but there would be nothing of any significance, only ash and blackened wood. Whatever rupture was there had been repaired as much as it ever would be.

May only had one short, animal life and she had spent enough of it with the order of things upturned. She would never set foot in Loveland or its shallows again. There would be details to consider and processes. Property, money, the body of a dead man, taxes. There were lawyers and families to deal with these. Lawyers paid by the hour. Families that were no longer hers. It would all resolve.

May had just that one animal life and she wouldn't hesitate.

Her son was waiting for her in his grandmother's spare room. Francis wouldn't yet speak to her though she'd called every hour. May's mother had been the one to tell him that his father was dead. Somewhere there would be a news item. Small and hidden. A man had set a house alight. A man had succumbed.

Rosie had told May that Francis hadn't reacted at first. Then followed hours of gentle tears like a much younger child. He wouldn't speak to May. He stayed in his grandmother's spare room and she brought him meals. He'd asked his grandmother to pass on a single message. That he wouldn't speak to his mother but he wanted her to come straight home. So May would go to Francis and face the failings and satisfactions to follow.

There were the wasted years to consider. The regret, alive and heavy in her chest. Things to consider and things to be abandoned or reclaimed. The regret would not shift entirely but it might lighten. May couldn't be sure. She knew only that there was a future and she would try to be grateful and proud.

The aeroplane and its staff went through their routines. May changed seats with a man so he could sit with his wife and screaming baby. He didn't thank her. May smiled at the upset child and settled into the white noise of departure. She'd thrown her headphones into a bin at the airport. She would no longer escape and May had lost her song, even if she'd wanted it.

She was a mother but not only a mother. She loved her son but not only her son. She was not made complete by him but she would pull their centres close.

It was what she determined.

The husband had hurt her for so long and in all the ways possible. This would go on, she knew and was sure. Maybe the ways could diminish. Maybe they would broaden still. She would care for herself, though, and ask the same of those around her.

This would go on, she knew. Her thoughts wandered to that vision of happiness. Her rose garden as the sun went down. It was a place of love and she could live in this place. The real work of life goes on inside and so she would work and laze and sleep in the garden of her heart. It was no escape. It was as real as any field of corn and needed as much care. She would be a creature of the rose garden, always, and she would feel no shame at this.

The plane's cabin was just human chatter beneath hydraulics and gears. Eventually they were flying and later all would turn dark. A universe without meaningful end. If an animal measures itself against this then it makes itself pointless. That night, flying over a churning ocean, May had the brief, minor thought that if she was only an animal, then what business of hers was a universe without end? She was a common, living thing and so she would measure herself against the span of living things. Life was all there was. All that mattered. And yes, yes, she did for now put the living things ahead of the dead. This was what she determined.

May closed her eyes and soon fell into a heavy sleep. In that night's ocean waves were rising up and crashing. Animals were scrambling for high ground. There was work to do. Protect and provide for living things. An endless universe to be defied.

LOVELAND, JULY 1958

Casey had known of the husband's time in Jean's bed since its beginning. This came to exist as weight and shame. He would leave to work on the pier but the noise of his hammer and saw wouldn't come for a half-hour. Later he would smell of sweat and sex. She had seen Jean's connection to her husband since its first days too. The way Jean stood with just the slightest tremble in his presence. A wink of fear she recognised. Later Casey had suspected the pregnancy, confirmed with Jean's changing body. The bond Casey made with Jean, their love, would never alter in its size but its shape could never survive. It had been deformed. Not by what the husband had done but by Casey's knowledge of it and her inaction. She knew and she was ashamed. She had failed to save Jean as she had failed herself.

This was how she had come to judge herself and how she always would. They formed a little horseshoe, the three of them. The husband at its centre, where he always placed himself. If he were ever to be overcome, if he could be removed, the structure of the horseshoe would have to break. Casey thought of holding Jean by the hand as they walked away from one another. Their fingers losing grip. There was love there and it was great but it must lose its shape. This was how it would always be remembered. Casey was ashamed at her failure.

When the husband returned from his work to find the final papers, the letter from the manager of the bank, Casey had been holding the baby. It was the moment. Casey told the husband that she knew about Jean, about the adultery—the word she had made certain to use. She asked him to admit it. Rosie was small, even for her mere four months, and in his impotence the husband grabbed the tiny girl and held her roughly by one leg. Rosie was silent at first, maybe wondering at this world upside down, but then was screaming with this first great pain of her life. Later that day a doctor would push the baby's hip back into place. He scolded Casey for her carelessness. Rosie would recover but for a time there would be pain and marks. The baby would wear stripes.

—

Casey had seen Jean moving across the bone-dry earth to the side of the big house. She called Jean over and the girl was startled at first and then bashful as she moved close. They hadn't spoken in weeks but they soon fell into their easy way of talking. Jean laughed as she told her story of the woman in the shop in town who had folded up the husband's bill and tucked it into the front of Jean's dress.

There was silence, then Casey asked Jean directly about the husband and the rape.

There were so many other words for it and other ways to describe the situation. Words and ways of putting it in a context so that it could be endured and ignored. Casey wanted to find the bravery she knew was still within them. There was a word for it and she would use it.

'He rapes you?'

Jean stared but only for a moment. 'Yes.'

'And me. He rapes me as well.'

Casey told her of the ways the husband had hurt her, and Jean did the same. The prison of this. They would nod in turn, knowing it all already but allowing it to be spoken. Needing it. The women clasped hands. Casey told the real story of Rosie being hung by her leg. How things carried on. That they would be buried in Loveland. Their babies too. The women clasped hands like a pair being married, making vows.

—

The husband was moving nervously from the moment he came into the house. He would need to be calmed. Casey would give him the sweetness. Though it was just on midday she would offer him a beer and she would put her hand at the place where his neck met his shoulder. The place he liked.

'It's hot already,' he said. 'There's a lot for me to do.'

She pushed more firmly into his neck and could feel the drum taps of his pulse. Something compelled her to make a final gesture. A confirming, last opportunity.

'We'll never leave this place,' she said, borrowing his tone that lay between a question and declaration.

She took her hand from him and brushed at some wood shavings on his shoulder. He wouldn't meet her eye and was inching towards a tantrum. He was a child and would find a way to centre himself in this. Casey calmly told the husband something true. It was nothing significant. Nothing any fair person could consider provocation. It was something she'd heard from the radio. That Elvis Presley had finished his basic training with the army. He was on a break and there was talk he might put on some concerts, maybe in New York City, and Casey would like to go.

It was said calmly, it was true, but it had been enough to send the husband wild. He had started on the new crockery and then on to her hips. He kicked the leg of the baby's cot and it broke away. Casey's throat had tightened. Bodies react in ancient ways. Her mind, though, was clear. She could think now because this was all coming to an end. She had made the decision she had always thought impossible and she would accept the consequences. A life would be claimed. It would complete things in a way. A horseshoe would become a circle.

The husband left, as he always did eventually, and headed to the bar on the near side of town. Or he went for a bottle of liquor from the big house. Whichever, he would escape the lake, as he always did.

Casey thought of what it might mean if she knew of the awful times of the husband's youth. The war that must have been beyond a nightmare. Maybe it was beyond explaining.

There is horror and circumstance but there is also fault and blame. He was in pain, he must surely be, but that could not be a full counterweight to his acts. There is circumstance but there is also fault and blame. She would not build him a way out of this.

She found Jean in the big house and they went to the gardener's shed and took the drums of petrol. No-one else remained so there was no fear of discovery. It took longer than they'd imagined to drag a wet line of fuel through the buildings. All the rooms. It was only the boathouse they left dry. Fuel spilled across the wooden boards of the promenade and pier, though Casey wasn't sure they would burn. They might be waterlogged at their cores. It wouldn't matter. Enough would take. One held the baby while the other emptied the drums.

All the structures of the lake were ablaze. The big house, the amusements, the boardwalk. The pier had caught in the end. Towers of black smoke. The women had waited at the boathouse, Jean in the covered darkness with the rowboats, Casey at the water's edge. Rosie was inside, asleep in her cot. They had fed her and sung her to sleep. Moses arrived dirty and torn from conflict. The little man had returned and found the creation of his family on fire and he had tried to fight it. He then came at Casey, cursing and demanding she explain. He screamed that it was all done, all gone.

When Casey had simply stood, calm and unmoving, he had been confused into silence. He waited but she would not speak. She never would again, not to him. This man she had never known. The blame he had earned would be at the centre of this, always, but not the man. Never again. Everything was the smell and colour of fire as if from a sulphurous lake. The act itself came as all things do. The water, the stars, the flames. Jean walked out into the light, barefoot on the sand, and called for the husband's attention. Jean called his name and so he turned his back on his wife.

Casey gave her sweet smile, the one her mother had taught her, and brought the knife up to the man's throat. She aimed the blade along the line where she suspected his life might reside and he fell without a fight or gesture. The act itself came inevitably, as all things do.

The women spoke, there in the water, and they clasped hands for the last time. Their bond could not survive this. Their great, damaged love. Jean would care for the house as an act of devotion and Casey would leave for the same reason. She would never return to her distant parents and siblings because she was no longer the person they had known. She was a mother too, and after this there must be a beginning for the child. She would leave everything behind.

The people of the town would be coming, drawn by the fires, and it would all fall on the man. The flames and the blood and the blame. It would fall on him as it should. All that he had done.

It had come so quickly in the end.

Their plan could never alter. The women spoke calmly, making vows. The ancient beauty around spoke of the coming of spring. The oranges and cinnamon and smoke.

BEFORE AND AFTER

All of this is real.

There are collections of particles in some particular and temporary arrangement and we assign them values for a time. We call them a body of water. The memories of a child. We might call the arrangement of our neural response love. Temporary arrangements and all of them real.

Love.

Love.

At the end is only boundless, living love.